Malcolm Knox is the author of fifteen books
including the novels *Summerland*, *Adult Book*,
winner of a Ned Kelly Award, *Jamaica*, winner of the
Colin Roderick Award. and *The Life*. His non-fiction
books include *Secrets of the Jury Room* and *Scattered:
The inside story of ice in Australia* Formerly literary
editor of the *Sydney Morning Herald*, he has twice
won Walkley awards for journalism and has been
runner-up for the Australian Journalist of the Year
Award. He lives in Sydney with his wife and
two children.

PRAISE FOR MALCOLM KNOX

'Knox is, quite simply, a fabulous writer.'

Literary Review

'. . . clear-eyed wisdom and startling, depth-charged prose'

Guardian

'one of the most considerable of our novelists'

Peter Pierce, *Sydney Morning Herald*

'Knox explores the inner life of men with both surgical insight and heartfelt compassion . . .'

Michael McGirr, *The Age*

'Page after page is radiant with the energy he brings to bear . . .'

Geordie Williamson, *Weekend Australian*

'Seductive, accomplished, intelligent and effortless to read.'

The Bookseller

'. . . one of our most exciting novelists'

Delia Falconer, *ALR*

'. . . there are not many men who can write like this, so poetically and with such immense complexity, about friendship, jealousy, insecurity, middle age and death wishes.'

Weekend Australian

'Knox writes with revealing and compassionate insight.'

West Australian

'. . . a knowing and satisfying craftsman with a deep, mimetic intelligence'

Peter Craven *AFR*

'Knox's great strength is his ability to get beneath the surface of his characters, into the dark, private recesses of their minds.'

Liam Davidson, *Weekend Australian*

'A combination of intelligence and punching power not always evident in Australian fiction.'

Qantas Magazine

'. . . a writer whose literary daring stamps him as one of Australia's bravest and best.'

Gold Coast Bulletin

THE
WONDER
LOVER

MALCOLM
KNOX

ALLEN&UNWIN

First published in Great Britain in 2016 by Allen & Unwin
First published in Australia in 2015 by Allen & Unwin

Allen & Unwin
c/o Atlantic Books
Ormond House
26–27 Boswell Street
London WC1N 3JZ

Phone: 020 7269 1610
Fax: 020 7430 0916
Email: UK@allenandunwin.com
Web: www.allenandunwin.co.uk

A CIP catalogue record of this book is available from the British Library.

Trade paperback ISBN 978 1 76029 112 9
E-book ISBN 978 1 92526 721 1

Text design by Design by Committee
Set in 13/19 pt Bulmer by Bookhouse, Sydney

Printed in Great Britain by TJ International Ltd, Padstow

10 9 8 7 6 5 4 3 2 1

For Jane Palfreyman

ONE
First Love
1

TWO
Soul Mate
119

THREE
Redeemer
237

FOUR
Fall
269

ONE

First Love

1

When we were very young, our father sat on the end of our bed to unload his sack of stories.

He clicked out our light. He would not begin until we had shut our eyes. The darkness confirmed his lack of scent, either animal or cosmetic, an absence that seems odder to us now than then. Being unable to smell him in the dark never struck us as unusual. Fathers had no aroma.

'I am waiting,' he said.

Scent was not all he lacked. He had no outstanding peculiarity of voice or appearance, no distinguishing timbre or taste, no *feel* that might embed him, like a splinter, in a stranger's memory. Neither coarse nor smooth, bitter nor honeyed, ugly nor handsome, a golden mean of averageness, he was, to the untrained eye, immaculately bland. Yet to us he was magnificently, simply, our father, as invisible and essential as the Equator, as vital and taken for granted as air.

'I am waiting.'

We might not have been able to smell, touch, taste or hear him, but he would hold his silence until we could not see him.

Need he have waited? We might have turned on the light and opened our eyes, and still not seen him.

But he did exist. He had heft. When he sat on the mattress, we rose on the wave that his weight pushed from his end to ours. Another sign of existence: his crossgrain of distrust. Even in the darkness, if he suspected that so much as one letterbox-slot eyelid was cheating and one of his own children was deceiving him, he would repeat: 'I am waiting.'

Or would he? Was he even speaking? He had no need to, and perhaps we were imagining the words. His silences were commanding, his absences unforgettable.

So, then: no voice, no odour, no mark on the senses, no feeling-tone, not even a trace of what might glibly be called personality. Why so many nos, nots, neithers and nors? Why remember him by what he wanted for? Perhaps, if you looked at it his way, these absences were not what nature had stripped away from him but what it had given. If he had exuded an odour, somebody might have asked him to change it, and if he changed it, somebody else might have noticed the change.

And then a third other might have been able to track him down, sniff him out.

Now we are not so young, we are inclined to look at it his way. In his phantomness, there was no lack, no deprivation. Nature had set him free. By giving him nothing, it had granted him his licence.

●

Our father knew things from the outermost stars of the universe, from the unseen core of the earth, from so many places that there was no doubt in our minds that he would surely know if we, at the other end of the bed, snuck a peek. Once, out walking at night on a steep rocky path, we complained that we could not see and asked him to carry us. Our father pointed at the moon and said, How far away? We trilled: Three-hundred-and-eighty-four-thousand, four-hundred kilometres. He nodded and said, If you can see that far, you can see the steps under your feet.

'I am waiting.'

He was warning us about time more than space. If we slitted one eye for the smallest instant he would stop his story and abandon us to the trials of falling asleep on our own.

'Not for one second,' he said of the disqualifying glimmer between our eyelashes.

'A half-second!' Evie cried, squeezing her eyes. Evie was the younger and considered herself very smart.

'A millisecond,' Adam cut in.

'A finity-second!' cried Evie, who had one desire in life, to exceed Adam. 'I won't open my eyes for a finity-second!'

Evie folded her arms smugly across her blanket and clenched her lips as tight as her eyes, wrinkling the blood out of them so that they puckered white.

Then, behind the curtain of one lash, a shining fissure.

He shook his head. 'I will stop talking and go back out to your mother if I see one eye open for—' he paused long enough for us to almost wet ourselves with excitement '—for an *atto*second.'

'Wow!' said Adam.

'Omigod!' said Evie, who had heard the expression recently and used it whenever Adam said 'wow'.

'OMG.' Adam, belying his belief that he was too old for sibling rivalry, tossed down a casual trump card.

'An attosecond,' our father continued, his tone matter-of-fact, 'the shortest unit of time that has been measured. One quintillionth of a second. An attosecond is to one second—' he paused again '—what one second is to the age of the universe.'

'Is it like . . . this?' said Evie, and clapped her hands before pulling them apart as quickly as if the clap had not happened.

'Shorter,' our father said.

'Will you *really* know if our eyes open for a . . . what is it called again?' said Adam, who had come recently to scepticism. Just the other day he had been overheard scorning Evie's belief in the tooth fairy. It's not a real fairy, he had said, tough with knowledge. It's just this man who comes around collecting teeth and leaving money.

'An attosecond, the time it takes for light to travel the length of three hydrogen atoms,' our father said.

'Three what?' said Evie.

'Close your eyes, Evie,' our father said.

We closed our eyes. We never cheated for long and the stories always, eventually, came.

Because we considered ourselves quite grown up and had been talking, that night, of marriages, he told us of the woman who had taken to her wedding seventy-nine bridesmaids, aged from one to seventy-nine, because the number brought good luck; and of her groom, who had been flanked by forty-seven groomsmen aged sixteen to sixty-three.

Evie had only recently discovered what a wedding was, and believed we, boy and girl, could marry each other. Our father's voice, the wondrous marriage ceremony, burst in the vividness beneath our eyelids. There were pulsing flowers, mushrooms, lattices, dancing supernovas, seventy-nine girls and forty-seven boys. Finity.

And then, because we were so still on our pillows, he told us of St Simeon the Stylite, who sat on a stone pillar at a place called the Hill of Wonders for thirty-nine years, only coming down once, so that his pillar could be extended in height. Just thinking of it (thirty-nine years—forever!) lulled us towards sleep.

His voice came flat and low, a monotone submarine cable. It could sound as if the back of his throat was covered by oilcloth and his words had to fight their way into the open. When our eyes were closed we had a strong sense of where he was, and where his voice was; yet marvellously they were not always in the same place. Sometimes his voice sounded as if it came from behind him, as if the man on our bed were a ventriloquist's doll controlled from outside our room.

'And, Dad,' Adam asked, 'who did you see today?'

'What did you do today?' our father, a reflective surface, replied.

'We learnt chess!' Evie said. 'I'm better than Adam, I beat him! And I learnt the hula hoop!'

'I played Lego,' Adam said.

Our father told us of the two men who played chess continuously for fifty-three years, the woman who hula-hooped with ninety-nine hoops, and the twenty thousand children who together built a millipede made of Lego measuring one thousand four hundred metres . . .

He talked us all the way into sleep, his filtered voice ferrying us across the river into dreams. Not for an attosecond did we open our eyes.

•

It was not every night that this visitation happened, only every night he was with us. When we were babies, our mother told us, he had been with us every night, every week, and he had talked us into sleep with his stories. But we couldn't have been able to understand him then, nor can we remember such a time. Telling his stories to babies, he must have felt he was talking to himself. Every night! We only remember him being an occasional visitor, like the man who comes to leave money for teeth. To have had him every night seems, like infancy itself, a marvel.

2

By daybreak, he was not the man we remembered from the night before. He was still the kindest and sweetest father a child could hope for, but he sat at breakfast with a stillness and such silence that sometimes we couldn't help wondering if we had done something wrong. He wore his ironed white shirt, a grey tie, suit trousers and polished black shoes. His hair, so blond it was grey or so grey it was blond, lost in a house-painter's colour chart between warm and cool whites, was combed and lacquered across his freckled pate. He was leaving.

Desperately, as if to hold him on a faint telephone line before it cut out, we tried to reach back to the magic from the night before. 'I heard the last story,' Adam said. 'The boy of my age who walked to the South Pole.'

'No,' said Evie, 'I heard that one, but there was another one after it, the hot-air balloonist who flew to the sun.'

The truth was that neither of us had heard these stories; instead we were pretending to have been the one who had stayed awake the longer. But these stories of ours were not false either, because even if they had not been spoken they grew from the truths he had sown and watered with his voice as we fell into a sleep that was not a blankness or an oblivion but a kind of fecundity.

He knew this, so he would not correct us or tell us we were making things up. He nodded along and spooned his Cornflakes from his bowl (servings of one hundred grams, levelled to the higher of two painted cornflower-blue circles at the rim of the bowl, milk poured precisely to the level of the lower circle). Thirty-three spoonsful per sitting. But while he accepted our enthusiasm for prolonging the game of the previous night, he wouldn't indulge fiction-making. He felt a responsibility to reel us back to the real. Bound by facts, married to truth, he said, 'What do you know about Cornflakes?'

'Invented in 1898,' Adam said.

'No!' said Evie. 'The current recipe, with sugar, was invented in 1903. The sugar was to reduce spoilage!' She beamed at our father, who issued a single nod.

'And, Adam,' he said to his now-sulking son, 'do you remember their world-first sales slogan?'

Adam hesitated. Our father, without a smile or any other expression, winked at him. Adam's face brightened.

'Wink Day!' he said. '"Wink at your grocer and see what you get!"' He poked his tongue out at Evie.

'And, Evie,' said our father, to be even-handed, 'you will remember the Cornflakes record authenticated last year.'

Evie was near to bursting with her facts. 'World's biggest breakfast cereal: one thousand three hundred and fifty-four people eating Cornflakes at the same time! Biggest cereal bowl *ever*: two point eight four metres long and four metres high!'

'And one point one one metres deep,' our father added for completeness.

Thus satisfied, he stood up, took his bowl to the sink, rinsed it, placed it in the dishwasher, and kissed each of us on the crown of our head. He shot his cuffs. He was a slim man and wiry. He ate terrible things: the most complex of carbohydrates and the most saturated of fats. He did no physical exercise, never ran or swam or even walked. He drove his car home and stayed home until he drove away. He did not spend any calories in superfluous conversation. But no matter what he ate, he never put on weight. Once he told us, 'It is thinking that keeps my weight down.' His thoughts used up more calories than a bee hummingbird, which we knew was the animal that burnt so much energy it was lighter, almost, than the air itself.

He joked that he might write a book one day: *The Thinking Person's Diet*.

Our mother Sandra, who thought as actively as our father and went to swimming squads and Boxercise and Zumba classes four times a week, who ate garden salads in the evenings after she cooked our slim, trim father his fatty lamb chops and his cholesterol-packed eggs and his mushrooms drenched in butter, carried weight enough for two. She was not fat, but could give that impression due to the spread of her shoulders and hips: she was, as she preferred to say, broad in the beam. Yawning and rubbing the dullness out of her eyes, Sandy shuffled into the kitchen in her dressing gown and foraged in the drawer for paracetamol.

Perhaps the difference was drink more than metabolism. While admitting to a glass of wine here and there, our mother Sandy consumed, with a cumulative slyness that bordered on turning a blind eye to her own habits, a quantum close to the nationally accepted public health threshold for defining alcoholism. Our father seldom drank. He had quit, more or less, after a sequence of youthful misadventures involving raw spirits, stomach pumps, blackouts and motoring accidents, stories so old and era-ending that they would come down to us with something of the flavour of epic folktales, a mythology Sandy resented, quietly, as it lent him the glamour (as she supposed) of a severely alcoholic distant past without (in her view) the payment of sufficient dues. He was not teetotal, however; our mother teased him into joining her for 'a glass with dinner'. He had the glass, of which he made much, to show he was still a drinking man; she had the bottle, of which she made discomfortingly little. To join her, even if in a token gesture, so she would not be stranded alone with the bottle, was one of his ways of showing marital love.

'All right then?' she said, and pushed her glasses back on the bridge of her nose. She wore glasses inside the house, so thick that they made her sky-blue eyes resemble scientific specimens, and tied her hair back into a thick ponytail. It was a source of constant surprise to us that she could transform herself from this into the perfumed, emblazered superwoman who would hustle us out the door an hour later. The glasses would be replaced by contact lenses, her eyes outlined and animated, and her hair would be tailored into a neat French roll. She dressed, to our eyes, with the elegance of high fashion, though she would later tell us that she 'made a little go a long way and a lot turn into a little'. That is, she seemed expensively attired and was able to conceal the largeness of her figure in public. In private, though, she let it go, for his benefit as much as for her own relaxation. Seldom enough for us to remember it, he would creep up behind her in the kitchen or the dining room and throw his arms around her wide waist, making her squeal. When we saw them cuddling like this, our parents, it filled us with a warm joy that burst and flooded us from inside.

He waved us a general goodbye. While we stayed in the kitchen and fixed our breakfast, our mother escorted our father through the living room to the front door. We heard their brief murmur of conversation and the loud smack of lips. He kissed our mother on the mouth if she was not wearing lipstick, considerately on the cheek if she was. We would memorise their kisses. She would come out of them with her mouth slack, the shape of an inverted kidney bean, and her eyes momentarily dazzled, as if zapped by an electrical charge and transported to another time. Sometimes, when she was wearing lipstick, he would give her a fairy kiss on her lips, light as a brush and so tender it kept us going, like fuel.

The rotary cough of his car starting, the whine backing up the driveway. The intake of breath as his car paused on the street—has he changed his mind? is he coming back?—but no, just trouble with the gear stick as he wrenched it from reverse to go forth, to the world.

He would be gone for weeks, to his offices in other cities and other countries. This was what his work required. This was its ironclad magnetism. He was a man of significance to people in the four corners of the earth. He was needed in so many places, for such important duties, that we counted ourselves fortunate to have our slice of his life. Our mother never demurred about the extent of his travels, and we accepted it as we accepted all the mysteries that our parents wore as naturally—easily is not the right word—as their very skin. He was our father. He did large things. We were one compartment of his life, the most important certainly, the one without which all the others would be meaningless, but still one among many. We needed him, but so did the world, so did history. He was such a scarce resource, we treated every day and night he was with us as a lucky break.

Our mother reappeared at the kitchen door and said, to herself as much as to us, 'Right, that's it, he's gone.'

3

At his office in the second city, the city which was his next stop after ours, a city thousands of miles away, he was just as important and respected and essential as he was in his office in our city. Some features of his work needed to follow a ruthless standardisation: everything in each office and in the application of his duties had to be reproducible elsewhere. Otherwise, the whole enterprise would have no meaning. Every last detail was regulated. Apples, he liked to say, must always be measured against apples. Laxton's Superbs must never be compared with Blenheim Oranges! (What other children could boast of a father who could not only name the seven thousand five hundred cultivars of the apple, but make jokes with them?) As the Authenticator-in-Chief for humankind's last word on extraordinary fact, the man who issued the final decision on what was fact *and* what was extraordinary, John Wonder oversaw this standardisation with an imperishable will.

Authentication (he practised but didn't need to preach) starts at home.

And so it was, at home.

At the end of each day at his office in that second city, he went home to a woman. She was also our mother, although she looked different from our mother Sandra. This mother in the second city was a dark, rounded woman with clear skin and no waist. He would go home and give her a perfect reproduction of the warm, familiar, loving greeting that he gave Sandy, the mother of ours with her fairer skin and weaker eyes and squarer shoulders. This second house was smaller and dimmer than ours, and rented. For all the importance of his work, our father was never rich. Or never rich enough. We were always struggling to make ends meet, no matter where we were, or who; while he, you might infer, was always struggling to bring those ends together without quite allowing them to meet.

In this second home, in this second city, he sat at the end of the children's bed each night and waited for us to shut our eyes and hauled out a swag of stories from his work.

The thirty-one thousand four hundred and twenty-four children who brushed their teeth in unison.

The two men who walked on the moon for seven hours and thirty-seven minutes.

The fifty-five elephants who danced together on a stage.

The train that ran as straight as a beam of light for nearly five hundred kilometres.

And in this other home he also had two children, a boy and a girl. They had our names, Adam and Evie. Adam Wonder and Evie Wonder. They attended, as we did, the free government school nearest the house. Our father and our mothers could not afford to be choosy. These children, Adam and Evie Wonder, are also us and we are they.

The morning he left, he ate his breakfast: Cornflakes levelled at one hundred grams, milk poured to where it was just visible beneath the float of the lowest Cornflake, thirty-three spoonsful. He kissed them, us, goodbye, and kissed his wife, her, the mother, our mother, goodbye, because his work demanded that he go off, as he must always go, to another city.

In this third base, he had an office that mirrored in every respect, down to the carpet and the wall paint and the furnishings, his offices in the first two cities. Apples with apples: he was the Authenticator-in-Chief. Once one detail varies, he liked to say to his staff, no matter how trivial-seeming, the whole edifice will fall. The enterprise is, he said, a house of cards. The principle of identicality is contained in every card. If you do not know which is crucial, you must treat them all as such.

Which reminded him of the man who built a house of cards twenty-five feet nine inches high, then added an entire city skyline comprising three thousand decks, one hundred and seventy-eight thousand cards in all, taking him a month of adding a dozen new decks a day. This man (invariably a man) called himself a 'card-structure specialist' . . .

The third city was thousands of miles and an ocean from the first and the second. Our father's work was equally important there. Hopeful applicants wrote to beg him to come and inspect them. To those seekers, John Wonder was godlike. He was the Authenticator. His work was essential there, as it was everywhere.

In this third city, each day he went home to a third woman. This one was yellowish and elfin, with black hair, pitted skin and a sensuous mouth parenthesised by a dimple in one cheek, a white scar in the other. Our mothers bore few physical similarities. There was no one type for our father, although, in another sense, the identicality of the women was another of the standardised cards of his existence and what we may call his sanity. The third house was smaller still, and unkempt.

His children of the third city toddled into his arms when he arrived. He lifted both of them at once. They were tiny: a boy and a girl. They had the same names as we. They had the same names as the two children in the second city. They, we, are Adam and Evie Wonder.

But they were not quite we. This third Adam had been born with a cleft in his palate and a bifurcation in his upper lip; this Adam needed doctors. And the third Evie, the baby, was unable to hear. Evie could hear none of his stories. Evie needed more doctors.

But still, at night, he sat at the end of Adam's bed while Evie squirmed in a cot. Our father waited until our eyes were closed so he could unload the sack of stories he brought home from his work.

And because we could not ask questions, he indulged himself, and talked us to sleep with the superlatives that he himself enjoyed the most.

The tallest mountain measured from its base in the bottom of the sea.

The planet's largest liquid body.

The largest subglacial lake.

The oldest continuous ice core.

The highest clouds, the longest lightning flash, the thickest density of crabs, the fastest fish, the rarest primate, the smallest burrower, the most dangerous pinniped. The superlatives that lived whether humans were here to measure them or not: his favourites.

Evie could not hear him. Adam could not understand him. But we went to sleep to the sound of his stories.

We sailed away on the ebb tide of his stories, and when we think about it now, when we see it his way, there must have been something Scheherazade-like, something desperate, in his telling his stories in a panic against stopping and, in the naked pause of silence, the turn of the tide, being caught out.

And on the last morning, he ate his one hundred grams of Cornflakes, kissed his wife goodbye and hugged his children. He gave them an extra cuddle because they were so little.

He would be back soon, he told our mother, but he was a busy man, an important man, he had work in his other offices. His wife, our mother, she loved him. His children, us, we loved him. He loved the mother on the doorstep of their small and shabby house. She never questioned the obligations of his office. He had come into her life in his guise as Ultimate Authenticator; if she might have wished their life together to be different—to be more *together*—the time for seeking adjustment was long past by the time she met him. She had accepted him for what he was. He started, as she admiringly told us, in the manner that he intended to go on.

With this third wife, however, he made exceptions. She was the youngest and the freshest in his memory. Something about the tininess of the children touched him in his marrow. Something about the differences in the younger ones, the babies.

As he kissed her goodbye, he made a slip: he promised her that one day things would get better and, thanks to all of this important work he did, he would one day be able to move his family into a bigger house.

'And spend more weeks with us?' the small black-haired woman asked him.

'And . . . yes,' he said, in his guarded, still, flat, oilcloth-covered voice. Sometimes it sounded noncommittal, like the voice you make when you are in a car and trying to communicate to a pedestrian. You mouth, 'You go first', and a sound is coming out of you, but you're not quite speaking either, because you know she can't hear you. A voice is coming out in spite of yourself. That's what our father's voice could be like.

And then he left them, he left us, and crossed oceans and countries until he arrived back where he started. Now it would begin again. His boy Adam and his girl Evie. He would end his journey by sitting at the end of our bed. He would bring us the stories he had gathered in his work. Which we knew were true, because he had authenticated them.

•

And so, this was how he went. This is the portrait of our father: it is easy to draw because it is perfectly (ruthlessly!) standardised. No matter what the city, the same perimeters surrounded him. That was how he built it. We are we. With his three wives, all unknown to each other, he had fathered a boy, and then a girl. The son was Adam and the daughter Evie. Little wonder he believed he held the secret of life. Little wonder he believed he had put an end to mystery, had deployed enough facts to crowd out the unknowable as a gardener will plant so much ground cover in a garden bed that the weeds will have nowhere to grow. Little wonder he believed he could do anything, *anything*, and get away with it.

And then—here is where our story starts—then calamity befell our father.

You know him now. To such a man, what is the worst that can happen?

No. No. No. Worse than that.

He might have believed he had space for one more. One last.

Or perhaps such a man, the keeper of the last word, will always keep reaching for the last love. Perhaps he had always been searching for the one who would ruin him.

Calamity struck our father. He fell in love.

4

He was trusted around women: by women, by their husbands and fathers and mothers and sisters and brothers, by their sons and daughters and nieces and nephews, by the process of authentication itself. He had had to dismiss a junior Authenticator for an impropriety involving a female claimant, a moment of weakness during the measurement of an attempt to break the world record for the world's longest kiss; three hours short of the record, this Authenticator had suffered an epiphany: after scrutinising the woman's lips for twenty-seven hours, he had fallen for them. Or not her lips as such, for they were invisible; he became besotted by the space he could not see, the gap between the woman's lips and her partner's (a friend, not a boyfriend; no passionate relationship could possibly survive a twenty-seven-hour kiss). That Authenticator underwent an explosion of feeling akin to a religious conversion. In the twenty-eighth hour he lunged, seizing the girl in his arms. One contact of lips on lips, his on hers, would conquer twenty-seven hours, conquer the world. In front of millions on live television and several hundred in the shopping centre where the attempt was taking place, the Authenticator was left without any excuse. Our father sacked him not for sexual assault (far from having charges laid, the woman pitied him and became his Platonic friend), but the more serious offence of interrupting a live world record attempt. Later in life, the erstwhile junior Authenticator attempted a comeback of sorts, jumping the fence from gamekeeper to poacher, or Authenticator to aspirant, by essaying the world record for the longest sequence of postcards (three thousand one hundred and twenty-seven) addressed to a cat (belonging to his Platonic friend, who still resisted his advances).

John Wonder, by contrast, was known to be as trustworthy around women as the day is long (which length increases, he would inform us, due to a slowing in the earth's angular velocity and rotational energy, by some 1.7 milliseconds each century). There was something transparent in his blandness of manner, depthless in the watery blue of his eyes, a void in the intelligence of his smile. No sooner had women met him than they forgot him. He exuded not an atom of sexual need, or appeal, or innuendo, or carnality—whatever it was that made a woman stop and look at a man twice. In his life, women had seldom even stopped to look at him once. That profusion of facts, which he exuded in lieu of tone or affect or scent or voice or personality, was to most women's senses an inoculation against sexual appeal. He lived on an aseptic plane, too ridiculously and boyishly trivial, too unapproachably earnest. He had none of the vulnerability or gameness that commonly attracted women or, for that matter, anyone seeking friendship.

There were times when the organisation needed an Authenticator who had no sexual weakness, who was, in that sense, something less, or more, than a man. If the task was to authenticate the number of sexual partners in a day (six hundred and twenty, set by the adult film actress Jasmine St Clair) or in a lifetime (one hundred and seventy-seven thousand five hundred, claimed by twin Amsterdam prostitutes Louise and Martine Fokkens); the most semen swallowed in one 'sitting' (1.7 pints, set by the adult performer Michelle Monahan); the biggest orgy (two hundred and fifty couples in an episode recorded, enigmatically, as having taken place 'in Tokyo'); the most garter belts removed with the teeth inside two minutes (twenty-six, by Ivo Grosche of Germany); or the numerous other records relating to the dimensions and singular attributes of sexual organs, John Wonder was the trusted Authenticator. It was our father's hands that ran the tape measure around the 177.8 centimetres encompassing the naturally-endowed chest and back of Annie Hawkins-Turner in New York City; it was our father's hands that poured the twelve hundred cubic centimetres (more capacity than a small car) of water into a plaster of Paris bust moulded by the adult stage performer 'Chelsea Charms'. Neither Ms Charms nor Ms Hawkins-Turner could later recall anything of the man who had immortalised them. The Fokkens twins would as soon remember him as they would any of the one hundred and seventy-seven thousand five hundred who came before him. The hands, eyes and pen of our father verified records with the same unmemorable blandness as he brought to his authentication of, say, the most gloves on one hand (twenty-four, set by a serial record-chaser, the New Zealander Alastair Galpin, who described John Wonder as his 'old sparring partner' yet invariably greeted him as if for the first time) or the tallest working windmill (33.33 metres, De Noord Molen at Schiedam in the Netherlands). Our father would have made a brilliant cardplayer, except that he had worked out the odds and rejected the pastime on mathematical grounds.

Our father did not take being forgotten personally. What world-record aspirants held in common, aside from their ambition, was their world-erasing self-absorption, which rendered them, in the heat of the moment of authentication, incapable of registering the existence of another human being. Just as John was perhaps the most unmemorable man on earth, he was in daily contact with the planet's most *unremembering* individuals. He and they, he had long concluded, were a perfect fit.

When he was with those world-beaters, he caught a glimpse of why he was a watcher, rather than a doer. He could not help thinking of the three times in his life he had fallen in love, and how none of those events had any connection with measurements or numbers. It was not that the record setters believed their dimensions made them, or their breasts, more beautiful than anyone else, or else's. It was that they had excised the intangible. For them there *was* no concept of beauty that could not be measured, just as, when our father met the fastest runner in the world, Usain Bolt, and asked him about style in athletics, Bolt said, 'There ain't no style; style is nine-five-eight for the hundred.' If our father had been able to engage Chelsea Charms in such conversation, he felt sure that she would have said there is no beauty—beauty is size 164XXX.

Over time, he had grown troubled by this missing sub-item in his line of work. Never had anyone been able to measure or authenticate what was said by the poets to be the sine qua non of the sexual sphere. His eyes, his instruments of authentication, could behold beauty and love, but he did not have the slightest idea how to measure them. He could record the duration of an unrequited serenade or the number of love-letters sent, but he would not fool himself that these results told him the first thing about love.

Love had happened to him (the passive, his voice of choice) three times, with such overwhelming force that all three tumbles had resulted in him promising to devote his life to the beautiful one (to the exclusion of all others, but we'll come to that). He was father to six children, three boys and three girls, and he loved us all. Clearly, love and beauty drove John Wonder as powerfully as anyone else. And knowing this—having apprehended it through the counter-experience of the sexual wonders of the world—drove him mad, as crazed with frustration as the astrophysicist who took his life after discovering the boundaries of the universe but not what was on the other side. The resistance provided by the unmeasurable threatened to invalidate, to *trivialise,* everything our father had done. He grew as obsessed with the gap between beauty and measurement as his colleague had grown with the gap between lip and lip. What exactly was the universal formula of physical beauty? How could he measure, and bottle, the love that could not be resisted? This need to entrap beauty had crept up on him slowly, but, like any illicit desire, ineluctably; in part it was what had made him fall in love those three times, or if it was not that, it was, after the fact, the story he told himself to set a frame of order and meaning around what he had done. He was, after all, a man without sexual weakness.

By the time he had sired his last child, our father harboured a secret wish: to find, and authenticate, the world's most beautiful woman. What a triumph that would be, what a crowning glory for a life's work! To authenticate the most beautiful woman alive! For years he was seeking her, as a veteran prospector keeps the corner of his eye open for that one culminating fortune, as a man who knows he has the abilities and powers that only he, on earth, possesses. Once he had found her, the world's most beautiful woman, and authenticated her, he could finish.

Yes, that was the prize: once he had found her, he could hear the last word.

5

The assignment was not to verify concupiscence or sexuality, let alone beauty, but longevity.

Our father was sent to authenticate two simultaneous feats, held in tectonic equilibrium against each other, a delicate situation that even he, with the Napoleonic metre bar he laid over life itself, found intriguing.

The first of the feats was the most ordinary imaginable: the world's oldest living woman, the exhaustively-documented and observed Dorothy Ellen O'Oagh, who had just celebrated her quasquicentenary. All our father had to do on that score was to visit her, to watch a doctor apply a stethoscope to her heart as she sat in her electric-powered armchair in her home and ascertain that she was still alive. And then our father would sit and drink a cup of tea with her, or, more precisely, take a few sips and pose answerless questions as Dorothy Ellen O'Oagh slept the sleep of the all-but-dead. Snoring in her chair, she wore a dress with a blue-black floral print, buttoned to her throat. The fact that Mrs O'Oagh always wore a dress, rather than a gown or nightclothes or a hospital garment, never failed to move him. Somebody, a nurse, had dressed her for the day and would change her for the night, as caringly as a child with a doll. It was an act both redundant and absolutely necessary; something about that persistence touched our father in his deepest recesses.

Mrs O'Oagh had not uttered a word to him since he had come to check she was alive on her one hundred and twenty-second birthday, when her eyes had opened and she searched his face with a look of panic and alarm. Her eyes were black, as if with age the pupils had eaten the irises, except for the pale arcs of her cataracts, which reminded him of plastic that had been bent so often it was whitened but not quite broken.

When our father asked her what was wrong, Mrs O'Oagh had burst out: 'Damn it!'

Our father repeated his inquiry.

With a tremor Mrs O'Oagh's head shook on its withered stalk. 'No,' she rattled. 'I wondered if you might be God.'

'God?' he said.

'But you're not, are you?'

He stroked his chin.

'Of course not,' Mrs O'Oagh said, her eyes falling shut again. 'He would not have forgotten me for so long.'

Since then, our father had returned to her chairside each year even though Mrs O'Oagh had not roused from her slumber. He noted her heartbeat, and stayed to finish his cup of tea.

He felt it would be rude to do otherwise.

The second part of the authentication assignment was rather more complex. In Mrs O'Oagh's province, a peculiar legal situation obtained. Under complex local property laws, and by way of lifting the growing geriatric millstone from the neck of the healthcare system, it was possible for a citizen to contract with another to buy her house outright on the day of her death. The vendor, uniformly elderly or terminally ill, would allow the buyer to take out a mortgage on the home, if necessary, and assume the burden of repayments. So the vendor would have her housing costs paid by the buyer, on the understanding that in exchange for the payments the buyer would own the title deed upon the vendor's decease. The result would be that asset-rich, cash-poor elderly people could stay in their homes and not crowd the retirement villages and hospices, the housing economy could be kept ticking over, and the buyer could own the property within an actuarially certified period.

Dorothy Ellen O'Oagh had been approached by a suburban lawyer, one Christos Economopoulos, when she turned eighty-five. Economopoulos, in his late fifties at the time, had expected to pay the mortgage on her twelve-bedroom residence and forty-acre parkland estate for five to ten years before he and his wife could move in, restore it, and enthrone themselves upon it as their family seat and nest egg.

Presumably. Actuarially.

But Mrs O'Oagh was now celebrating the fortieth anniversary of the day the late Christos Economopoulos had signed the deed of transfer.

While Mrs O'Oagh had continued in rude health for those forty years, the Economopoulos family had fallen on harder times. Christos Economopoulos, his nerves ruined by the anxiety brought on by the long wait for Mrs O'Oagh to die, had consoled himself with heavy gambling when he entered his eighties. His wife, under intolerable stress caused by the outflow of funds both to Mr Economopoulos's habit and Mrs O'Oagh's mortgage, had developed an inoperable cancer and died when Mrs O'Oagh was one hundred and six. Mr Economopoulos hanged himself and his broken heart six months later.

Once it was apparent that Mrs O'Oagh had fooled such an astute pair of operators, no local was game to take over the mortgage. Instead it was bequeathed, by default, to Mr Economopoulos's son, Menis, also a lawyer in the same

town. Menis was in his fifties, just as his father had been
when he took over the mortgage. Like his father, Menis
anticipated soon being able to occupy the O'Oagh house,
which was large and perfectly situated by a lake, to restore
it and rebuild it, or perhaps to subdivide and sell off the
land. Menis Economopoulos was a different beast from his
father, though. Whereas Christos Economopoulos had bent
his disappointment inward and punished himself for Mrs
O'Oagh's astonishing longevity—how could he wish for
the death of a helpless and kind-hearted old lady, who had
entered the deal in full expectation that she was going to
get far the wrong end of it?—Economopoulos Junior, Menis,
was a man sliced, diced, seasoned, salted and steeped in
second-generation disappointment. Never having had any
personal relationship with old Mrs O'Oagh, knowing her
only as the sloughed-snakeskin enemy of his late parents'
happiness and the destroyer of their hopes and indeed their
lives, Menis Economopoulos was consumed with rage. He
made no secret of his wish that Mrs O'Oagh should expire
at the earliest possible date, and if not then, at some date
that could be brought forward by human agency.

The O'Oagh estate lay in the centre of a village that had,
in those two-score years, become a medium-sized town.
In normal circumstances, the estate would already have
been consigned to history. On its former grounds would
stand tower blocks, schools, post offices, and perhaps a street

named O'Oagh. The original estate would be a note in the municipal archives. But because of the legal preservation of Mrs O'Oagh's ownership, the estate, and the town that now engulfed it, were held in counterpoise. The forty acres of the lakeside property and the palatial home were preserved as if in amber, waiting for the progress that only death could bring.

History hates a vacuum; as, with history on his side, or so he thought, did Menis Economopoulos. In a town that clung expectantly around such a large and unchangeable estate, with such a famous resident, it was not long before people heard about Menis Economopoulos's desires. He had never uttered any threats against Mrs O'Oagh in person, but in his golf club, in his masonic lodge, in his law society and in his extended family, he was so outspoken in his wish that Dorothy O'Oagh be dead and so intemperate in his rages that an ex parte injunction was taken out against him, as a class action by the membership of the town's local history association, to restrain him from bringing his desires to fruition. He could not be jailed, as the threats had not been direct, but nor had he recanted. Menis Economopoulos, a furious little man eaten by time, by clocks analogue and digital, had ranted about how much he wanted old Ma O'Oagh to pass away. Given his family history, he certainly had a motive. As a lawyer, Menis knew he could not be placed under arrest for merely expressing a wish. But the injunction, granted by the courts and renewed each year, placed him under constant surveillance by law enforcement officers. So likely was it deemed that he would kill Mrs O'Oagh (a likelihood increased by the surveillance itself), that he could not be left to his own devices for as long as the five minutes it would take him to drive to the lakeside house, burst through the front door, charge up the stairs, and stove in her skull, so paper-thin that he would need no more than the wind to blow out the candles on a cake. Or worse: so threatening and hot-blooded was his nature that the local historians and their magistrates thought he need only enter the house and materialise in front of Mrs O'Oagh, in the guise of the angel Lucifer himself, to provoke cardiac arrest and cause her demise without the use of any weapon other than his own mottled pop-eyed visage. And then he could be charged with nothing, not even trespass, as it would be his own house he was breaking into.

The risk was seen as too great, and so Menis Economopoulos was still, in his late seventies, after fifteen years of the angriest mortgage payments ever known, under surveillance.

Our father, as well as annually certifying Mrs O'Oagh's continued life, had the secondary task of authenticating Menis Economopoulos's record of being under the longest temporary restraining order known in human history.

When our father visited Menis Economopoulos, it was always a tricky affair. How politely to certify a curse? Furthermore, a curse brought on Menis by an accident of nature against which there could be no legitimate complaint? Accidental death was an ordinary thing; accidental life, Mrs O'Oagh's in this case, was a rarity, but did it leave any lesser devastation? Our father sympathised with Menis Economopoulos. Molten cores of disappointment hit a certain point inside our father's soul, and he was probably the only person in the town who felt genuinely sorry for the man. There really was no need for a sleeping human to live so long. Even Mrs O'Oagh had acknowledged that, with her disappointment that John Wonder was not an extinguishing and merciful God. Perhaps, our father had said on his first meeting with Menis Economopoulos, the lawyer was the agent of redemption and Mrs O'Oagh would welcome him.

'Exactly!' Economopoulos had yelped, writhing in the fine Chesterfield he occupied, under house arrest, in his study. Like Mrs O'Oagh, as if they were facing off across some empyreal courtroom, Menis also dressed formally each day. In a dark three-piece suit and club tie, he looked ready for a funeral. Menis had a whiskey-bruised voice and a face the colour of almonds, except for the crow's feet that spoked out of the tails of his eyes, wrinkles a poignant white against the brownness of his skin, as if he had done all his smiling in the days when he was out in sunshine. He embraced our father on that first visit, a fellow traveller, a man who understood the epic scale of his frustration, a man who knew the agonies of waiting.

It had occurred to everyone familiar with the case that Menis Economopoulos could execute Mrs O'Oagh by proxy. The likeliest assassins were seen to be his four children, by now adults aged between twenty-six and forty-four. Unable to walk the streets of their town without a veil of suspicion over them, the three eldest had left to make their lives elsewhere. By all reports, they were harmless individuals. The eldest had gone into the law but been disbarred for misappropriation of clients' funds and now worked as a clerk on another continent. He had never married. Nor had the second, who had become a primary school teacher and also lived in a faraway place. The third, a hothead like his father and grandfather, had quit school at fourteen with hopes of becoming a professional football player. He had moved away to the nearest capital city but his career had not progressed beyond a bright apprenticeship cut down by disciplinary infringements and hamstring injuries. He now worked as a personal trainer and Pilates instructor.

When our father visited Menis Economopoulos in his study, on the afternoon of Mrs O'Oagh's one-hundred-and-twenty-fifth birthday, the two men shared their customary glass of whiskey and Dad, pursing his lips and pretending to drink, willing the ice in the glass to dissolve faster and mask his amber shame, invited Menis Economopoulos to update him on news of his family. What else could one talk about in this situation? Discussing the weather seemed too cruel.

As well as the three sons, Menis had a wife, Helenna, who seemed to have been whited-out by the cares and woes of Mrs O'Oagh's duration. It was years since our father had seen Helenna Economopoulos, and he only had Menis's word for it that she was still alive. The woman, in Dad's memory, was so erased by disappointment, as if Dorothy O'Oagh was sucking out her vital juices, that she, Helenna Economopoulos, might well have simply faded away without giving notice.

'Life is nothing but sitting on the shitter without ever squeezing one out,' Menis said, settling into his Chesterfield and his Laphroaig. Unlike his wife, he was a human of boundless determination. His thwarted energy found outlets in his features: a fat rosy mole at the crease of his nostril, the bulge of a subcutaneous cyst on his neck, the spiralling riot of black ear and nose hair, the tumescent strawberry of his nose, the defiant enormity of his ears (should I have those lobes measured? our father sometimes wondered). All of these enlargements seemed direct outgrowths of Menis's imprisonment, his homicidal vigour having nowhere else to go. At seventy-eight he remained as zestful, tanned and toned as he had been at thirty-eight. His family had capitulated around him. He would maintain his rage until the last day.

Which was why he had been under house arrest for so long. It was obvious. Our father wanted to ask him, as they sat there in the dying light of the afternoon, why he didn't just give in like his wife, like his sons, for his own good? But there was no other way for Menis Economopoulos. He could either live on as an untamed threat to a defenceless old lady, or he could perish. Without his anger he was nothing. He loved his house arrest as he loved life itself. Dad's visits, certifying the arrest (he took his annual statements from the local head of police, whose identity had changed, now, six times in the course of the restraining order), were to Menis Economopoulos a badge of honour. His place in the world was defined by the threat he posed to Mrs O'Oagh. He was in all the record books. He had put up framed certificates on his study walls.

After the whiskey, Menis insisted on Dad staying for baklava and koulourakia. They were carried in on a silver salver by Menis's youngest child, Cicada, who was still living in the family home at twenty-six.

Although he had been aware that Menis had a daughter, Dad had never taken any notice of her. He had made a career from not being distracted by pretty girls. Hyper-focused on his task, his attention was monopolised by Menis. From one year to the next, our father would be able to tell you if Menis sported a new wrinkle in his forehead, yet not have registered if the house had been knocked down and rebuilt. Our father's eye, during these visits, was trained upon age, not youth. Menis never referred to the daughter in his family bulletins. Perhaps she was self-evident. Perhaps she was invisible. She certainly had been unseen, for all those years, by our father, who, at best, if he had been asked, would have described her as a rather mousy individual, discreet and shoeless, sliding like a droplet of water in and out of her father's study.

Cicada slipped in with food and drink and a fresh ashtray for her father. She neither spoke to the visitor nor acknowledged him in any way, and Menis Economopoulos did not invite her to.

The extraordinary thing (our father ruminated later, when all he had left was to ruminate) was that Cicada Economopoulos had been coming in and out of her father's study, in her discreet way, blossoming from childhood into womanhood, for so many of these annual visits before our father's eyes opened. Why now? He acknowledged that the change must have occurred in him rather than in her. What was it that year, the year of Dorothy O'Oagh's one hundred and twenty-fifth and Menis Economopoulos's fifteenth in their respective captivities, that had altered in our father, what was it that pulled the scales from his eyes?

There would be an answer to that but it would come to him later. He was not a man who could easily admit that the grail for which he had been searching had been in front of his eyes if not every day, then one day a year. For the moment, as he sat braced in the usual tension between hazy unaccustomed whiskey-filtered contentment and unbearable discomfort while eating sweets in Menis Economopoulos's study, as he went through his usual rigours, ticking boxes on forms both concrete and imagined, as he did what he did in his life, our father opened his eyes to the presence gliding across the room.

She was astonishing.

In profile, her face had the lines of Attic aristocracy, from the wellsprings of classicism: what Plato might have called the ideal form of the female face.

Her hair was the colour of autumn sunshine, emanating its own light, in a knee-trembling contrast with the unbroken olive tones of her skin and the trefoil arches of her black eyebrows.

She walked like a ballet dancer, with poise and grace, her spine immobile over her feet, which, invisible beneath a flounced ankle-length crimson damask skirt, carried her like casters across the carpet. The proud angle at which her head sat on her neck. Nine-tenths of beauty is in posture, our father had read—and, at that moment, *learnt*.

Her form, tight-packed into no more than five feet in height, was some kind of natural miracle, capturing both plenty and slenderness, a fertile figure that was also skin-tight and athletic, rounded yet compact, her secondary sexual characteristics not large but dominating the room, occupying, for that revelatory instant, the entire field of our father's vision.

Not only vision but memory; not only his memory but, somehow, the human race's.

She pivoted, took five sprung dancer's steps and pulled the door behind her with what John Wonder imagined to be a slam. She had not looked at him, he was sure, even though he had not dared look at her. Nobody ever looked at him. But he also felt suddenly sure that the ferocity with which she had ignored him was a heavier form of recognition than any mere look.

She was *superlative*.

Our father's throat was made of sand; he gulped down his watered Laphroaig, flattened the front of his trousers, and stood to take his leave of Menis Economopoulos.

Across the room, as if shaking himself from a dream, his host offered a grimace that John Wonder initially took as a wolfish, disgusting leer, but he soon realised he was only projecting his own shock. The man under the world's longest temporary restraining order, this benighted soul who had lost both of his parents to the cause of life itself, pure life, the unalloyed, uncomplicated continuance of the human heart, was, our father believed, suffering a coronary infarct. Menis Economopoulos was twisting and wriggling, bent back in his armchair, his arms trembling, his whiskey hurling itself against the maddening wall of his glass. Gasps came from over the horizon formed by his upturned throat, his Adam's apple a bulge surging from his stiff collar as if being given birth.

Our father looked around in terror, not so much of Menis dying, or of having to ask himself whether he was equipped to administer mouth-to-mouth resuscitation or CPR on the old lawyer—no, not that, but of having to leave the room and summon the apparition. With this man convulsing in front of him, our father was terrified of having to talk to her.

'Mr Economopoulos!' he let out, shrilly, it seemed to him, in the fluting voice of a young girl.

Menis Economopoulos continued to choke. Had God remembered him, in the end, while still overlooking the ancient fossil up the road? Had God, in His old age, simply grown forgetful? Was Mrs O'Oagh going to outlive yet another generation of Economopouli? Was our father going to be able to certify, by means of personal witness, and measure, to the minute, to the second, the end of the world's longest temporary restraining order?

'Mr Economopoulos? Menis!'

John Wonder's body unbent before the lawyer's. Worry ran out of our father and pooled on the floor around his feet, and for an unnerving moment he could not remember where he had been for the last hour, who he was, or what he had seen. He was adrift, helpless in a strange house in a foreign country, caught in a trap into which he had no idea how he had wandered.

Menis Economopoulos's hairy left hand rose and wiped his eyes. His head assumed the vertical for long enough for him to drain his whiskey, which—telltale sign—had remained, throughout his seizure, in the secure spirit-level grasp of his right hand. Then his head fell back again and the choking sounds resumed.

Our father walked out of the study backwards, almost bowing, like a supplicant or a courtier, to Menis Economopoulos, who continued laughing, laughing as though he could laugh for another hour, revealing the medicine, laughter not rage, that kept him alive; laughter at men, a life force that owed nothing and yet everything to the tragedy of his father and his mother, his sons and his wife, and to the persistence of old Dorothy O'Oagh, laughter at our father above all, as if the old lawyer had been waiting for this inscrutable blank sheet of an official to get the punchline of a prank Menis had been playing on him from the start.

6

As if it had never happened before, it was happening again. As if, each time, he could not remember or recognise the signs and the symptoms. As if he was born anew each time, our father fell.

But not into her arms, or any other cushion that Cicada Economopoulos was equipped to provide. Indeed, he would not see her for another year, three-hundred-and-sixty-five sleepless nights, replaying his vision of Cicada, embroidering the finest detail, flinching from the sting of Menis's laughter, obsessively striving to recall, assess and calibrate her beauty. His yearning would, however, have faded, as it does with time, had it not been mixed with a preservative, which in his case was a crisis of confidence. If he had missed this most central thing, the presence of a defining beauty, for so long, what else was he missing? Was he losing his mind, or, if not his mind, his touch? If he had not been able to authenticate this, was he capable of authenticating anything?

From that date, our father had one year left to give us, a twelve-month pause while the penny dropped.

He came to us, every third week, every second week, every week. To us, his children. His families.

We will be accused of horrors, none of which is greater than our forgiveness of our father. Nobody wishes to believe that such a man as John Wonder, traitor, liar, coward, could have been anything but a monster. We do not deny that, to others, that is how he must seem. A man who keeps separate families is swimming in a sea of untruth, and like a shark he must continue swimming or else he will drown in his own perfidy, suffocate on his own excretions.

But to us he was our father, the only one we had, and he was all we knew about fathers. He was all fathers, and as far as we knew we were the only children he had, and we were, we are, two of us in triplicate. We are all his children, all six of us, and we never had reason to beg for his kindness or his mercy or his reassurance because he gave without being asked. You could never find a more generous father. And we know that by saying this, we will stand condemned. Condemned for the crime of love. Condemned for forgiving him. Yes, while he was the only father we had, he chose not to give us the same exclusivity. But he must have loved us if he wanted to keep reproducing us, mustn't he?

And so when he came to stay with us, for our turn, he talked us to sleep each night with his stories. In the morning he dressed us and made us breakfast and played with us. He made the sandwiches and baked the cakes for our birthday parties. He drove us, kissed us, and picked us up again in the afternoon. When he had time free, he would do a load of washing and clean the house for our mother, whichever she was. He did not simply talk the talk of modern fatherhood. In truth, he did not talk the talk at all. He *did*. He helped us with our homework and our projects, he taught us to swim and to play sports, he made sure our little friends did not come to grief when they visited our house, he drove us to our extracurricular lessons and activities, and when we hurt ourselves we would scream and cry not *Mummy*, but *Daddy*. His depthless blue eyes would crinkle up and drink away our pain, and we would curl into his scentless arms.

He never lost his temper; he never had a temper to lose.

You will think we are idealising him. This is what neglected, betrayed children do, is it not? They remember only the outbursts of good in their parents, not the routines of bad. And perhaps there is some truth in that: because our week with our father was a treat, because it was rationed out, because it was never ironed flat by habit, our time with him remains special in our memories, it keeps its outlines. But even so, he was a good father in every way that he could be. Remember too that it was a trebled routine for him: he was also a good father to the others, committing himself to different stages of development, each of them overlapping, so that he was living all of young life at once. He transported his kindness and generosity as if they were thriving on the host body of his terrible guilt and loneliness; he took them all with him.

It was necessary, also, for him to be a good father because of our mothers; and let us talk here of our first mother—Sandra—with the thick glasses and the long rope of dark-blonde hair, the broad beam and the fair skin. Our mother Sandy was a doctor, but no ordinary doctor. She worked in research, studying paediatric oncology: childhood cancer. She went every day to a university laboratory where she battled the tumours that ate children. She had won a university medal in medicine, just as she had been the dux of her school and the winner of every scholarship and prize she had ever been eligible for. Her parents, a couple who had owned a home-building company, had both passed away from asbestos-related lung disease when Sandy was in her teens. Self-reliant and academically brilliant, she had been raised by boarding-school mistresses. Neglected as a child, our mother Sandy had found a redemptive calling: to save all children. We understood intuitively that we were the children of a very important mother, a mother of multitudes.

We had to share her. When our father wasn't around, we were raised, largely, by nannies. 'It never did me any harm,' our mother Sandy said, her true meaning impenetrable. And so, when our father returned home, he could never pretend he was not needed.

The difficult times for them must have been social, the rare occasions when we were together as a family among normal families. We remember school concerts and barbecues—easy to recall because so rare—when both of our parents were there and our family was, for the moment, a table with four corners. As children, we scampered about with our friends. We were as adaptable as water, flowing into the spaces, while for our parents, these must have been times of stiff self-consciousness. Inconspicuously, Sandy slaughtered bottles of white wine, glancing impatiently at our father's ever-full cup. They stood at the class picnics, off to one side, clutching their plates, our mother smiling and nodding and trying with all her might to fit in, our father summoning the chameleonic energy to disappear against the background.

Inevitably, some Samaritan souls viewed social awkwardness as an invitation to do good, and there was one mother at our primary school, Linda de Lisle, who took it upon herself to draw our parents in. *And what is it you do? And your husband? Oh, what an exciting life you both lead! No wonder you're so busy! Come over here and let me introduce you to the others . . .*

With the thrusting blondeness of the once-pretty, Linda de Lisle tried her best to force the square pegs of our parents into the round hole of the social circle, with the same willpower that she forced herself into her size-ten dress. While our now quite drunk mother entered the spirit of forced conviviality and our father edged silently again to the margins, helpless against his own entropic shyness, Linda de Lisle moved on to other conquests. She had a reputation as a 'helicopter mother', hovering around the schoolyard each morning, unable to fly away, and she loved to be one of the kids. Even we recognised the tragedy: she missed being our age. She was the type of adult all children loved, until they turned thirteen. At this particular picnic, she saw us gathered near a statue, which we were using as bar in our chasings game.

'So, kids,' Linda de Lisle said sunnily, 'do you know who this is?'

Because we were still little and she was a parent, we had to listen to Linda de Lisle's Let's-make-history-fun! lecture about the bronze man in the tricorn hat. She glazed our eyes with dates and events. We were wriggling with impatience, wondering how to get away from a parent who makes history *so cool*. But it was our father who released us.

We, only us two, Adam and Evie, saw it coming. Having detached himself from the group of parents, he had been standing alone until Linda de Lisle's twitter of facts, wars, personages and historical timelines drew him like a moth to a flame. He didn't want to talk to Linda de Lisle, let alone make an enemy of her. Being noticed was, to him, a social death worse than social death! But when it came to trivia, he could not help himself. He was powerless against the magnetic force of Linda de Lisle's lecture. Once she had reached the end of tricorn hat's career, our father was by her shoulder, chewing his lip furiously, his paper plate trembling in his hand.

'Fascinating, isn't it?' Linda de Lisle beamed at him, welcoming an ally in the struggle to improve the children's general knowledge.

'And even more fascinating when it is accurate,' our father said. His foggy voice seemed to be coming not from him but from the statue.

'Oh yes?' Linda de Lisle said, her smile intensifying ominously.

Our father proceeded to rattle off a string of corrections. Linda de Lisle had been wrong, wrong, wrong. We could see he was trying to do it pleasantly, but there is no such thing as courteous humiliation. A flush rose on Linda de Lisle's chest. Her grin grew so broad it crackled. Once she fell silent, the kids, who didn't really know our father, ran off and played again, leaving just Linda de Lisle and our father, and us two, loyally waiting for him to get to the bitter end.

'And so he died, a heroic pauper,' our father concluded. 'Truth is always stranger than fiction, wouldn't you say?'

This was the last straw for poor Linda de Lisle, who replied to us, 'So nice to see your father show up,' and tottered back to the security of the adults.

Oh no, our father was not good socially. Because accuracy meant so much more to him than politeness, he had just sabotaged his goal of remaining invisible. He had made a nemesis. The episode formed a turning point in the attitude of other parents towards ours. Until then, Linda de Lisle had held her views of Mum and Dad in tolerant abeyance, but now she was ready to pounce. Fuelled by the humiliation our father had visited upon her, Linda de Lisle spread poisonous gossip and ruthless assessment. When parents want to judge each other, they redirect to the children, their children, your children, and condemn vicariously under the cloak of concern. 'You have to feel sorry for the kids,' Linda de Lisle said. Sandy was not a bad mother because she led an important field of medical research; but she was a bad mother because her poor children were picked up by their nanny. The father was not a bad father because he was away so often; but his absences explained and defined the slightest trouble his children got into, hints of learning difficulties, talk of playground stoushes. Never mind that Adam and Evie showed no sign of deprivation or neglect. That would come, that would come. 'The resentment is there,' Linda de Lisle pronounced, 'it's a time bomb that will blow up when they're teenagers.' For now, the burden of our coming resentment had to be carried by the piteous premonitions of our friends' parents.

And behind his back, because he was so awkward and gave so little information about what it was he did—in truth, he was too used to the punishment of being questioned, by patronising adults, about their own investigations into *trivia*, so he preferred to say as little as possible, to make himself a reflective surface—because he had left a vacuum waiting to be filled, and because his irresistible need to correct the record had given Linda de Lisle an opening, she began a rumour, not maliciously but with 'the best of intentions', that 'the Wonder man' was a low-life of some kind, a private investigator, a double agent, a spook for some unsavoury foreign government, even, she ventured, a 'hitman'.

That also suited the other parents. They needed some intrigue in their lives. At their tight little school-parent dinner parties and barbecues, to which our parents were no longer invited, the subject of Sandy and John Wonder was soon a gushing well for entertainment and speculation. But it was his fault. He shouldn't have humiliated Linda de Lisle at the statue, and he shouldn't have been surprised if the other parents turned on him. 'A foreign spy,' they nudged and winked with smug television-fed worldliness, 'is not a man in dark sunglasses and a fedora. A spy is an invisible man, impossible to remember, the blandest of the bland.' And the other parents could not possibly disagree, because at that moment, when they tried to picture John Wonder, they could not remember what he looked like.

We heard Sandy and our father argue, late in the night he turned Linda de Lisle into his foe. The sound of raised voices was so rare in our house, we crept out of our room and crowded at their bedroom door. Sandy's tone as she spoke to him was more pleading than berating.

'Why?' she asked. 'Why couldn't you let it go?'

'Because what she said was incorrect.'

Our father's voice was not, in fact, raised. Whenever he was tense or angry, he spoke flatter, like a threatened echidna balling up with its spikes outward.

'Do you not realise, John? Do you not understand that when you speak like that to other parents, it has consequences?'

'The only consequence was that the children were being misinformed by that woman, but after I spoke to them, they knew the truth.'

'Oh, you drive me crazy sometimes! How can you say you do things like this for the children, when it's the children who end up as outsiders because all these people begin gossiping about their father?'

There was a long silence after this. Our parents were moving around in their room, probably preparing for bed. When they next spoke they were further away and quieter, and their voices bounced off the ceiling, so they must have been lying down. We were ready to go to bed when our father spoke.

'Still, what that woman said was absolutely wrong.'

Our mother made a noisy sigh. 'Don't you see that in these parents' groups, there has to be some yielding, some give and take?'

'The facts do not yield. The facts do not give and take.' His voice was so low it was almost underground.

'Oh darling, I'm not talking about the facts.'

Her words were still contesting him, but her tone was giving up. We waited a long time for our father to speak again. An argument between our parents was exciting! But there was only silence, and eventually the absence of words and then a stifled female giggling drove us back to our room.

•

The surface of John Wonder's life, at this point when he was old enough to be looking with less concern at what he might achieve and more at what he might lose, could be said to resemble the surface of the planet Earth. His domestic life, once a single land mass, had broken into continents which drifted apart.

Between them was ocean, flowing continuously and keeping each of the continents unknown to each other. This ocean was his work.

Water and earth, incompatible substances, knowing nothing about each other.

To the people he worked with in his offices and met with in their search for authentication, his private life was even more mysterious than the term 'private life' implies and conceals. His colleagues and associates knew nothing of his family, or families. Some said he had a wife and many children. Some said he was a hermit, a bachelor. Some said he was a hermit and a bachelor but also a sexual deviant who travelled to poor countries once a year and committed unspeakable acts, an ascetic's purgative. Some said he lived, monk-like, in the hotels and airports that were the connective tissue of his professional life, that he had no home, no place of residence.

Three homes, or none—was there any difference?

'Some said'? Most said nothing. Our father had a life, he had three of them. He went to restaurants and frequented cafes. When he went to the counter of a shop, he was ignored, the last to be seen. He would stand at a counter and place his order. When he went back to check why his order had not arrived, the staff looked at him as if they had never seen him in their lives. Even when he went to the same place every day for a week, the staff still didn't remember him. He was perfectly—immaculately—forgettable.

And just as the life of birds in the treetops is a mystery to the fish in the sea, to us on the land masses the ocean was a frightening enigma. We have spoken of his work as 'Authenticator' with a hint of deeper knowledge, but the hint is all we had. In truth, we didn't know what our father did. This is not unusual for children. When we were first confronted with school or holiday camp administrative forms where we had to fill out a line relating to 'Father's profession', like most of our schoolmates we suffered the kind of panic that leads to improvisation. Once, in copying the answer of a neighbour child, we wrote 'Accountant'. Another time, because we heard of a word that was a catch-all to cover any work that didn't have a name of its own, we wrote 'Consultant'. That sufficed until the day we found one of our father's business cards. It had his name, a column of phone and fax numbers and email addresses, and a business name. The business name was Norris McWhirter and Associates. Norris was a man we had heard of, who had some important connection at work with our father. When we asked our father what all of this meant, he smiled and patted our heads and indicated the card and said, 'See that? That's me.'

And so for father's profession on those forms we would write 'Associates'.

This phenomenon, of not knowing what a man does for a living, is not confined to children. Unless someone is a doctor or schoolteacher or bricklayer or house painter or garbage collector or tailor, often lifelong friends have no real idea about each other's job title, let alone what keeps them getting out of bed (or keeps them in bed) each day. None of us knows much about what our friends do when they start their working day, who they call, who they meet with, what they produce, who they help, what wheels they grease. Even less how they do it. We are islands of mystery to those who love us.

But what was most unusual about our father was that, buffeted by the crisis of confidence and unappeasable longing that had engulfed him since the day he last saw Cicada Economopoulos, even *he* knew less and less about the thing that he did for his work. He was Authenticator-in-Chief, but of what, and for whom?

In the beginning he had worked for *The Guinness Book of World Records,* having come to their notice as a kind of child-prodigy record freak, if not a record holder, himself. In those days the book was collated by English twins, Norris and Ross McWhirter, Cambridge graduates who had been given the task by the Guinness brewing company because of their own encyclopaedic knowledge of sporting records. As the book grew it attracted a kind of cult of application, and its main editorial task became to distinguish between two types of human hope, the *Guinness*-worthy and -unworthy. On the fringes of this behaviour, and as a kind of meta-*Guinness*, were readers, mostly young boys, such as our father, who were not interested in setting records but in overseeing their integrity. This oversight was initially the preserve of the McWhirters themselves, but when Ross was killed by an IRA bomb and Norris became swamped by management duties, standards began to slip, not only in the liberalisation of the notion of *Guinness*-worthiness (throwing phone books, growing fingernails, throwing the book itself) but in the grammar, style, typography and punctuation of the production. In his capacity as a rather avid twelve-year-old, our father had submitted a sixty-seven-page catalogue of errors personally to Norris McWhirter, to which the chief compiler replied in a handwritten letter and which errors, to our father's prideful astonishment, were corrected in the book's next edition. Encouraged, our father repeated his exercise with each new issue of *The Guinness Book of World Records*, and became a kind of adjunct teenage subeditor, working purely for the pleasure of correcting error, his relationship not with the organisation but with McWhirter personally.

When John Wonder turned eighteen, McWhirter asked if he would like to come into the offices and work as an unpaid intern. John was not seen for dust. When he finished secondary school he was given a subeditor's position. He rose through the ranks to become the direct personal assistant and adviser to the Keeper of the Records, as McWhirter was styled.

This was the position John Wonder held when he met Sandy, a medical student in a carapace of thick lenses, defiant brilliance and world-changing work. Throughout, long after she had lost interest in the minutiae or even the maxitiae of his work, she thought he still worked for *Guinness,* as McWhirter's successor as Keeper of the Records or some equivalent entity.

But he did not. In the 1980s McWhirter had become disillusioned with the freak-show illustration-heavy tendencies of *Guinness.* His first 1955 edition of the book had opened with Everest, the world's highest mountain. That was the kind of permanent memorial to which McWhirter's soul cleaved. By the 1980s the book was opening with the world's largest breast implants, and McWhirter was off, to tilt at his own windmills, more 'purist' versions of a book of records such as *McWhirter's Book of Superlatives* and *The Book,* simply, *of Records.* As his relationship with our father had always been personal first, almost paternal, McWhirter took him into his new ventures. It was while working as Chief Superlative Officer for the McWhirter breakaway group that our father met his second wife, the darker woman in the smaller house.

The McWhirter splinters, founded in a spirit of purist text in an age of heretical illustration, inevitably failed. McWhirter retired and died, but our father's skills were of such unique value that every challenger to *Guinness* knew of him and made him the first man hired. He was the culture carrier for every fundamentalist assault on *Guinness* and its trashiness. He worked on record books which were published by companies that were bought and sold, bought and sold, until he grew indifferent to whom he was authenticating for. Amid so much reorganisation and restructuring, his actual job had an unchanging priestliness. Just as, when he was the Keeper of the Records for *Guinness*, his role was to oversee record attempts, lay down the rules of integrity and authenticate the results, his role in successor bodies, be they cyclopaedias, books of lists, books of firsts and lasts and in-betweens, almanacs and compendia and miscellanies and, eventually, online encyclicals, remained essentially the same. The nature of the facts he was authenticating changed, generally in the direction of the bizarre and the gross that were thought to be the key interests of the teen and preteen boys who subscribed to such publications—the ultimate irony was that every purist, text-based, old-school, nostalgic venture he ever signed up to had ended up, after high initial hopes, chasing the same lowest-common-denominator sensations as *Guinness*, due, of course, to the iron fact of the western world that the type of adolescent male who craved fundamentalist texts was not the type who was buying *Guinness*—but his role as Authenticator was perfectly static. When he met his third wife, the scarred woman with the special-needs children, our father was Authenticator-in-Chief for an online project, named The Last Word, that was so clandestine that not even he knew who was behind it. Some said The Last Word was a massively-funded project that would supersede both Wikipedia and Google. Others said that it was far more ambitious: it was an attempt at an Encyclopaedia of Everything, of all human knowledge, and it was already employing thousands of Authenticators of which our father was just the most experienced and top-rung, each working in independent 'cells' unknown to each other and financed by a cartel of software tycoons, bankers, media barons and mafia bosses. The Last Word was certainly, judging by the offices, better funded than other breakaway groups our father had worked for. But its ownership and aims were only rumours. The scarred woman, if asked what her husband did, said he was 'a kind of fact-checking guy for like Wikipedia or something, but don't ask me any more'. And nobody did.

As for our father himself, it had been years since he had ceased caring who he worked for. As long as his fortnightly salary payments appeared in his account, enabling him to undertake the byzantine task of secreting the proceeds into three different banks and pay the bills for three different households with watertight privacy, he was content not to ask questions. He had enough going on without worrying about who he was working for. The final product, be it The Last Word or whatever came after it, was decreasingly a part of his consciousness. What he worked for was a set of values: memory, trustworthiness, authority. He was the greatest expert in trivia the world had known, the heir to Norris McWhirter. Even *Guinness* acknowledged that; *Guinness* had an entry on him. But he was a secretive individual whom few, outside the confines of the trivia industry, had heard of. He could have made himself a millionaire several times over if he had played television quiz shows. But he preferred the shadows. Without suspecting what motivated him to shun the limelight, his employers and colleagues ascribed to him the most generous interpretation. They said he lived not for personal aggrandisement but for the facts themselves. He resisted lucre because he bowed to eternal values, they surmised. To a degree they were correct, but only to a degree.

He had another prime motivation. He was so trusted he had no direct boss. He prowled the world from one authentication to another, a lone wolf. He would receive an assignment and his travel papers, go off and execute his task, and report to one of his employer's standardised global headquarters. He never failed in the diligent completion of his duties. And the price of this, or the reward, was that he did indeed live, as those workmates guessed, in a rootless world of hotels and airports and places of transit, except that there was something that could never be accounted for, tallied up or authenticated in this arrangement.

Which brings us, brings *him*, back to Cicada Economopoulos.

7

In the three hundred and sixty-five days of Dorothy Ellen O'Oagh's one hundred and twenty-sixth year, three hundred and sixty-five days of Menis Economopoulos's continuing confinement under the increasingly lackadaisical surveillance of his municipal police department, a new chunk had broken away from our father's three continents of domesticity. He became convinced, during that year of rumination, that the superlative young woman he had seen in Menis's study merited some kind of pedestal in the compendia of universal fact over which he was the lord and master and humble recorder. Most Beautiful Woman on Earth did not quite specify it. For one, he was not so besotted as to be blind to the subjectivity, and hence controversy, in such a claim.

To record Cicada as the Most Beautiful Woman on Earth would bring unwanted scrutiny both to John and the girl. And besides, there was something crass in the claim. Wasn't the very currency of popular culture, of Hollywood and gossip magazines and television and everything, a kind of street brawl over the Most Beautiful Woman on Earth? By staking such a claim for Cicada, he would be lowering her beneath her dignity.

Already he was thinking—not thinking, but in some purring workings beneath the thinking self—less of recording than of possessing.

As the date approached for his return to her home town (formerly the home town of Mrs O'Oagh and Mr Economopoulos, but now indisputably the home town of the hermitic daughter), our father grew agitated. He had to make some sort of direct personal approach, but how? To broach the subject with Menis Economopoulos was inconceivable. The man's great gouts of laughter the previous year contained as much murderous threat as merriment. To ask Menis, *May I have a moment alone with your daughter?* was to risk not only expulsion from the house and a refusal of access to one of the world's most fascinating records, but also physical harm. If Menis couldn't take out his ancestral pain on Dorothy O'Oagh, perhaps he would find the pale, unprepossessing, middle-aged form of John Wonder an irresistible substitute. And John wouldn't get the girl.

As John Wonder was a man of little constructive imagin-ation, a man of fact and veracity rather than of hope and dream, he was stumped. He could not force his way covertly into the Economopoulos house. What, if he managed a break-in, would he say to her? Nor could he see how he could steal away during his interview with Menis for an unsanctioned word with her. (Again, what exactly would he say? Where to start?) He had too much on his mind. And so, like a mouse in a wheel, he was trapped inside his energy. During the last month before his return to Mrs O'Oagh and Mr Economopoulos, our father was even more reserved than usual. A part had, truly, split off inside him and he did not know whether to hold onto it or let it go.

When he travelled to the town where Mrs O'Oagh and Mr Economopoulos lived, our father chose to stay, as always if he could manage it, in the most anonymous commercial hotel. The more generic, the better. Such places were the pathetic fallacy of his self-image. Ensconced in a hotel chain that travestied the word 'Inn'—a Holiday, a Quality, a Comfort, a Travellers'—he could vanish against the background of the wallpaper, make himself indistinguishable from the bathroom tiles and the watercolour prints. There he could breathe.

He checked into the Holiday Inn the night before his prearranged interviews with Mrs O'Oagh and Mr Economopoulos. Usually he would arrive on the anniversary morning. This time he took an extra night to stabilise himself.

Every other year, he was nowhere more comfortable than on his own, reading a biography or watching television, in such a hotel room, leaving no trace. This time, this long insomniac evening, he needed to go out.

If there was one thing John Wonder was less likely to do than drink alcohol, it was drink alcohol on his own. He had lost his taste for the stuff when, as a teenager, he had experienced drunkenness with systematic meticulousness. He had measured alcohol by volume against price per litre and, with two school friends, found an optimally corrosive and cheap rum, secured four bottles, and then become delirious with laughter, prone with vomiting and, finally, comatose, within the space of half an hour. Once he had done that, he had alcohol pretty much figured out. Though he continued to have a drink—one drink—in social situations where it suited his overriding imperative of anonymity, he had never, since the age of sixteen, been drunk. As he only ever had a drink to fit in, there was no need when he was alone.

But this night, unable to sleep, he needed a circuit-breaker. The Holiday Inn receptionist, a young adult male with a factory-made beard, told him that by happy coincidence the only bar in the vicinity that remained open at this late hour was in the Holiday Inn itself. The bar's piped neon sign proclaimed it the Lakeshore, though its aluminium-cased windows faced away from the water and towards the copse of firs behind the O'Oagh mansion.

Wearing a business shirt buttoned at the wrists and suit trousers, our father conducted himself gamely to an automated glass door, which slid open. The Lakeshore beckoned. Seeing nobody inside, he lurched to the bar and asked for the lightest of the available low-alcohol beers. The barman, the same featureless boy who had hovered in from the reception desk, made a great fuss of pouring it from the tap, emptying it several times in an elaborate quest for perfection. Dad noticed that the fellow did not have much else, except touching his beard, to occupy him.

Settling onto a bar stool, our father dared to look around. The Lakeshore was as generic as the rest of the hotel. The light was both uncomfortably dim and too bright: too low to read by, not low enough to hide in. The seats, varnished cane enclosing panels of turquoise leatherette, clustered around circular glass-topped tables. Tall laminated cocktail menus stood at attention among perspex salt and pepper shakers. The carpet was the same as throughout the public areas of the hotel, indeed probably the same as in every Holiday Inn, a design he had once heard described as 'technicolour yawn'.

There were no patrons at the tables.

Along the bar, previously concealed by a mirrored concrete pillar, a man in his forties with wavy brown hair drank a glass of red wine and watched the wall-mounted football game in the corner of the bar above Dad's head. As the man's face was unavoidably turned towards him, Dad blinkered the corners of his vision. The last thing he wanted was eye contact.

In the nervy blur of his first glance, our father had missed another few patrons. Beyond the wavy-haired man, voices, male and female, mingled beneath the jukebox's low pulse. Dad could not risk looking towards these other people—too great a chance of collaterally engaging the wavy-haired man—but he guessed that there were six or seven men and maybe two women. Young, yet old enough to have shades of grey in their hair and laughter barked raw by use. No matter how much he drank, there was not enough low-alcohol beer in the town to persuade him that he and they were of the same species. He regretted being in this bar so intensely that his heart ached, but he considered that to swig down his beer or, worse, to leave it undrunk would attract more attention than he wished. Like a Martian trained to impersonate a human, he was a stickler for normal behaviour. So he set himself to drink in even sips over a period of eight to ten minutes, the world average for the public male consumption of three hundred and seventy-five millilitres of light beer.

'Smell anything?'

Our father was two hundred and twenty-five millilitres of the way through his beverage. Oh, why did he have to present himself to the world as such a planetary loneliness, drawing lighter bodies towards him with a gravitational ineluctability?

Why did there have to *be* other people? he thought, possibly the most frequently asked mental question he had posed himself since the age of eight. Why did there have to be solitary drinkers with wavy hair who were not, in the end, solitaries but rather confessions brimming to be made?

Our father could not ignore the man, who had bounced along four bar stools like a frog coming at him one lilypad at a time. Our father lived on the line of least resistance. His nose made a polite pretense of sniffing. 'No, sorry, nothing.'

He could not bring himself to look at the man. He stole a peek into the mirror behind the bar, between the modestly stocked liquor shelves. There, piercingly, were the wavy-haired man's eyes.

Dad looked down into his beer.

'You know, I can't either,' said the wavy-haired man, exposing himself thereby as a patron who was not here for inquiry but for exposition. He proceeded to tell our father that the appeal of Holiday Inns was that they did not smell of anything aside from nylon and, periodically, cleaning products. 'Ozone,' he said as if answering a question. 'They pump them with ozone to make us feel at home.'

'You live in ozone?' The pause in the man's monologue was quicksand, sucking our father in.

The man laughed, running a hand through his wave. He wore a thick wedding ring. His laugh had an ugly triumphalism, as if having drawn Dad into the conversation was a win for him, a loss for Dad.

'Both metaphorically and literally,' the man declaimed, before pausing. 'You know what they mean? I mean, those words?'

Dad nodded pliantly, surrendering to the inescapable bond of autodidact literacy.

'Places, you see, are like bodies. They have a smell of their own. Oh yeah, sure, I know you're thinking; of course, India smells like garbage, Mexico smells like adobe, England smells like soot, the USA smells like treated pine. Romania—ever been to Romania? Smells like shit.'

'No. I was not thinking—'

'Don't argue, you know it's true. I've been everywhere and I've been making a study of it. Every country has its own smell and every city within that country, every town, every house, every open square of space, has an absolutely unique unreproducible scent. Did you know that? I've actually tested it out. New Zealand smells like mud, but there are places in New Zealand that smell like clay mud and others that smell like volcanic mud—obviously Rotorua, but that's not what I'm meaning. Some places smell like jade mud and another place in the same town is going to smell like jade mud with a hint of male BO and a dash of lime. And the incredible thing is, you know—'

'They are all different?' Dad said, taking a long and, he hoped, conclusive double-draught of his light beer.

'Well, yeah,' the wavy-haired man said, and with a flick of his finger beckoned the barman to bring another. The man was drinking something that smelt to Dad like the eighty-six per cent proof rum he had titrated into his bloodstream forty years ago. His head was ruddy and meaty, the superannuated pretty-boy features hemmed in by the encircling flesh, as if his future were chasing his past down a hole in the middle of his face. But when they look in the mirror, the sociable see what they want to see, what they remember: this man would see the coppery pomp of that splendid wave breaking across his forehead and his memory would be sparked by his long, fair, feminine eyelashes, which some girl had once scorched his soul by pronouncing beautiful. People's one true marriage is to themselves, and this man's life partner would forever see him as a twenty-one-year-old.

'But no!' the man continued, as if to catch himself out in a debating misstep. He was playing both hands of a conversational card game, our father the croupier. 'The incredible thing is, like I said before—you gotta listen, you know?'

He waited until Dad acknowledged him with a nod: yes, you have to listen.

'The incredible thing is, like I said before, places are like bodies. They all have their own smell but the one that you can't smell is your own. You ever noticed that? Your own body odour is so familiar to you that you can't smell it. And so, my friend, this is the only way you know you're at home.

You know you're at home because you can't smell the place you're in.'

Dad politely drank the first third of his light beer, then let out a burp redolent of the room service chicken tikka he had regrettably ordered two hours earlier.

Covering his mouth with his hand, he said: 'I beg your pardon.'

'No need to beg for it, my friend. Consider yourself pardoned. Tom Dews.'

He introduced himself with a nod rather than a proffered hand.

'John Wonder.'

'Dews and Wonder.' The wavy-haired man nodded approvingly. 'I can see our shingle on the wall. Or on a billboard, eh!'

Dad said: 'Wonder and Dews, I think it would be.'

And he gave a little chuckle at his pun before considering whether it might not be a little too obscure even for a man who knew the words 'metaphorically' and 'literally'.

A cloud came over Tom Dews's slightly battered face, which Dad was looking at in the mirror behind the bottles. Dews said, challengingly: 'So, John, you reckon you should be first cab off the rank in our little operation, eh?'

Dews threw an arm out towards Dad, who ducked, but to show that he meant no harm, didn't take it personally, Dews was throwing his arm around Dad's neck and hauling him into a headlock-cum-hug that felt every bit as ambiguously friendly-yet-menacing as, Dad sensed, it was intended.

'So I guess that means because I can't smell anything here,' Dews said, 'I must be at home. Holiday Inn, your home away from home!'

Dews laughed, and Dad joined palely in. He desired only to get out of the Lakeshore in one piece. The price of that desire was to condemn himself to Tom Dews for two rounds of drinks.

Having divested himself of his opening monologue, Dews moved back onto surer ground, telling our father his life story, unbidden. He was twice divorced 'and on the brink of my third', with six children. Thinking, *Three wives, six children*, Dad furiously steered his mind away from common ground. Dews said he was in town selling pharmaceutical products to hospitals and general practitioners. Dad wondered if he was the man who provided life-prolonging drugs to Dorothy Ellen O'Oagh. Dad wondered if Tom Dews knew he might be keeping Mrs O'Oagh alive, unknowingly stumbling, by virtue of a cocktail of medications for the extremely geriatric, on an elixir of eternal life, and thereby helping to set two world records. Dad wondered if, should he tell Tom Dews this, the man would embrace him or hit him. Why would he hit him? Why not fall at his feet in astonishment and celebrate the Eureka moment with the most expensive drink on the laminated menu, and then pull out the contacts book that

Dad was sure was warping the seat of Tom Dews's chinos and begin to map out the business plan, titled 'How to make a killing out of eternal life'? Why not? But our father was too scared to speak. The prospect loomed over Dad, in his profound innocence of the world of humans, particularly of thrice-unhappily-married travelling salesmen, that Tom Dews had reached a stage of intoxication where his only reaction to any kind of shock, whatever its nature, would be to lash out with his XXL fists.

'So what do you do, Johnny?'

Dews was ordering two more beers, even though Dad had barely started his second. Dad tried to stop him, but Dews misunderstood.

'No, no, man, I won't let you pay, it's my thanks to you for letting me bore you for so long. The least I can do. Unless you tell me you're in the health industry. Then you're picking up the tab!'

Dad shook his head. He had always resisted telling adults what he did for a living. It went beyond the school parents. Adults in general could not take seriously, to the point of refusing to understand, his explanation of what he did. Children he could tell. Children loved to know. He loved to tell children. But adults had outgrown the ability to comprehend the existence of an Authenticator of the world's outer limits. For children, The Last Word was most natural; for adults, it was a childish fantasy.

'I represent a publishing company,' our father said concisely. In all conversation, he spoke in the way that a fastidious dresser clothes himself: not a wasted syllable, not a single error in grammar or syntax. He might have seen his mode of speech as distinguished, or elegant, a matter for pride, but in the real world, his verbal pedantry had the effect of doubling the erasure already begun by his odourlessness, his immaculate beigeness.

Tom Dews, who had tuned out, was looking to the other end of the bar. Having played his opening hands—the quirky observation, the potted history, the pro forma but uninterested inquiry—Dews then cut to the chase and talked of his real subject, which was, in his word, 'pussy'. Tom Dews on pussy was something of a blend of Tom Dews on places and their unique smells, and Tom Dews on Tom Dews. Our father switched into his default mode (and how well we knew it) of outward attentiveness and inward drift.

Although he lived very much like a travelling salesman, and indeed among them, and although commercial travellers would have understood the soul of our father better than anyone if he had only let them have a glimpse, his desires and instincts were as far as can be imagined from those of the knight of the road. He thought about what Tom Dews had said about smells and home. Dad, as we knew, had no scent. Did that mean that when we couldn't smell him, we were in a kind of home of our own? Were we absorbed into his scentless familiarity, and if so, where were we when he was away from us? Homeless?

Or (he wondered) did it mean that home, and one's own body, was a kind of sensory death? When you can smell nothing, and by extension hear, see, feel and taste nothing, is that not death itself? Or is it a transition, a forestalling of death? Somewhere in Dorothy Ellen O'Oagh's desiccated shell, was she travelling at such a speed that she could see, smell, taste, feel and hear nothing, thereby keeping death at bay? Was she sprinting from death, or to it? Or was she the opposite—standing so still that death had run past without seeing her? Was utter nullness her secret?

As Tom Dews rambled through his remembrance of pussy past, it struck our father that he and the salesman, both as types and as individuals, were polar opposites on the question of change; that is, on the matter of life and death. The salesman restlessly and relentlessly wanted transience. In the way he spoke of women (in the way he started to glance predatorily over his shoulder, away from our father, to the other end of the bar, where the laughter of the two or three women was rising), Tom Dews was making it clear that his position was a desire for transience and nothing else, the disposable body without any lingering connection, either emotional or physiological or (God forbid) pathological. Tom Dews, in short, was only interested in what he could use up and leave behind. Our father, by a contrast so complete that it struck him, in his creeping tiddliness, as earth-shattering, was only interested in what he could come back to. He had thought, in spite of himself, that Tom Dews's monologue on the scentless self-projection of the ozoned Holiday Inn was an expression of camaraderie, for didn't Dad himself love Holiday Inns because they were the acme of nowhere and nothing? But now he saw that he and Dews were opposites: Dews was chasing transience, self-erasure, death, while Dad was chasing the ever-more-elusive vanishing point, reproducible life: home.

He was tempted, in the spirit of the moment, to interrupt Dews and expound his own theory of change and scent and life and death and transience and permanence—the story, in other words, of how one man can be married three times consecutively and another man three times concurrently. But he was not so squiffy as to have lost his restraint and his lock-hold over his secret. So he kept his silence, nodded along, and relished his own counsel.

Change! What better expert on change, the need for change, in the human soul than John Wonder!

Our father's soul was split into two perfectly twinned parts, in equipoise. One part resisted change implacably, and the other part craved it with a megalomaniacal force. The cocoon part of him was in thrall to changelessness: his work never altering, the processes engraved in stone, the constant comfort of never having to wonder where his next dollar was coming from. The more rapidly the world he worked in changed, the more tightly he was wedded to stasis. When he looked around him he saw a corrosive demand for entrepreneurialism. Lawyers could no longer read and write contracts and offer advice, but had to conjure new business. Publishers could no longer read and edit books; their livelihood hinged on discovering and selling new ones, without editing or reading them much at all, unless unpaid and on their own time. Academics had to forget about teaching and researching, and instead sing for their supper as fundraisers. All branches of working life, it seemed, were infected by the virus of business development. To a man such as our father, a born technician, the very idea of salesmanship terrified and revolted him. His work was a bastion of assurance, none of his income 'at risk'. He performed tasks, he received money, he was left alone. In the end, that was all it needed to boil down to. And beyond that it granted him something more existential: because he no longer knew who he was working for and *for what* he was authenticating, because he was as invisible as he was essential, he needed some reassurance that he existed, and that reassurance came in the form of an absence, for his job, and let's get down to the bottom line here, offered a temporary exemption from the fear of being exposed as a fake. This plague-like terror, from what he could see, had spread to anyone who had achieved anything at all of any magnitude: they were all scared they would be shown up as a fraud. He knew this because it was largely his job to try to show them up. To debunk as much as to—what was the antonym?—to bunk? He was the man who brought down imposters, and in this capacity he had intimate acquaintance with the fears of imposture. It was a horrible thing and it ruined lives, it shattered sleep, it destroyed conscience.

So it was a new thing, this disruption to sleep that had beset him this past year. He was not an adventurer, but a regulator. As he produced nothing new and made no mark of his own, as he was a checker in the shadows, he had lived without the fear of being exposed as a fake. What a marvellous freedom—now that it was gone, he longed for it. Primarily it was his job's exemption from this fear that got him out of his bed each morning.

Wherever that bed happened to be.

•

'I am, aren't I?'

'I beg your pardon?'

Tom Dews was batting his glossy eyelashes desperately into our father's face.

'I told you, you don't have to beg me. You're pardoned, okay? Damn. I'm boring you. This always happens between the fourth and fifth glass.'

'Not at all,' Dad said. 'I was about to say—'

'Don't apologise,' Tom Dews said fiercely, his maudlin turn veering back to menace. 'I'm boring you. There's only one way out. We go get some pussy.'

Tom Dews got up, his shirt sweat-puckered, with a certainty that told our father more eloquently than words that the salesman had been here before. Not just here in the Lakeshore but here in this conversation, here in this scenario, here at this endpoint. He was a stage performer contracted for a long-running one-man show. And here was act three: he rose from his bar stool, cuffed his silently-suffering interlocutor by the wrist, and dragged him to the part of the bar where, he had already ascertained, his quarry lay. Having gone through bluster and self-pity and desperation and overcompensation, Tom Dews now passed into benevolence, taking John Wonder to the other end of the bar not only because Tom Dews needed a woman's body but because his role required him to owe it to John Wonder to get one for *him*.

'Come on, man, I'll sort you out.'

Still entangled by the line of least resistance, Dad allowed himself to be dragged.

For the first time, he took in the other group. It comprised five men, late thirties to late fifties, in business shirts and slacks like those worn by himself and Tom Dews. At least he was fitting in. And it also comprised two women. One, a putty-nosed green-eyed gamine with spiked dark hair, young enough to be quite attractive in her ugliness, was perched like a budgerigar on her bar stool and enjoying being a seller in a seller's market. She forced laughter, said little, and inspected the men haughtily and brazenly, knowing the rules and the balance of power, all out in the open here, making her choice. If indeed a choice was to be made. Notwithstanding the loudness and reeking frustration of her audience, as plain as she was, this girl still retained the prerogative of, first, being able to choose whether she would be a chooser, and, second, if she chose to be a chooser, who she would choose.

The second of the women had skittered towards the bathroom as Tom Dews brought our father into the circle.

'Oi!' Dews shouted after her with the rudeness of long and familiar acquaintance. 'Where's your manners?' Our father could hear a shadow intimacy protruding from the end of Dews's question like a phantom limb, which so terrified him that he had to physically turn away from it. As a consequence, when the door of the female toilet swung shut, our father had not been able to see her.

But we know who it was, don't we? We are his children and we know everything about him. He was our father and he knew everything about us. We are not locked in the moment. We can jump forward to another, later that night, when our father would be lying on his bed fully clothed and too wired to sleep, when out of the paralytic excitement of the intervening hour he starts to remember how she must have fled to the bathroom when she saw him coming, and he starts to speculate on how she must have been feeling, hiding in there from him, knowing full well that there was no other exit, that unless she was prepared to wait the unknown hours until our father left, or until her spike-haired friend (whose name was Bucky, or Becky) grew concerned and followed her into the bathroom and somehow hatched a viable plan to get our father out of the bar before Cicada emerged from the toilet. But such a plan could only involve Bucky, or Becky, seducing our father and somehow luring him out of the Lakeshore for long enough to give Cicada the opportunity to escape . . . which was unlikely, as not only was John Wonder absolutely not Bucky's or Becky's type, but in all likelihood she was not his, he just didn't seem a sex kind of guy . . . and anyhow, why should she, Cicada, need to hide from him anyway? Why cower in a horrible over-lit bathroom making up her face endlessly, for that was what she was doing, counting her imperfections that were so painfully exposed in this horrible light, why do this all night when she was getting a nice enough buzz on and these guys were okay—not that she'd made her mind up to, well, you know, but that Tom guy was back and last time he'd . . .

And so Cicada Economopoulos decided to come out of the bathroom, without waiting for Bucky or Becky to wonder about her; she strode out under her own majestic full sail, her jaw-dropping bust thrust forward, clad in tight jeans and cork wedges and a figure-hugging electric-blue cashmere sweater that evaporated moisture from the back of men's throats, her anguish-producing buttocks thrust counterbalancingly back, Newton's law in motion, what goes forth must weigh back, freshly made-up and restored to full vigour, her hair, this year the colour of an adult raven, so black it was almost blue, falling across her left eye, a hand drawing that one tress aside only for it to fall straight back, into the darker corner of the Lakeshore bar of the Holiday Inn, where she seized the half-drunk glass of wine from Tom Dews's hand.

As great as was her love of theatre, she did not throw it back. She took a demure sip and returned it to Dews, who had sat, since her entrance, as immobile as Lot's wife. The end of her pink tongue dabbed the corner of her mouth. She swept the lock of hair out of her eye. It fell back again. She wanted to be drunk, fast, but not that drunk and not that fast.

And having observed this dumb-show, our father experienced a renewal of the sensation he had undergone when he had *recognised* her three hundred and sixty-four days earlier in Menis Economopoulos's study. He did not know who he was, what day or year it was, how old he was, how he had got here, what he had been doing for the last little while, or how to get out of here. While in Menis Economopoulos's study the disorientation had come upon him in a brief flash and left him with a headache, like a minuscule stroke, this sense that her beauty was something that opened voids, something that made him question his very substantiality—for beholding Cicada was to double the sensations of discovery and recognition, seeing his ideal for the first time yet also knowing that she had been in his sights for so many years—on this occasion, in the Lakeshore, the disembodying effect sent him into a tearful panic from which his only escape was . . . escape.

'I beg your pardon, I . . .'

Being John Wonder, he could not leave even this gross company without apology. His face afire, he stumbled towards the lift lobby.

Tom Dews let his new friend go. Dews had forgotten his plan to use this pale sexless man as a stalking horse, for he was too smitten by Cicada Economopoulos to have access to any residual presence of mind and instead sat, nonplussed, disarmed, desolate. Had he been capable of speech, Dews would have had a different word for Cicada's effect on him: Dews was pussy-blinded.

Our father, meanwhile, space-walked towards the lobby. Dramatic imperatives demanded that Cicada follow him and ask why he was leaving, what was wrong with him, and finally they would *talk*, at last, after all this time, he and she could talk; but the imperatives that occupied Cicada Economopoulos had an altogether different trajectory, or centre of gravity. When she saw the pale man stumble from the bar she breathed a sigh of relief. The night was both young and old, she didn't yet know which, but in any case she was pleased to see that strange guy leave. She could do without the complication.

The next day, crippled by a one-in-forty-year hangover, our father missed appointments for the first time in his professional life. He did not oversleep; he did not sleep at all. As ashamed as if he had committed some unspeakable atrocity, he packed his bags before dawn and waited until a reasonable hour to call a taxi. Throughout the eternal night he had fancied he could hear laughter, and rough sex, from other rooms. At seven o'clock in the morning he contacted Dorothy Ellen O'Oagh's personal physician and delegated the duty of measuring her pulse on that day, her one hundred and twenty-sixth birthday. Then he called the local police sergeant and asked him to write a letter certifying the continuation of Menis Economopoulos's temporary restraining order. It was cheating, it was bending the rules by which he had lived his life, but our father cared only for getting out of that hell.

And yet, when he descended to the lobby, he stopped his lift on every floor and put his head out, in case she should emerge from one of the rooms, dusty and defiled. In the lobby he waited for a telescopic time, lingering in and around the breakfast room. In the taxi his eyes were as alert as a sniper's. In the little airport terminal he imagined her racing up to ask why he had not come to the house, because she had been waiting all year, and that day, that day she had asked her father to allow her some private time for an interview with John Wonder, and with her having gone to all that trouble, why was he leaving? Why? Where did he have to go in such a hurry? And she would stamp her foot in disappointed rage. Twenty-seven, and still stamping her foot.

As he sat in the terminal, its only retail outlet a machine screwed into the floor, he noticed an odour both cloying and earthy. Its sweetness reminded him of an overripe pear. Its earthiness brought to mind the cool damp spaces underneath an old house. The smell also had what he could only describe as a humanness, and the word that adhered to it was one of colour, not odour: the smell was dark brown.

He had never smelt this aroma, and while powerful it was not unpleasant. As he glanced around the terminal, which was mostly empty of people and furnished with metal, plastics and other synthetics, he could only come to the conclusion that this smell was the smell of himself. And this was the strangest thing, not only because, as Tom Dews had reminded him, a person can never smell his own odour, but because, as our father's three wives had often remarked, he had no odour. But here it was, revealed, his own smell, rotting pears, under-house crawl spaces, and something dark brown, not shit or chocolate or wood, but perhaps leathery, a remnant of tanned hide.

And he asked himself, thinking of Dews's theory: What does this mean, that I am now smelling myself?

His flight was delayed. But it came and lifted him up and carried him on thin air back to us.

8

Our father might have been fleeing from the captivity threatened, or promised, by Cicada Economopoulos's beauty. Surely many had been trapped before him. He knew that without needing to test it empirically. Some truths, he willingly accepted, can be taken a priori.

We incline to a more generous view. We are his children. We think he was fleeing from the spectre of wrongdoing. We think that our father's gut instinct was to do right, and his only way of expressing, or obeying, that reflex was to get out of that town before he could find himself in the morass his lesser parts most desired.

But we could be wrong. Perhaps his morality was not as firm as we trust. Perhaps his obeisance to doing right had been corrupted long before, and he didn't need Cicada to bring him down.

We have always been unfairly biased towards him. We forgive him too much.

Just ask our mothers.

The next week, he was at home with his first family. The week after, he was with his second family and the dark-skinned woman. The following week, he was back with his third family and the scarred woman and the child who had been stricken with an incurable genetic disability. His sixth child, his third Evie. Perhaps he was always pushing his luck until it ran out, and he was merely a reckless and stupid gambler without any care for the welfare or wellbeing of others, least of all those who needed him.

During those three weeks, he was as kind and caring as always. His bedtime stories, though, tended to fall into a steady stream with a common element.

The change in his heart was producing a change in the nature of his stories. He was less concerned with records and feats and measurements than with stories of love gifts.

The Ottoman king, Suleiman the Magnificent, who freed his Russian slave Roxelana and made her his empress, all for love.

The grief-stricken emperor of the Moguls, Shah Jahan, who built the Taj Mahal for his favourite wife, Mumtaz Mahal, who had died giving birth to their fourteenth child.

Diamond Jim Brady, who gave Lillian Russell a gold-plated bicycle with mother-of-pearl handlebars and spokes encrusted with chips of precious stones, and a case of blue plush-lined morocco so that the bicycle could travel with her wherever she went.

Joe DiMaggio, who delivered fresh roses to the graveside of Marilyn Monroe three times a week in the twenty-five years between her death and his.

We understood nothing of the names, only the sadness in his oilcloth-covered voice. Hearing the change in his tone, each of our mothers, at various times, came to the doorway of our room and quietly listened to him.

'You're getting soft in your old age,' said the mother with the thick glasses.

'Sentimental nonsense,' said the mother with the dark skin.

'Stop crying, my love, you'll scare them,' said the scarred woman with the disabled Evie.

But our father did not hear. His inner ear was ringing with a new sound, and new truth.

Love is the desire, simply put, for beauty. Plato. This was what might scare them.

What, anyway, did he know about the final mystery? Our mother Sandy, with the thick glasses, was so consumed with protecting children from terminal illness, so overwhelmingly *busy*, that she had long ceased thinking about what passed through her husband's mind. To her he now occupied the role of a steadfast if part-time collaborator. In her mind, she was the essential person in this family and our father had reduced himself to an auxiliary. Harsh but true. Sandy took care of the children of the world; John took care of the children in the house, one week in three. When he was home, no husband could be so thoughtful, so useful and so fastidious a supporter of her work by way of his inconspicuous contribution to getting the children fed and clothed, keeping the household ticking over, making the home, for her, a place of rest and recuperation; but she was not a woman for illusions, and suspected that he was only such a considerate father and husband because he was around in fits and starts. Familiarity, and dull routine, did not have time to set in.

But when they had first met, she too had been fascinated by the question of love. Or rather, specifically, by the question of what love meant to him, how it resided in his soul.

Sandy had been a final-year resident in the emergency unit at a large city hospital, working the tail end of a thirty-six-hour shift, when a child was brought in bleeding from his ears, nostrils and into his own eyeballs. At first Sandy did not notice the man who had brought the nine-year-old boy in his arms. The triage demanded action. She stopped the blood flow and performed a thorough examination while the boy's escort stood by the gurney.

The man was in his late twenties or early thirties, not much older than Sandy herself, which did not rule out his being the bleeding boy's father. But the boy was brown-eyed, dark-haired and olive-skinned, whereas the man had papery white skin with dusty freckles and the palest, shallowest blue eyes, which crinkled in a kind of innocent guilt as he confessed to her that he was some kind of agent for *The Guinness Book of World Records*, and had been supervising the boy's attempt to break the record for stuffing the most plastic drinking straws into his mouth when the bleeding had started, first from the nose, then the ears and finally in the eyes, and he, the blue-eyed man, had deemed it necessary to call the attempt off and bring the boy to hospital.

'Where are his parents?' Sandy asked, still unsure what to make of this man's bizarre tale. *Guinness Book of World Records*? Plastic drinking straws? As a young emergency resident, the onset of world-weariness came early in life. She, like most of her colleagues, took only a few months in the job to come to the conclusion that she had seen it all. But this was a new one. She administered coagulants and sedatives to the boy and asked that he be moved to an in-patient ward.

'They, ah, were unable to attend,' the man said.

Sandy didn't want to look at him. This sounded like trouble. It sounded like fantasy, and it sounded, possibly, like police and a lot of paperwork.

'Wouldn't come to hospital,' she said, 'or wouldn't come to the . . . attempt, you call it?'

'This is not unusual,' the man explained. 'It is the parents who have entered their child for a record attempt, and it is the parents who persist with it even when it becomes dangerous. Our biggest battle is with the parents of child prodigies. We, ah, we are in dispute at this moment. His parents opposed my decision to halt the attempt and bring him here.'

Sandy didn't want to be involved. The boy, though traumatised, was not seriously hurt. She suspected that he might have a history of haemophilia, but of course such history could only be solicited from the parents, not from an agent for the—for *The Guinness Book of World Records*? Was this real or some kind of *Candid Camera* stunt?

While pretending to make notes on her clipboard, Sandy appraised the man. Really, his eyes and hair were unnervingly colourless. When he smiled, as he did now that he saw she was spying on him, his teeth were yellowish and gappy. He was not an attractive man, with his stiff way of talking, yet he seemed oddly comfortable with her.

'Four hundred and ninety-seven,' he said.

'Pardon?'

'You were on the point of asking what the record was. It is four hundred and ninety-seven straws. Young Paolo here had reached four hundred and twenty-two. I suppose his parents were thinking just another seventy-six and then he can go to hospital.'

Sandy directed the man to the appropriate administrative officer and got on with her work. Only later did she hear, second-hand, that the parents had arrived in a terrible flap and, having come to their senses, far from accusing the *Guinness* man of sabotaging the record attempt or kidnapping their son, were grateful to him for putting Paolo's welfare above their temporary madness.

It was at the end of her shift, as she was walking out of the hospital, that Sandy ran into the man again. A long footbridge connected the hospital with the railway terminal, and as it was late in the evening the man asked if he might join her on the walk. He didn't phrase it as a chivalrous offer, probably fearing her reaction. Instead he said what a beautiful night it was and, as he was going the same way, perhaps she wouldn't mind sharing the stars with him.

The walk took half an hour, and Sandy did little talking. The man seemed to need to explain the bizarre circumstances of Paolo's injury, and by way of explanation give a short history of his own life, telling her how he had been a '*Guinness* aficionado', had monitored its accuracy and 'editorial cleanliness', had established a friendship with and almost filial reverence for the founder of the book, and then, on leaving school, had been offered full-time employment.

Hearing all this, Sandy felt that she was talking to a preadolescent boy, not Paolo's guardian but his playmate. John's enthusiasm was so unquestioning and the love he manifested, not for the book so much as the idea of record-setting behind it, had such a purity that she could not help being touched by it. He was five years older than her but had none of the bone-weariness she was used to seeing in the men, mostly doctors, she dated. Indeed at the time she was seeing a cardiology intern, a university medallist like her and on the fast track to all the honours that the medical profession was capable of bestowing, who was, nevertheless, so direly disappointed with everything he did and so cynical of life's promises that she had privately, silently, diagnosed him as clinically depressed. But it seemed that every doctor, nurse and orderly she knew socially and worked with was lurking somewhere on the spectrum of depression. They were all sleeping with each other and all diagnosing each other. This callow, strangely formal *Guinness* guy was a breath of fresh air, and by the end of their walk she did feel, literally, invigorated by his company; she could not but say yes when he asked if, on her next free night (which was two weeks away and feeling like a safe eternity into the future), she would mind going out to eat at a restaurant with him.

Sandy was so busy in the meantime that she more or less forgot his invitation, but afterwards she reflected that she must have been preparing with more care than she allowed herself to admit, because during those two weeks she broke off her relationship with the overachieving cardiology intern, the rupture setting off a ten-year chain reaction of events that would see him—he knew hearts, and now he knew heartbreak!—become, as if in vengeance or mourning, the youngest cardiology specialist in the state's history, the youngest president of the cardiologists' professional body, married with three children, the youngest chairman of his children's private school council, diagnosed with chronic depression, retired from all the positions he had held, treated with numerous versions of psychotherapy and drug therapy and finally electroconvulsive shock therapy, returning to university to retrain as a stage-one primary school teacher, entering the workforce as such, and coming out gay on his fortieth birthday.

Sandy could have quite an effect on men.

She dressed modestly for the dinner with John Wonder, in a long skirt and wraparound black cotton top. It was late summer yet quite cool the evening John picked her up, on foot, from the terrace house she shared with an older woman, an aromatherapist, naturopath and masseuse, who was six months pregnant with the child of a married television producer with whom she had been having an affair that he had now, on discovery of her pregnancy, broken off. Sandy told John about her flatmate while they walked to an Indian restaurant to which she had been a number of times.

Sandy went into the evening without expectation. After the tumult of her breakup with the cardiologist and the in-house soap opera involving her flatmate, she felt, almost, that she was going out with a young boy, and she need only sit back and let him entertain her until he began to bore her, and that would be the end of the date. She felt no sexual attraction to him, so was free in her consumption of the white wine she kept ordering. He sat on his one glass. The warmer she watched his wine growing, the more thirsty she grew for her own frosty tipple. She had no fear of losing control, as there was no way she was going to sleep with this odd, papery, overgrown boy.

To her surprise, he did not bore her with endless facts and figures. 'I am the one person you will meet who will never be offended if you say my concerns are trivial,' he said, making her laugh. Instead of nervously filling the space across the table with an almanac of ephemera, he limited himself to a few surprisingly interesting observations on the origins of okra and the molecular processes of the tandoori oven, before asking her about her own work and life. Sandy was unused to this kind of attention. As, for the past six years, she had dated no-one but fellow doctors and other narcissists she had known from university, no boyfriend had ever shown the least curiosity in her past or her work. They knew it already. She was a fixed quantity: forbiddingly brainy, serious, ambitious. Now, with this intense man picking her brain (as it felt) across the table, as she grew increasingly drunk on white wine and attention, she felt her mood elevate. He was treating her as a star, which, to her momentary surprise, she realised that, to a stranger, indeed to anyone other than the men she had known, she was. Why was it that every boyfriend she'd had would make a personal crusade of putting her down, mocking her seriousness, apparently in the interest of 'keeping her feet on the ground'? Why did everyone want her to forget she was special?

Nor was John Wonder ingratiating. He seemed genuinely interested not only in her, but in the processes of her work, the discoveries of medical science (or those she could talk about with any claim to authority), her routines, her hopes, her disillusionments. As she still felt no trace of sexual interest from him, and had none in him, Sandy was liberated into honesty, and from honesty into candour, and from candour into roguish indiscretion. What did it matter? Not at all!

She didn't think it mattered at all when, to be polite and to thank him for such an easy evening, she responded to his timid loafing at her door and invited him in for coffee. Her flatmate was away for the night, Sandy explained as she prepared the espresso machine.

John and Sandy would dispute what happened next. He said that he was standing innocently in her dank little kitchen when Sandy 'took me by force'. In Sandy's memory, she was grinding the coffee, with her back to the room, when a pair of grey-freckled hands materialised under her ribs, 'hauled me up and turned me over like a shearer with a sheep'. Whatever it was, they were soon rolling on the filthy linoleum, crawling out of their clothes and making love, heads cracking the kickboards, toes getting caught in the drawers. For all of his impressive, even lunatic, energy, however, John was unable to have intercourse with her that night. 'I want you everywhere,' he said, trying to reassure her, himself, both of them, he didn't know who. 'In my fingers, in my hair, in my toenails, I want you with every cell. Just—it doesn't appear that I want you *there*.' He nodded accusingly at the offending, or non-offending, object. Sandy didn't mind. She told him, once she had got him up and led him to the more forgiving carpet of the living room floor and they lay in moonlight streaming through the venetian blinds, that it was a common effect of abnormally high adrenalin flow. The blood was rushing everywhere else, the body's needs were too urgent. Down there was not—in a decision made by his body, not his mind—a priority. 'You're too excited to get excited,' was the way she put it. He said tenderly, 'If there was a God, I would thank her that you are a doctor.'

When she continued to see him, for coffee or dinner, Sandy was always surprised by the avidity of his lust. He seemed so boyish, so thrilled by knowledge, so taken with the intellect, and so physically dry- and weak-looking, that she was continually off her guard when he ambushed her in her house or, when her flatmate got back, in the flat he was renting on his own. John was a frenzied lover, she had no other way of putting it. The first-night nerves dissipated and she grew used to a desire as red-blooded and sweaty as his external shell was white and dry. This was, too, a reflection of her own low self-esteem. Although she had had no trouble attracting boys, Sandy knew she was not a particularly pretty woman and had seen her advantage, in the marketplace, as her maturity and willingness rather than any physical attributes. She was heavy-boned and her face, while pleasant, was large and fleshy and unrefined. Her hair was uncared for, pulled back into a ponytail with a fringe over her forehead. The largeness of her breasts had dismayed her ever since, at the age of thirteen or fourteen, they had headed southwards. On her deathbed, her mother had matter-of-factly broken Sandy's heart when she had asked her to consider mammary-reduction surgery, something Sandy had too much personal pride to contemplate, even if it was her mother's dying wish. What is the saying? There are two types of women: those who crave love and do something about it, and those who crave love so much that they refuse to do anything about it. Sandy's chest was her cross to bear. While she could make it presentable with the right trussing and cantileverage, she knew she was selling a bill of goods, and had gleaned as much from the disappointment concealed in a sharp intake of breath and diversion of attention in her previous boyfriends. Her breasts looked enticing until she let them fall like fatty jowls across the base of her ribs. When she lay on her back, they cascaded into her armpits. None of this mattered to John Wonder; in fact, he made love to her and paid attention to what she thought of as her many flaws as if God had delivered him a bounty permitted only to heroes. For months, he set upon her so hungrily, arriving at her house like a missile, launching himself through the doorway to tackle her onto the floor or the couch, or molesting her halfway through some important task, that she felt a shy gratitude. For the first time, her body was adored. As a creature of the intellect, she was thrilled all the more by this unexpected hunger. To be loved for her mind was something she expected, but to be *devoured* was a surprise she had never felt she deserved. She had to do so little to excite him. With her, he turned from the Clark Kent of his trivial pursuits into a Superman of sex.

And so their first years passed.

As Sandy grew to know John Wonder, she saw two sides that each begged questions about the other. His sexual voracity prompted her to speculate about the other part of him, the part she saw getting up every morning, dressing in his methodical manner, chaining one simple act to the next to form a day. She watched him lace up his shoes with full concentration, each aglet equidistant from the eyes, each loop of precise shape and equality, as if he was carrying out a demonstration of exactitude in a 1950s instructional film clip on etiquette. He did not deviate from the energies required for knotting his tie, like a machine of mass production, the same every time. She thrilled to see such *presence,* such a containment within the act of each moment, as if nothing more important could ever be taking place. He seemed so complete and calm: the finished article. He pursued his professional work in a self-sufficient way, knowing what he did not know but also what he did not need. Nor did he need another person, as he seemed to draw his own counsel and commonsense from within, a deeper place than she could reach. Did he really need her? Only in the way that she needed him, bodily, avidly. In the other ways he travelled with his own possessions, so much like herself that sometimes she felt they were so well-fitted a couple, so perfectly complementary, that she grew terrified by the thought of losing him. And by this she knew she was in love.

•

Once when he sat on the end of our bed, our father said, 'Did you know you are descended from a queen of England? From a knight of the Crusades? From Kublai Khan *and* from Julius Caesar?' We shrieked in delight at the prospect of a story, but our father was talking mathematics, not fantasy. 'You have billions of ancestors,' he said. 'They double every generation. You have two parents, four grandparents, eight great-grandparents. Time travel back to the year 1750, and you shall discover one thousand forebears. When you arrive in the middle ages, a possible four million people carry your blood, take away a million or so to allow for interbreeding. Go back to Caesar's time, and if his ancestors have lasted through the ages to ours, then it is more likely than not that we are related to him.'

It was exhilarating to hear our father speak like this: mathematics *was* fantasy, facts *were* fabulous. The heroes of his stories were our family! (And now, too, there are six of us, with more than the usual allotment of parents and grandparents!) It is something of an anti-climax, then, to know so few. We might be descended from kings and wizards, but the ancestors we know are decidedly common.

Sandra met our father's parents early in the piece, when she had him invite them to her house for dinner one night, about six months after she and he had begun seeing each other. Sandy tried to hide her curiosity and busied herself with helping John make Mr and Mrs Wonder comfortable, rather than sit facing them and having to inspect them (and suffer their inspection of her). So Mr and Mrs Wonder were left alone in the dining nook while John mauled her in the kitchen. He took her against the fridge before she could get the soup off the stove. The need for silence—only the breeze under the back door was allowed to moan, only the boiling soup was permitted to gurgle and gasp—heightened her pleasure like some exotic restraining device. She didn't get a chance to give his parents a good look until dinner.

Physically Mr and Mrs Wonder were innocuous. Their most noticeable feature was their age. A quick calculation told Sandy that they must have been in their mid-forties when John, their only child, was born. They were now in their seventies. The father was pale like John, quite bald with silvery tufts above his ears, and clearly the donor of John's long nose and chin and thin dry lips. He seemed a wry, good-humoured fellow, his mouth turning down as he smiled as if to suppress the perpetual absurdity of life. He went out of his way to be gallant to her, and even though she was wearing a thick dark sweater she could see him sizing her up. If there was one type of man Sandy could instantly identify, it was the boob man. 'We Wonders are all sex maniacs,' John had once told her, and she believed him, though she had asked him how he knew this, and he had replied: 'It is what my father always says. Though I do not know what evidence he is basing it on.'

Mrs Wonder (they only introduced themselves as 'Mr' and 'Mrs', unusual in this day and age, but then they weren't really of this day and age) was handsome rather than beautiful, a stern, intense, long-faced interrogator with forbidding cheekbones and china-blue eyes that seemed to bathe in their own bright cleverness. She must have been twice Mr Wonder's weight, and from the way she led the conversation, asking Sandy exhaustive questions about her background, throwing out quick orders to John, declaiming her opinions, Sandy would have guessed that she was the dominant force in the family. Certainly John deferred to her, and Mr Wonder's chucklesome attitude, as if there was a potential laugh in everything his wife said, struck Sandy as a yielding protective membrane. Other than that there was little for Sandy to remark on or to put aside to think about later, when she had time for reflection, except perhaps that Mr and Mrs Wonder had a morbid obsession with personal appearances. When discussing someone, the subject was always either 'beautiful' or 'no oil painting' or 'frumpy' or 'gorgeous' or 'absolutely stunning'. About people, Mr and Mrs Wonder seemed interested only in judging their looks. It did not seem a particularly unusual or sinister or repulsive quality to Sandy, but it was noticeable nonetheless; she could guess what they would say about her. But she did not care. Their son had just finished devouring her on the other side of that wall. John's lust was her suit of armour.

Late in the dinner, which had been as pleasant as possible in the circumstances, something happened to jolt her view. Mrs Wonder was saying how she had forbidden Mr Wonder to climb up his ladder to fix their chimney, due to his age and a stroke he had suffered six years ago. Rather than simply telling the story, Mrs Wonder was using the opportunity to mount an argument, expecting John and even Sandy to pipe up and agree that it was insanity for Mr Wonder to climb a chimney at his age. But midway through, the thin little man let out a torrent of truly fearsome abuse, calling his wife a 'fucking harridan' and 'an ignoramus' and a 'control freak', spitting out the words with none of the deference to social niceties that he cloaked, in all other conversation, in jauntiness.

His outburst was parried by Mrs Wonder—'Oh shut up, will you, I've heard it all before,' she said with a flick of her square-fingered hand—but it embarrassed Sandy, who was not well-adapted to domestic venom and could not quite believe what she had heard. It was not that the conversation or the evening was spoilt, and indeed, after their bizarre eruptions, Mr and Mrs Wonder carried on to the next topic as if nothing had happened, so that the rupture seemed all the more like something she had imagined. Which was more strange, the outburst or the cordiality that followed it? Sandy so needed to sit down alone with John and digest the event that she hurried the rest of the dinner along.

After a hasty dessert, Sandy and John took the plates to the kitchen. John looked ashen. For not taking it in his stride, for being shocked and embarrassed, for sharing her emotion, Sandy loved him all the more. At least to him the outburst (soon known as The Outburst) wasn't as normal as it evidently was to his parents.

John clattered the dishes and cutlery, an ostentatious washing-up coda to the evening, and his parents were tactful enough to take the signal. Mr Wonder came to the kitchen doorway and said, 'We'll be off then.' John dried his hands, fetched his mother's coat from Sandy's bedroom, and ushered his mother and father to the door. His gratitude for their compliant departure was cut short when, as she gave Sandy a peck on the cheek, his mother stage-whispered, with a nasty leer, 'Now look after him, dear, you know you're the first.'

Sandy noticed that John froze. Sandy kissed Mr Wonder goodnight and suffered his close and extended hug, which he clearly did not realise was inappropriate. She went to the window and saw that Mr and Mrs Wonder were able to get their car out of a tight parking space. Muffled shouts floated up from the vehicle. John had returned to the kitchen. When the parents were safely gone, Sandy followed John and said, with a nervous giggle that she tried to make playful:

'The first?'

John thrashed at the dishes in the sink.

'Of course not. It is typical of her. Whenever she makes a fool of herself, she diverts attention to someone else. She was getting back at me for their appalling behaviour.'

Sandy moved close behind him and put her arms around his waist. He was as splintery as a fencepost.

'It wouldn't matter to me, you know.'

He shrugged her off, rougher than necessary. 'I am thirty-one years old, for goodness' sake. Do I do things to you like you are the first girl I have touched?'

Sandy said nothing, and went into the dining room to tidy up. She was returning the napkin rings to the drawers in the kitchen sideboard when she heard a handful of cutlery crash into the metal drainer. Before she could turn, she was being crash-tackled to the floor. Perhaps this was a Pavlovian response to the act of washing dishes and making late-night coffee; she tried, while it was happening, to think back to the first time, but John was unusually crude and clumsy with her.

As they lay in overheated silence on the linoleum, she tried to caress him back to normality. Then, getting everything out of order, John got up, changed into his pyjamas, put on some soft late-classical music, lit the living room with candles, poured red wine and beckoned her to curl up in his arms on the couch. She complied, cautiously.

She waited for him to speak, and when he did, his voice was clear and grim with words stored past their use-by date. He spoke of how distorted and involuted his parents had become in old age, the ferocity and hatred that had curled back and penetrated their forty-plus years of marriage, like an ingrowing hair infecting and inflaming the flesh. 'What surprised me,' he said, 'was not to see the way they have become to each other, but that they felt comfortable enough to do it in front of you. Obviously,' he gave a weak laugh, 'they saw no need to do a sales job.'

'I don't think they could help it,' Sandy said. 'It seems to have reached the point where they don't care if someone else sees this or not. Were they like that—but, you know, behind closed doors—when you were younger?'

Rather than answer her question, John spoke of the massiveness of their disappointment in him. He was their only child, born late in life, long after they had given up hope of children. They had both been reasonably successful in their careers, Mrs Wonder (a girls' school principal) more than Mr Wonder (a government town planner), and to have a child in their mid-forties was both a bonus and a burden. Mr Wonder, whose progress in the bureaucracy had stalled, would, they agreed, step back from work and become the main parent to John, who remembered him as 'present but absent, always with me but with his head in a book or the newspaper or stewing over something that made him boil'. John quickly emerged as a prodigious child, reading advanced books at the age of four and five, doing high-level mathematics and science ahead of everyone else in his school, quiet and well-behaved and the envy of other parents, excepting those who pitied him, believing he was raised by his grandparents. So he had slipped through school, rising without trace, his successes applauded yet also on the margins, too eccentrically brainy to be a threat to anyone.

'They must have been proud of you,' Sandy said, thinking of her own parents: what they had missed out on, what she had missed out on.

'They might have been pleased with my achievements,' John said, 'but they misjudged my character. My mother thought I would be a leader of government, or on the high court bench, or a chairman of companies. My father dreamed that I was going to invent some miraculous device or cure a disease. They both thought my talents, which could be measured in so many ways, were an indicator of my potential to do something entirely different. But standing out from the crowd, leading, that was not me. I hated the spotlight and began to deliberately finish second in tests so that I could avoid getting a prize and becoming the centre of attention. They thought this shyness was a quirk I would grow out of. They still do. They still hope I might wake up one day and realise I have wasted my so-called gifts. They resent what I have done with my life . . . working in *trivia* of all things. You should hear the way she says it. She makes *trivia* sound like *paedophilia*. She thinks I pursued my career expressly to spite her.'

Sandy could picture it. Mr and Mrs Wonder felt that they had nurtured the crown jewels, a child who would come to a family once every five generations, and then, out of his own perversity, he had shrivelled under the shadow of Norris McWhirter and frittered his promise away.

'They have never realised that the feats I could achieve as a child were not an indicator of some higher adult abilities,' he said. 'Doing quizzes and tests and gathering knowledge—those *were* my abilities. That *was* what I loved, and what I was good at. Trivia was not a pathway through childhood. It is my adult life. They have never accepted that. But I suppose you will say that their disappointment in me is the only way I can know for certain that they care.'

Sandy watched the candles burn down. She did not feel in the mood to drink the wine he had poured her. Oddly, he was into his second glass. She still felt a coldness in the room; the rough way he had been with her, like he was impersonating some other kind of man. He had hurt her. If he had offered to leave and go back to his own place, she would have let him.

But then he did. He pushed himself to his feet, tipping her onto the couch, and said, 'I am leaving now.'

They say that the moment a suicide's feet leave the edge of the cliff is the moment he changes his mind. At the moment our father announced his departure, Sandy changed her mind about wishing for it. He stomped into her bedroom and changed from his pyjamas back into his clothes. Going from clothes to pyjamas and back to clothes, without a night's sleep in between, accentuated his emotional disarray. She felt a stab of pity for him; he only seemed to become angrier. He brought out his overnight bag. Minutes earlier, Sandy had wanted to be alone to take everything in. It was all too much for them to absorb together. Now, she felt it was all too much for her to absorb alone.

When John reached the door, Sandy's chin was trembling and she could hardly speak. If he went, she was convinced, he would never come back. But she could say nothing. It was his exit to make.

He yanked the door: in the humidity, it had expanded into its frame. Perhaps he took its resistance as a sign. Her door did not want him to go. Her door knew what was at stake.

As he turned around to face her for the last time, she thought: People who are dry and cold, when they let go and cry, they really let it all out.

He was struggling to summon a farewell. She took a step towards him. He held up a hand to stop her. He choked as if hyperventilating. He steadied himself by hugging his overnight bag to his chest.

'I lied to you.' His voice was a distant croak, a dying man's gasp.

Sandy felt herself dissolve.

'I know.' She felt her arms go out. His bag fell on her foot.

•

'You don't seem to feel any love from them,' Sandy said.

An hour had passed, and they were back on the floor. John had transited, in the course of the night, like a stage actor in a quick succession of scenes, from clothes to naked to pyjamas to clothes to naked again. But this time it had been right. His shirt and pants were strewn on the furniture and his overnight bag was back in Sandy's bedroom.

'Was that what you saw tonight?'

'I'm not quite sure what I saw, but I get the feeling that the longer I think about it, the stranger it's going to seem.'

'And the stranger I am going to seem.'

She didn't mind that. 'I'm strange too, John. We can be strange together.'

Then he opened his heart and told her how, since his earliest memories, he had felt utterly bamboozled by the idea of love. Although he knew his mother and father loved him, in their way, and he felt safe and secure and happy in his home, he also scrutinised expressions of love in the outside world and feared that love was a cult or a special language that was known to others but not him, a club into which he had never been invited. From social exclusion at school to his rejection by any girl he had approached, he figured that love was a mystery in the possession of others, and that when anyone looked at him the first thing they realised was that he was outside the world of true passion.

'I've felt that way myself,' Sandy said. 'It's hardly unusual.'

To himself, John maintained, it was more existential than mere teenage and young-adult sexual longing. But he was determined to overcome it, and he still had enough energy to hope that he could break in. Rejection had not embittered him, but had pushed him onto a platform from which he set himself to observe and learn. If he couldn't be inside the party, he decided, he could at least press his face to the window. Through a decade of failed attempts to find love, he promised himself that if he ever got his chance he would not waste it. He would not be offhand or casual or *habitual* with his lover. He would maintain his hunger. He would never forget his loneliness. If he had squandered his other gifts, as his parents and most of society seemed to think, then love, if he ever found it, was the one gift he would set himself to cherish. And yes, he confessed with a shuddering sigh, his breath catching in his throat, at thirty-one he was still, when he met her, a virgin. His soft fingertips played across her nipple until it tightened and hardened. 'I am making up,' he said, 'for lost time.'

Sandy folded tighter into the space he made for her between his arm and his ribs. Although it would be another five years before they moved into a home together, another six years after that before they married (both delays brought on as much by her career commitments as their mutual shyness and indecision), Sandy would remember this conversation and this night as the moment when their partnership was sealed, the moment when he convinced her that he was her kindred spirit, her fellow traveller. They spoke their own language, and if it was a language of outliers, of strange, determined, obsessive seekers, then the fact that they were the only ones who spoke it was their fortress. They would never stop being lonely, but they could be lonely in company. She understood him now. Or rather, she had the story by which she would understand him. In that night, in those first years, he had frozen himself inside her, implanted himself, the lost only child, both lonely and solitary, primed and bursting with love.

Her lurking regret, in those years of professional advancement, material prosperity and conjugal happiness, was that she and John were unable to have children. They passed forty together, making love perhaps too wild, too recreational, to permit procreation.

We can bear to imagine that she could have been fully satisfied without us.

TWO

Soul Mate

9

As powerful and necessary as was our father's need for it, inertia can imply movement as well as stillness. We have observed our father's resistance to change. In his inertia, he moved constantly. Now it is time to talk of his equal and opposite, constant and unchanging, a restlessness so deep that it was itself a form of rest, a kind of stasis. In his need for change, for novelty, in his lifelong process of embedding and enclosing and disguising this need within himself, in embracing the newness of life that only love can provide, like a new season, we wonder if he believed he had conquered the fear of change.

After the unfortunate incident with Cicada Economopoulos, or without her, accurately speaking, at the Holiday Inn, our father fulfilled his commitments to his families and his work for another twelve months. His three lives were so busy that he had little time for anything but the logistics: he authenticated claimants and refused others, he received his salary, he divided his income into the complex beehive of accounts and blind trusts he had set up to maintain three families, and he patrolled the high walls he had erected within himself to keep his lives separate. Every now and then he would lapse, or the walls would spring a leak. From his first family, a car, a Hyundai, disappeared. He came home one day and told our first mother, Sandy, that he had decided, on a whim, to sell it.

'Why?' she asked.

'I cannot answer that accurately,' he said. 'I suppose I just felt like it.'

In fact he had had the Hyundai transported to his third family, who owned no car; this family had to be shifted upstream on the financial priority flowchart, due to the children's health needs and his third wife's restricted ability to work. But then, when he transferred an end-of-year bonus directly into the third family's account and purchased a car that was better suited to their needs, he had the opportunity to return the Hyundai to its first home. Transporting it both ways by sea cost him more than the value of the car, but there were some emotional attachments not even his rationality could surmount. Ninety per cent of the man was coldly logical, calculating every cent and every consequence, and the other ten per cent was utterly insane. Did we ever mention that he was a man who could not let go?

'What happened there?' Sandy asked him at dinner one evening, when she saw the Hyundai in the driveway.

'I missed it,' our father said.

'You missed it?'

'I missed the car. I tracked down the fellow to whom I sold it and I bought it back.'

'Well I hope you got a good price.'

'The worst at both ends,' Dad said, making her laugh.

But then, his second family's Ford station wagon gave up the ghost. His second wife was having to take her Adam and Evie to school via a tortuous route involving buses, minibuses and trolley cars. So the Hyundai disappeared once more.

'What now?' Sandy asked. 'You've sold it again?'

'The car is not the same,' our father replied. 'Since I sold it, it came back changed. I could not abide it.'

There must have been a base load of complication, not to mention high-maintenance deception, in our father's psyche that left no room for anything else. Keeping three families ticking along would have been a full-time job. And what about the fear of being caught? There was a story in a newspaper about a man who kept two separate families. He was a commercial jet pilot; apparently, the story said, pilots were specialists at maintaining second families. The pilot was caught when a cousin of his, who lived in the city of his second family, went to an open-house real-estate inspection. The cousin caught sight of a family photograph of the inhabitants. To her confusion and eventual horror, she saw that the father in the photographs, smiling in a group shot with a woman and two children, was her own cousin, the pilot. Another story told of how a wife of forty-five years' standing, with a terminal illness, was sorting through her business papers and discovered that her husband was keeping a secret bank account that led to evidence of another wife, another family, also of nearly half a century's duration. The man was not only a husband and father twice, but a *grand*father to two parallel clans. His response to getting caught was to attempt a reconciliation by bringing his second family to his first wife's funeral. It did not end well.

Ridiculous coincidence? A one-in-a-million stroke of bad luck? For our father, there would have been nothing of the kind. There must, our father realised, be an infinite number of ways for such a man as himself to get caught out, and therefore an infinite number of details of which he must keep track and possibilities for which he must be ready. The porousness of the walls in the human heart is the natural state; it is sealing up that porousness which is unnatural, which kills a man, and our father, as he grew older, was fighting a battle that, it must have dawned on him, was only going to become harder to keep winning.

His slip-ups with the Hyundai might have owed something to age, as he turned fifty-six that year. But the leakages were statistically twenty-five per cent likelier, given the fourth continental chunk of concupiscence now drifting into its own oceanic zone. Not for one moment could he forget Cicada.

He resisted contacting Menis Economopoulos for the year, but Cicada was a constant presence in our father's heart, and he spent that year planning to speak personally to her. He had no idea what to say, but baby steps, he told himself, baby steps, one word at a time.

He would stay in the Holiday Inn the night before Mrs O'Oagh's birthday again, and retrace his steps late at night to the Lakeshore bar. His plan was based on equal parts superstition and empiricism. If she had been there last year, why shouldn't she be there this year? Cicada's captivity—to Menis, to stasis—was no less avoidable than our father's. She might be as much a creature of habit as he.

So on the eve of Dorothy Ellen O'Oagh's one hundred and twenty-seventh birthday, our father checked into the Holiday Inn. He ordered chicken tikka on room service, asking the kitchen to hold the onions. He removed his tie, brushed his hair and rode the lift down to the reception desk, where he asked a featureless young woman where a man could get a drink in this town at this time of night. The featureless young woman, nodding over our father's shoulder, said the only open bar, as luck had it, was the Lakeshore.

Our father padded towards the sliding glass door beneath the neon sign with blood beating in his ears. He felt as if he was wearing socks. He had no sensation below the level of his waist and outwards from the points of his shoulders. He felt he might faint.

He crossed the technicolour-yawn carpet and arrived at the near end of the bar, where the featureless young woman materialised to pour him a light beer. In the mirror behind the bar, our father saw a slick-haired man—a salesman, but not Tom Dews, thank God—sitting four stools along. There were no patrons in the lounge area. At the far end of the bar a noisy bushel of five men and two women had gathered. The men were indistinguishable in their uniform of business shirts rolled halfway up their arms. Both women were perched on stools, as if on display. One was the Bucky or Becky of memory, although it might not have been, as she had the same hair but a different voice and a different laugh, or possibly it was the same voice but a different laugh and different hair. He did not dwell for long on the Bucky, the Becky.

There was no change in Cicada, except that her hair was the colour of Japanese maple leaves in their dying throes. She perched on a bar stool with her legs crossed at the ankles. She sipped red wine. She was wearing a faded orange T-shirt stretched across her bust. She was in the worst bar in the world, entertaining the worst men in the world, cawing like carrion birds. The bar wasn't distinguished enough to be dingy; the men weren't ruined enough to be rakes. It was a thoroughly modern setting, clean, franchised, synthetic. Its awfulness lay in its insipidity.

Her deep red hair hung over her left eye. She flicked it aside; it fell back.

Bored and disengaged, she let her eyes wander around the mostly empty bar. Suddenly her hair gave a violent jerk, as if from an electric shock. By this, the iota of emotion in that jerk, our father told himself that she had seen him.

He waited. He drank in millilitre-sized sips. He would be the vacuum for eternity.

The slick-haired salesman approached him, but our father, who was never rude, ignored his greeting until the man took the hint and left the bar, thus clearing a line of sight to Cicada Economopoulos.

He could wait just as long as she could.

Fear of doing wrong, or of doing right?

Fear of blowing his chance, or of not blowing his chance?

Fear of the Most Beautiful Woman?

Fear of his own smell?

He tried to tell himself he was running an experiment. Perhaps, he thought, he was running for a place in history.

And just as a vacuum knows no enemy, only friends, when her boredom got the better of her stubbornness Cicada went to the bathroom. When she emerged, freshly made-up (but why? He ached. How do you touch up the *Mona Lisa?*), she swept up her half-full glass of red wine from her corner of the bar, moved away from the group of salesmen, leaving in her wake a complex potion of blatant longing stares and the shrill glee of the now top-of-the-dungheap Bucky or Becky, gliding across with her figure-skater's posture, her Attic features carved into stony perfection by years of servitude, bearing her perfection as if on a tray, she stopped behind John Wonder and waited for him to swivel on his bar stool.

He had exhausted his supplies of patience. He swivelled.

Her eyes, he saw, were the green and brown and red of pistachios.

'Have you heard the one about the snail?' she said.

Our father ducked his head. Literally, he ducked. His hand flew up to his face to protect it. He felt the slap coming before it arrived. He felt the wine sting his eyes before it was flung. He felt his head ring before it was concussed.

'This guy finds a snail in his living room,' she went on. Two fingers went to the lock of hair over her left eye and tucked it behind her ear. 'He goes to the back door and throws the snail out into the garden. He shuts the door and sits back down. A year later to the day, there's a knock at the door. He goes to the door and opens it. Nobody's there. He hears, *Ahem!* He looks down. On the step is the snail. And the snail looks up at him and says, *What was that about?'*

John Wonder uncoiled. His mouth and throat had turned to sand. Cicada seemed preposterously angry with him, furious in fact, but she had kept her wine and her slapping-hand to herself.

'So,' she said. 'What was that about? Why did you walk out of here leaving me with those cunts?'

Our father's heart burst with happiness. She remembered. But he was choking. He had nothing to say. Two, three years of exhaustive rehearsal, and not a single line. To stop himself from falling off his chair, probably into an epileptic fit, he responded to Cicada's question like a bad author; that is, he forgot the text and grasped for the subtext. He forgot the play and went for the meaning. He said: 'How is it that you are in this place and not on a yacht in the Mediterranean being waited on by some handsome young billionaire?'

How indeed? It was what he had wondered every day since he had recognised her for what she was. A world-historical beauty surely needed a world-historical setting, just as a perfect diamond needed to be set into jewellery rather than left rough and unseen in the earth.

Cicada Economopoulos tossed her chin. As she put her mouth to her glass of red wine, she muttered to an invisible third conversant: 'Men!'

He had heard the phrase 'turned on her heel', of course, before now. But he had never seen it enacted in one simple movement with the eloquence of feminine centuries. Cicada

Economopoulos turned on her heel, went back to the group of salesmen and, to Bucky or Becky's savage but somehow inevitable and therefore comforting chagrin, threw her arms around the tallest and youngest of the men, pressed her chest against his, and began to slow dance.

No music was playing.

John Wonder left the Lakeshore, went to his room, and fell into a deep sleep. It was over. He could visit Menis Economopoulos in the morning and hold the customary interview and receive his drink and his snack, and never again give Cicada a moment's thought. When he woke in the morning, fresh as a child, he wished he could have thanked her. It was over.

And so he visited Dorothy Ellen O'Oagh with a small pound cake for her one hundred and twenty-seventh birthday. She wore a cream blouse with a ruffled collar, a navy-blue skirt, stockings and pumps. *Stockings!* he thought. She was asleep, of course, or adrift in her customary vegetative contemplation that outwardly resembled sleep. He placed the pound cake on the nightstand beside her electric armchair and followed his standard procedures for verifying her world record, taking down the observances of the white-coated doctor who measured her heartbeat and blood pressure. The doctor hummed 'Happy Birthday'. Our father, having spent the requisite fifteen minutes by her side, was readying to leave when Dorothy Ellen O'Oagh almost caused him to suffer a fatal heart attack of his own.

'You!'

Her eyes opened.

'Mrs O'Oagh,' he spluttered, blushing as if caught in some criminal act.

'You were not here.'

Our father cleared his throat and sat back down.

'I brought you some pound cake for your birthday,' he said, feeling that he was making excuses to his mother.

'You were not here,' she whispered again, her mouth a frill on a heart monitor, a seismic tremor. Lipstick had been applied expertly. Lipstick! 'Last year.'

He could not suppress a smile. Mrs O'Oagh, as people loved to joke, was sharp as a burr and never sharper than when she was unconscious.

'You remember?'

'I remember 1936,' she said. 'I was already a grandmother. Of course I remember last year.'

'I apologise,' he said. 'There were circumstances.'

'I condemn you,' she rasped.

There was nothing our father could say to this; he mutely bowed his head.

'I thought—' she took a rattling breath '—if you were not here then I must have passed on. God had remembered me at last. But now I see you were only deceiving me.'

'It will not happen again,' he said.

'Another cruel lie,' she wheezed.

He waited for more, but she was asleep again, or had passed into her other state, or had lost interest in him.

•

Menis Economopoulos showed no sign of remembering that our father had missed a year. As they sat down for their one-hour interview Menis picked up on subjects left fallow for two years as if the conversation had barely paused for a moment. He vented his bitterness at his enemies and lamented the tragic death of his mother and father. He cursed the health of Dorothy O'Oagh and bemoaned the downward trajectory of his existence. His giant ears glowed. There was nothing self-pitying about his tone, which was as energetic and combative as always, while slightly perplexed, as if he couldn't quite understand how the facts of life had treated him so badly while the temperament he had been given was so cheerfully belligerent. He carried on as if our father were not there, ranting and raving and plotting all the ways he would like to bring about what he called Mrs O'Oagh's 'timely demise'.

Our father was not listening to Menis Economopoulos. All our father noticed was that the tray of drinks and snacks that was usually carried into the study ten minutes after the interview had started was present on his arrival and was unremoved when he left. He even prolonged the interview, encouraging Menis to go on more than usual (an encouragement Menis did not need), to see if Cicada would come in and take the tray away. But she did not. And our father left in a state of both nervous exhaustion and triumphant euphoria. He needed no further proof that he had had an impact on her. He did not ask himself what that impact might be, positive or negative. It was enough that something he had done had caused her to alter her behaviour. He felt as warmed and flattered as if some eternal sculpture, the *Venus de Milo* or the *Winged Victory*, had come to life for him alone, and smiled upon him. Beauty, the ideal form, had noticed him.

'Men!' One word.

And her absence from duty this morning.

His virtue, such as it was, had been preserved. He had done nothing wrong. He had overstepped no lines. He had, in some way, warded her off. He had stayed faithful to his marriage. Marriages.

Enough to keep him going for another year.

10

After Dorothy Ellen O'Oagh's one hundred and twenty-seventh birthday, our father followed his normal routines with a sense of gratitude towards the hand of fate. The way he saw it, he had dodged a bullet. Life was busy enough without the complication of a fourth woman. Busyness, in fact, was the defining trait of his existence, or existences. He did nothing but rush from one of his lives to the next, fulfilling his commitments to the best of his abilities, unappreciated of course, but to be unappreciated was just one of the mounting deposits in the price he had to pay, for to be appreciated was to be understood, and to be understood was unthinkable.

So he permitted himself a private pat on the back for being a conscientious father and husband. He had excised all other distractions. He had no friends, no siblings, no relations above the procedurally cordial with his workplace and workmates. We think of the years that passed by, grooved into identicality by the constancy of his routine, one year slipping through his fingers much like the next; and yet he, our father, had to live through the days. And the days were infernally complicated. Any situation he was in, any person he met, had first to be subjected to a private assessment: Can this be a threat? Can it escape from its compartment? Once it had passed that test, he could admit it to his orbit. Otherwise, the practicalities absorbed him. He had not only three wives and three Adams and three Evies in three different places. He had three dentists, three doctors, three accountants. He had three solicitors. He had three local butchers and bakers, three car mechanics, three home handymen, three plumbers, three electricians, three separate diaries. The maintenance of each of his three lives was not as risk-filled as it had once been, as he had grown used to its demands and was something of a past master. But it was terribly, and increasingly, tiring. Its exercise of his faculties of memory and keeping track, which he had convinced himself over the years was good for his health, like a forced fitness regime, now seemed to be depleting him. Can you imagine what all that keeping track must do to a mind? Can you imagine?

No, he had no room for another. And by not falling for Cicada, he could tell himself that he was acting with honour.

Three of this, three of that, three of the other. But he had only one set of parents, and it could seem to him, looking back, that if his parents had been a little younger and able to stay alive a little longer, the effort of keeping his existences compartmentalised would have been too daunting for contemplation.

The death of Mr and Mrs Wonder, in the year that John turned forty, had been the first domino to fall.

He and Sandy had been together for nearly ten years. While regretfully childless, their life together was otherwise fulfilling. Sandy's medical career was stellar, John had established his reputation in the trivia world—now television game shows and board game makers were paying him to compile and verify their questions—and their romantic life, constricted between their obligations, was if anything more vigorous than ever. The more successful Sandy grew as a world-leading medical researcher, teacher and mentor to the best and brightest youngsters in her profession, the more she developed a taste for wild sex acts. She would fellate him in graveyards, tear off his pants in stairwells, present herself naked in a disabled person's bathroom, frilled gown at her ankles, in the middle of a scholarly formal dinner. John accepted all this with the usual relish. Sandy was a woman of spasmodic but irresistible needs, and he was here to satisfy them.

His contentment was shaken by the death of his parents. Coincidentally, he and Sandra had just endured another of the unpleasant occasional dinners with Mr and Mrs Wonder. During the dinner, an argument had arisen over a dog. John said, 'When I was young, you bought me a dog.'

'We most certainly did not,' Mrs Wonder said. 'I loathe dogs.'

'And I get allergies,' Mr Wonder said to Sandra. 'I don't know where John gets these ideas.'

But John insisted. 'It was when I was three or four years old. He was a golden retriever and his name was Hedley. Whenever someone was hugging or showing affection in the house, Hedley would try to squeeze between us, to be part of the hug. I called him Jelly-Bags, for Jealous.'

'What piffle,' John's mother said. 'You have dreamt it up.'

Later, after the parents had left, Sandy said, 'Did you really have a dog?'

'You do not believe me.'

'Well, I did until you said there was affection shown in your house.'

John was troubled and upset by what Sandy had said. Not because she was wrong, but because she was right. When he thought about it, he couldn't remember hugs at home. So what was the story about the dog? Had he imagined it? He couldn't remember. At length, it was more believable that he had made Hedley up. His memory was that unreliable, his wishing that constant. He concentrated his mind away from memory, towards fact. Golden retrievers were first bred by a Scottish landowner,

Sir Dudley Marjoribanks, or Lord Tweedmouth, in 1868, when he crossed a yellow Wavy-Coated Retriever with a Tweed Water Spaniel. Golden retrievers are the most popular breed of dog in our country. Our father breathed again. He knew that much.

Very soon after that night, Mr and Mrs Wonder had been driving home from a symphony orchestra performance, Mr behind the wheel, when they had sped through a stop sign and been wiped out by a semitrailer. John was overseas with work at the time, and the disclosure of the news was staggered, or muffled. He had a phone call from Sandy saying his parents had been in an accident. She knew no more than that, but he suspected the worst while changing his travel schedule to get straight home. He was on a fifteen-hour flight before he could receive any further information. By the time he landed, he was braced to hear that his parents were no more. And so, when he called Sandy from the airport and received not her voice but an answering machine message saying, 'John, if this is you, I know this is irregular but I had to leave urgently and you will be wanting to know, but unfortunately the news about your parents is the worst.'

How much does the way we learn of a catastrophic event shape our reaction to it? When the event would have happened regardless, and was beyond our control, does it matter at all how the news was broken to us? Or is it of paramount importance—for the living, is our *learning* of the death the real moment of extinction and devastation? Our father was drip-fed his parents' death by one inconclusive phone call, a day of private speculation, and an answering machine message that delivered anything but an explanation. It was a sudden, shocking event delivered to him in opaque slow motion. As a result, once he arrived home his attention was diverted from absorbing the fact of their deaths to an inquiry into the circumstances and reasons. He was dealing with the after-effects of shock without, somehow, experiencing the shock itself.

Sandy, who had been unable to break a long-standing commitment to a research conference, had left a list of phone numbers: a doctor, a police officer, a counsellor, a morgue, a funeral home. John called the police officer and when, a series of recorded messages and dead ends later, he got through, the sergeant told him that 'unfortunately' his parents had died when his father disobeyed a stop sign, but 'fortunately' the driver of the fatal pantechnicon had survived without a scratch. Our father held the phone thinking that these adverbs were inserted to soften the brutality of the facts, to show that the policeman was a human being too, but they had the directly opposite effect. When our father contacted the doctor, he was told that an autopsy had been carried out by a state medical examiner whose number he could obtain if Dad wished. When our father got through to the medical examiner, he was told that there were 'signs of struggle' on both victims: scratches on his mother's face and pieces of skin and traces of blood under the fingernails of both of his parents.

'It appears,' said the examiner, who sounded blocked up, like he had a cold, 'that the cause of their running through the red light was that Mr and Mrs Wonder were having a strenuous physical altercation. This is also backed up by the truck driver's statement, which was that their car had already spun around and was side-on as it came through the stop sign. When elderly motorists are involved, we often find that the driver has suffered a stroke or a heart attack that causes the accident. But this time, it does actually appear that Mr and Mrs Wonder were, ah, I think the only way to put it is, they were wrestling.'

Between sniffles, the medical examiner could not hide a remnant of humour, as if he had told this story already to colleagues, and a part of him was unable to remember that now he was telling his story to the only child of the deceased.

'Thank you,' our father said. 'Since I can remember, my mother hated the way my father drove.'

'Well,' said the examiner, 'not every couple gets to go out together.'

'They did everything together,' John said. 'Even their fighting.'

'At least they went out doing what they loved.'

He went about the business of taking care of funeral and legal and medical and financial arrangements, and was then into the packing of their possessions and the selling of their house, and the practicalities steered him away from himself. Sandy was greatly comforting, as he would expect, but she was nothing if not honest and did not attempt to pretend that she had loved or even liked Mr and Mrs Wonder. Ever since the night of The Outburst, John had, he now realised, emotionally abandoned his parents.

It was only on their death certificates that Sandy learnt the first names of Mr and Mrs Wonder.

Adam and Evelyn.

•

A subtle difference, there was, in John Wonder's new life as an orphan. Although his work was standardised to the last attometre, after his parents' death it seemed to our father that he was speaking and hearing in a slightly different accent. That his skin was registering changes of temperature and humidity, even atmospheric pressure, with a new sensitivity. That he was hearing and smelling the world not better, not worse; just differently. He could not put his finger on it. He had changed. Everything had changed. But only by one degree, not enough for him to be able to draw any conclusion about the nature of that change or what, if anything, he could or should do about it.

The answer, and for that matter the question too, had to come from another. If John's consciousness were an ecosystem at that stage, it would have resembled the continent of Australia in 1787, at the last moment before European settlement. He was sheltered, contained, isolated, in perfect and more or less eternal equilibrium. He was ripe for invasion and heartbreakingly vulnerable to new strains of disease.

His work, when he was forty, had morphed from the verification of records to the composition and administration of trivia games to the authentication of what might be described as urban myths. The almanacs and compendia of the world had been through their wild adolescence, when it was no longer enough to know about the height of Everest and the depth of the Marianas Trench, nor to know the heaviest weight lifted by nothing but a beard. The fad for trivia board games had peaked. By the 1990s, the taste for new facts tended increasingly to the obscure and archaic and disputed, which suited our father, firstly because he had not liked the direction in which his work had taken him over the previous decade of 'Guinnessports' and their tabloid ilk, and secondly because the requirements of his job became not so much to dream up and verify new records as to consult the past and authenticate old ones. In trivia, the advent of the Internet had brought on an attack of self-doubt. Everything was questionable. Every 'known fact' was back in play. Every truth had to be re-checked, gone over, before the world could start turning again. In the strangely tilted mood brought on by his parents' death, this suited our father just fine.

So, for example, in the new age of miscellanies, he was assigned the task of personally verifying Pi to one thousand decimal places. He had to investigate the thirty-three degrees of Freemasonry, from Entered Apprentice all the way to Sovereign Grand Inspector General. He had to measure the world's standards for egg sizes, envelope sizes, boxing weight divisions, airport marshalling signals, care symbols on clothing labels and the deities common to at least seven ancient cultures. This is, to say perhaps even less than the least, not even to scratch the surface of what his work entailed. He had to travel to Hong Kong to verify the truth of the story known as 'The Eaten Cremains', in which a family living in the far east had annually sent a jar of spices for their mother in England to stir into her Christmas cake and remember them by, until one year the old lady had gone to Hong Kong in early December to spend Christmas with them herself. A week before Christmas, a jar of spices arrived back in the old country, where the lady's second daughter had stirred them into her own Christmas cake, which she and her family enjoyed greatly until they received a letter, delayed mysteriously in the post, telling them that the matriarch had died in Hong Kong and the relatives had sent back, in a glass jar, her ashes. 'The Eaten Cremains—fact or myth?' was the heading of the briefing note our father received from his organisation, which was suddenly worried that it had been publishing the story for years as factual. Now, it was being questioned by this impudent new agent of scepticism, the World Wide Web. (Dad was able to ascertain, by means of tracking down not only the family involved but the old lady herself, now comfortably resident in Hong Kong, that it was a myth. This did not worry his assignment-givers back at work, who divided his task into 'Urban Myths Confirmed' and 'Urban Myths Busted', published in companion hardback editions two years later.)

In tracing the origins of urban myths, our father had to consult with many more human beings than when his work had concentrated on trivial facts. Very often the culture carriers of myth were journalists and other writers, and it was in this capacity that he met a woman of north South American extraction—Guyanese/Venezuelan/Ecuadorean, to be precise—who gave him some aid in investigating a myth involving a factory worker who had inadvertently caused his contact lenses to weld with his corneas, and when he removed his lenses at the end of the day became either permanently blind or permanently clear-sighted (there were two versions of the myth). The journalist who first reported the story, from a bureau in Caracas, was named Paulina Morelos, and our father was able to locate her at the newspaper where she worked. When he arrived to interview her, she invited him to a small Mexican restaurant situated in a car park that served what she claimed to be the best chicken mole poblano outside Oaxaca.

Paulina explained with swivel-eyed whispering urgency, as if she were Deep Throat and our father Woodward and Bernstein, how she had come across the story and run the gauntlet of factory owners, vested political interests, and 'the powerful contact lens lobby, otherwise known as Big Vision'. Even though the event involving the factory worker had occurred eight years earlier, Paulina was still looking over her shoulder, literally, saying she feared reprisals from the multinational stooge network employed by Big Vision. Dad said little, taking notes and trying to keep down the challenging pieces of chicken in brown sauce.

This woman had the coarse coconut-fibre hair, beaked nose and bow-shaped mouth of her racial origin, John observed as he blinked away the tears brought on by the fiery confrontation between chilli and chocolate. Paulina was about five years younger than he, in her mid-thirties, with mocha-coloured skin. Her manner was brusque and her speech laden with pat journalistic phrases, although those could have been an artifice of her imperfect English. She spoke with a strong Latin-American accent and verbal tics, such as a penchant for the present tense and a habit of confusing 'because' with 'that's why'. So she would say something like, 'The corporate affairs lobbyist from Big Vision is parked on my front lawn, that's why I break the story the day before.' Conversely, she also said, 'The mayor's office is too corrupt to trust. Because I tell the whole world.' Until our father had analysed and corrected for the transposition, put the verbal cart back behind the horse, he thought she was slightly mad.

Paulina was wearing a sleeveless singlet and grey sweat shorts, as if on her way to the gym. On her right biceps was a pink scar the size and shape of a eucalyptus leaf, contrasting brightly with the darkness of her skin.

'You're not listening,' she interrupted herself. And he wasn't. But it was not something people normally said.

She gave her conspicuous scar a hard flick with her index finger, both to arrest his eye and to show that it didn't hurt.

'When I am twelve, I have a boyfriend I will love for my whole life. He is criminal and my parents hate him. That's why I want to shit them, I go with him to a tattoo parlour and have the same symbol as him tattooed onto my arm. It is the yin and yang. Don't laugh,' she commanded, though Dad wasn't and nor was she. 'Yin and yang, it is cool at the time in Georgetown. But by the time I am thirteen, that's why he is an asshole, I am not going to stay with him for another day, forget the rest of my life. There is nowhere to do tattoo removal. So I do it myself. I heat a steak knife and cut it out. I never forget how it hurts. And the worst thing is, when I bandage it up and cry myself to sleep with the pain, my parents chew me out and the only person who is nice to me is the asshole, my ex-boyfriend. Because we then start going out again. I think he love me more for cutting it out than for getting the tattoo in the first place. I offer to have it put on the other arm, to show I love him forever, but he says no. When we get through all my healing, he run off with my best friend.'

John Wonder averted his stinging eyes. The meal was finished and although he was fairly sure she was a reliable witness to the story of the man whose corneas were welded to his contact lenses, he was not sure about anything else. It was as if he had come to see a reputable source about authenticating a doubtful story, and instead had found the story authenticated by a source who, in every other way, was disreputable.

'So you are able to take me to the man himself?' he said.

'My ex-boyfriend? He still in Guyana. He been in jail for thirteen years. Drugs, you know? Asshole.'

'No,' our father stuttered, 'I mean the blind ma—'

'I know who you mean!' With a dry cackle, Paulina punched our father, unnecessarily firmly he thought, on the point of his shoulder, leaving it throbbing.

'Sure, I take you,' she said, and led him out of the restaurant by the hand. Hers was tiny, a child-sized hand, even though she was a stocky five-foot-four.

Her car was a half-destroyed Mustang. She drove like a maniac and made him think of his parents. He still wondered why he had not only not cried over their deaths, but not even felt any sadness. It was as if his parents had served their evolutionary purpose and, from the time of The Outburst, he was already outliving them.

On a strange compulsion, as Paulina threw them down the wrong side of broad but whimsically-paved roads to the outskirts of the Latin megalopolis, our father decided to tell her about his parents. He could not discern if she was listening or not. She was focused on the road like a rally racer, her lips opening and closing as if giving herself directions. Her frizzy black hair was pulled into a failed kind of chignon, and for driving she wore blue-tinted sunglasses. The car reeked of stale cigarette smoke and the back seat was covered with papers, compact discs, folders, notebooks and other journalistic flotsam.

He finished talking about his parents before they arrived at a dismal blue-painted concrete house in a treeless estate on the edge of the city. Paulina had said nothing in response to his confession about his parents. The car skidded to a halt on the concrete apron in front of the house and she jumped out urgently, as if the Mustang were about to catch fire. She had a chunky but firm figure, curveless and utilitarian, like a martial artist's.

She took him inside the house and introduced him to an elderly Spanish-speaking woman in black, who guided them through a labyrinth of shadowy rooms in which indeterminate other women and men sat, until they came into a bright courtyard. Among the weeds, sitting with his face to the sun, was a man wearing a Continental Airlines sleep mask and a pair of basketball shorts. His greased black hair was trained back off his forehead. He looked like he was sunbathing, but the day was more than forty-five degrees.

Paulina barked at him in Spanish. The man smiled and shook hands with our father. On Paulina's request he removed his sleep mask. Dad saw his scarred and indubitably sightless eyes. The man began to talk.

'He just bullshitting on about the injustice and the compensation,' Paulina interjected. 'He never get it. He never has a lawyer. They say it is his own fault that's why there are warnings against wearing contact lenses without goggles in the factory?'

'I can see how they could argue that,' Dad said hesitantly, not wanting to take sides.

'You can see that! Well good for you! At least you can *see*! Because you are an asshole like the rest of them!'

He was still trying to work out if she had really meant 'because' or 'that's why' when his head was painfully ringing.

She had punched him. Not slapped, but punched him with a closed fist.

'I beg your pardon,' he said. That was not what he wanted to say. That was what he wanted her to say.

'You *will* be begging my pardon,' Paulina said, lighting a cigarette she had cadged off the blind man, who was smiling and nodding away as if enjoying a radio play.

She spoke with him in Spanish for a while longer, sounding intolerant and irritated, though whether at him or at someone else our father couldn't tell. They stayed until Paulina finished her cigarette and then, after she'd low-fived the blind man, slapping his hand as it hung by his shorts, she took our father back through the dark warren to where her Mustang was still ticking in the sun.

Her temper subsided as quickly as it rose. 'It prove nothing. That is a hospital we go to. You see the conditions? Life is shit.' She thumped her steering wheel. 'And it still doesn't prove nothing.'

'Prove anything?'

'You know, I just show you a blind guy. He talk to me in Spanish about his case. Does that prove that the story is true? See, this is *always* my problem.' She smacked her steering wheel again, inexplicably furious with herself. 'You don't need to believe me. That's why I could be making it all up.'

Because she could have been making it all up, our father thought.

'But I do believe you,' he said. 'I trust you.'

'Why you trust me?' She flicked out a hand, dismissively. 'That's why I hit you?'

Because you hit me, our father thought. Yes, yes, that probably is why I trust you. Because you hit me. That's why you hit me.

'You think you know so much,' she said with an intimate viciousness that hit him again, a closed-fist smack in the jaw. 'You know your facts. But what you know about real facts, eh? Anything important?'

'I never said anything about importance.'

'No, you never say. You never say nothing about nothing. You want facts? Here is your numbers. There are three hundred thousand children fighting in wars around the world. And even after all the people who are killed in those wars, there are more deaths from suicide. That not enough? In my country, bribery payments make up a half of what a family spends every week. Eh? You want important? Three and a half million people in this country is HIV-positive. Girls, they want to leave this country. Why not? Every year twenty thousand of them go from here to the USA and Europe to work as slave prostitutes. Children in this country, they three times more likely to suffer mental illness than children in yours. One in five people in this country live on less than a dollar a day. Every milking cow in your country is subsidised more than double that. Every year, six thousand three hundred women in my country die in domestic violence. We have half a million men and women in our armed forces. We have six hundred thousand girls who are pregnant before they are fifteen. You want numbers? You want to fill your books with facts? Go and authenticate something that matters! Eh? You are a fool. And you never say nothing about "importance", like that is your defence. It is not your defence, amigo, it is your last words before you go to *hell*!'

Our father sat, throughout this tirade, disembodied, on a cloud. He struggled to hear the facts through the beating of his pulse in his ears. He might have been the Queen of Sheba floating away on David's songs.

'So anyway,' Paulina said, careering through a busy intersection, 'you see enough? You flying out this afternoon?'

'Not until later tonight,' our father said, his voice a watery croak.

'Eh good,' she said. 'That's why I take you to your hotel and you gonna fuck me.'

•

If it had happened like that, John Wonder's fall from grace, we would still have forgiven him. How could we not? Without Paulina Morelos Sanchez Garcia Bustamente Marcos, two of us, two of his children, one third of his complications, would never have been given the gift of life. How can we look back on the seduction of John Wonder as anything other than a biological, evolutionary triumph? What are the odds against . . . *us*? To ask us to condemn him is to ask us to erase ourselves. We cannot regret his fall. We, above all.

But . . . but it didn't happen like that. Our father had been faithful to Sandy in deed, word and for the most part even in thought and dream for ten years. Sandy, with her planet-sized brain and world-changing conscientiousness and secret sexual adventurism, with her heavy hips and her breasts that sometimes he looked for but couldn't find, because they had poured into some cranny where he had never thought of looking for them, with her busyness that matched his and her dedication to her research, to saving the children of the world, with her unyielding energy and her borderline alcoholism, was his first and only love. He might have been a sex maniac like his late father said all the Wonder men were, but his mania had only found its target in one woman. As dazzled as he was by Paulina's effrontery, our father was not a fast reactor, he was not an opportunist, he was not a womaniser, he was not impulsive. There was an infinite list of what he was not. He was the opposite of all the things that would have made him say yes to her invitation, or command, or whatever it was. He made his excuses.

'You lie,' Paulina said. 'You just tell me you have six hours to spare. Six hours not enough for you? You want more? Cancel your flight. Stay a whole night. That's why you can. You know you can, only you never dare anything. You are weak.'

Dad's head trembled on the end of his neck like a leaf in the wind.

'I am strong.'

'We will see,' said Paulina.

'No,' Dad said. 'We will not see.'

She pulled over. They were at a service station in a coastal desert, midway between two industrial parks. For an instant she regarded him with such pure brown-eyed Third World anger that he thought she was going to headbutt him. She had never asked if he was married. He sensed that to her, his being married was immaterial, both to her proposition and his response. What mattered to her was what she felt like doing now.

'No!' she spat. 'Your favourite word. Get out of my car. But you make sure you say *yes* one of these days. Say *yes* to my story, that's why it is the truth! Get out! *Vamos!*'

11

As you know the ending, we see little point in drawing out the sexual tension between our father and Paulina, the darkest-skinned of our mothers. Their genesis is too important to deploy as a rhetorical tease. This was our father's first infidelity, the one that cut the pattern. What you do not know, and should not have to wait for, is the beginning. Something of our second mother's impulsiveness is taking hold of us. Like Paulina, we cannot wait.

A few months after their first meeting, Paulina heard on the journalistic grapevine that John Wonder was going to be visiting another city, a short flight away, to do what she thought of as his pathetically secret-squirrel work as Chief

Superlative Officer of whatever it was. She didn't care. She had to see him.

In her experience, if she wanted a man, all she had to do was make it harder for him to say no than to say yes. It wasn't a matter of seduction. It was a matter of strategy and manoeuvre, of harnessing natural forces, more like judo. John Wonder had said no, but he wasn't the first and she hadn't wanted him so much anyway. It had seemed that with six hours free in a hotel, waiting for a flight, making love might be as good a way as any to pass the time. And hotels made her horny. The word *hotel*. Sometimes just the word *lobby*.

But she didn't pursue him to the other city out of an ambition to even the sexual score, or break him down, or leave him hanging blue-balled, or teach him a lesson. She wanted to see him because she had news. Things had changed. What she couldn't explain was why, in particular, it was so important to tell *him*. But she was not one for explaining or understanding. Paulina was one for acting.

She found him where her contacts had promised, at another hospital verifying another urban myth. Paulina didn't care what it was. She didn't care about other scoops, only her own.

She waited for him outside, and he soon emerged with his stupid briefcase containing his stupid notebook. She walked up beside him and said: 'Boo!'

He jumped and yelped and his white face went as red as a raspberry, and from that she knew that her trip was worthwhile. The blood spoke: he had been thinking about her as steadily as she had been thinking about him.

'You want to go somewhere?' she said.

'Ah. I have checked out of my hotel,' our father replied.

'I don't mean that, asshole.' She punched him in the ribs, bringing a tight wince to his face. 'I mean take you to lunch. I owe you. This time it's my shout. That's why I got some news.'

Over lunch, another fiery Mexican affair, this time featuring the regional tamales of Veracruz, Paulina told him that she had sold a novel for fifty thousand dollars to a New York publisher.

'I didn't know you dealt in fictions,' Dad said. 'But congratulations.' He raised his frosted plastic glass.

'Of course I'm a novelist,' Paulina spat angrily. She was already angry on this point. 'Everyone thinks journalists is frustrated fictionists. I am too bored to take you through that story. I am a novelist first, I am a fictionist, and it does not need someone to publish me to announce that I am an artist. I already know it! I am an artist first and then a frustrated journalist. I want to write truth. Because I then become a journalist. And then I sell a novel and I am a fictionist again!'

She knew she had made a hash of this, but her blood had risen too fast.

'So what is your, ah, novel about?' the very white man said after a long eating pause.

'I wish you don't ask me that,' Paulina said. 'Everybody gonna ask me that, and I'm sick of it already. Oh, it's about this and about that, and now I told the story. Boring! You wanna know what it's about? You read it! That's all I got to say!'

'Well congratulations anyway,' the very white man said. 'I am proud of you. Ah, assuming this is what you wanted.'

Man, the only thing she wanted more than to shut this man up was to shut herself up. Paulina could feel she was botching this whole thing. She went to the bathroom and had a line of coke to quieten herself down. She didn't know why, but coke calmed her. It sped everyone else up but slowed her down. Strange world. She was regretting coming here and making a fool of herself in front of this ghost, who was, after all, just nice and harmless and calm and kind. So white he was invisible. He didn't have a sun tan, he had a moon tan. He hadn't done nothing wrong. She wanted to burn him and pinch him and puncture him and break his invisible man's cool, but she didn't want to hurt him. Did that make sense? She didn't know. She was hungry. Another back-to-front thing about coke: it made her hungry.

Returning to the table, she talked very calmly with him about why she wrote fiction. She talked about her impatience with only having one life to lead. Since she was young, she'd fantasised about different universes where she could lead hundreds of lives in addition to her own. She led these lives, for years, through her reading, and then decided that there might be a way through the door, into a different dimension, one with more substance than reading could give her. This was why she was a fictionist, she said. She was greedy. She wanted more lives than her own.

'I thought you were more interested in facts than fiction,' he said.

'Eh. You tell people facts, who listens? Eight hundred million people every day go to sleep at night with not enough nutrition. Three in four people in my country never make a telephone call. But who cares? Who listens?'

'More people in my country vote in television talent shows than in the national elections,' our father said. 'More people recognise the Golden Arches of McDonald's than the cross of the Christian church. My countrymen spend more money on pornography than on foreign aid.'

'Uh-huh,' Paulina said approvingly. 'You are a man of hidden shallows. You fit in with your countrymen. You all swim in trivia, it is your natural water. And for me, you know, the facts is too painful to tell. For my countrymen. Who want facts? Too much pain. The only way to open ears is to invent. The only way to escape my pain is to escape me, and live in other lives.'

'I think that is what has driven me too,' he said, surprising her. She hadn't given much thought to what had driven him. But then he spoke with some emotion about the life he had led, enclosed in his world of trivia. It's strangers, she thought. People are such assholes, they can never unburden themselves to those they love. They unburden themselves to complete strangers. And then, by sharing the burden, they turn those complete strangers into those they love. And then they can't unburden themselves, be honest with them, anymore, because they are no longer strangers. May I always be a stranger to this strange man.

The very white man with the see-through eyes said that when his parents had died he started to believe that they were right when they told him he had always been a failure. In his life, trying to deny he was a failure, he had sought escape in the achievements of others and the greatness of human hope. Every time he met someone who had done something extraordinary, he said, he learnt something from their capacity for hope. Even if the range of their hope was tawdry celebrity, he said, they were inspired to act.

'We live vicariously,' he said, 'people like us. I know I am not a creator like you, but we are not a million miles apart. When you said you were greedy for more lives than the one you live, I thought: I know you. I know who you are. I apologise. I am talking too much.'

'Why you apologise? You hardly say nothing,' she said quietly, patting his hand. Now she was stroking the back of it. He didn't move it away. It felt like paper.

She told him she wanted him to read her novel, 'that's why I wanna know your opinion'.

'What is it called?'

She swallowed. She knew he was about to take his hand away. She had no title for the novel.

'It's called,' she said, thinking hard and then giving up, allowing the first thing to come to her head to keep going out of her mouth, 'Wonder of Wonders.'

His hand was an old man's hand, even if he was not much older than her. She had made love with men a lot older than him. And younger too. And middle. And why was she going on this random thought stream?

'You got no hotel,' she said. 'But I do got one. With a lobby.'

•

It couldn't have been easy, Paulina's seduction of our father, but it was quick. They had spent a few hours together the previous summer, and now, in the autumn, they were going to a hotel where she would cut them some lines of cocaine and John Wonder would discover, in the following hours, why its consumption was a trillion-dollar industry. He had fallen, without for a moment feeling that his love for Sandy was one grain lighter, in love with Paulina. She possessed a force that he could not resist. Yes, perhaps it was just that for the first time in his forty years an attractive woman was chasing him, flying from one city to another to ask him for sex, and he was undone by the sparkle of the drug and the flattery of the woman, the grossest and weakest of weaknesses. Yes, perhaps this was the outcome of the tilting of his world, the change in accent and tone and affect and sonar clarity, caused by the death of his parents. Perhaps he suffered from a loneliness so profound that his happy marriage with Sandy, as satisfying as it was, as comfortable as was their mutual independence, would always leave a great part of him untouched and still seeking to be loved. Sandy was, really, when you boiled it down, very self-sufficient. But he couldn't let himself follow that line of logic, for to compare her with Paulina might lead to finding her wanting, and he could not find Sandy wanting in any way. The problem, the lack, was his. And now he had compounded it. Irrevocably.

Paulina rammed her fingers into his eyes and prised them open while they made love. She dared him until his gaze met hers; she studied him through his eyes, to see if somehow he might betray himself. She also wanted him to be watching her as she climaxed. Her back arched and she lost her voice and her legs stiffened around his hips and she went into an electrical kind of spasm. It was quick and simple and stunning. There was none of the envelope-pushing voluptuousness of his lovemaking with Sandy, none of the soft padding. Paulina's body was functional and linear. It knew what it wanted, and took it from him.

He lay on the bed and watched her walk to the shower. Perhaps this was the moment when he really did fall in love with her, for the sight of her figure, chubby and even dumpy yet uncurved, with no waist or bust, just a compact little nut of pleasure, moved him to tears. The smallness of her feet. Her confidence in her nakedness. Sandy conquered her shyness by brave endeavour, by pushing herself out of her comfort zone, by trying things that she knew were out of character. Sandy used lovemaking to explore new boundaries. Paulina, he saw then, had found her boundaries at a very young age and would be happy living her entire life naked. Clothes were the imposition. Sex was exercise.

When she came out of the bathroom she found him hysterical, literally broken down, sobbing into his soaked pillow. Paulina, not knowing what to say but knowing how he felt, sat and stroked his back. She did not talk. She had not asked him if he was married. It was none of her business. He had given nothing away, but she didn't care. She didn't want lies. She wanted silence. And she could see, in his grief, that he wanted silence too and the comfort of her hand in the loose papery wrinkles between his clenched shoulder blades.

Later, after they had made love again and showered and dressed and resumed the professional duties they had been performing until a few hours ago, she explained—or, rather, declared—that she did not want him to change his life in order to see her. She just wanted him to let her know if he was in her region, and to make an effort to clear an afternoon for her.

He shook his head. 'I love you,' he said. 'I am not going to abandon you.'

'I not afraid of being *abandoned*,' she sneered.

His face furled in on itself. 'Sorry, that was not what I meant. I put it the wrong way around. What I meant was, I am not going to let you abandon me.'

And this was how it began. When he was with Paulina, something crumbled inside him, in the solvent of happiness. He had found his soul mate. Paulina was a woman of facts and greed, a counterbalance to his universe of facts and self-sufficiency. She was his identical twin and his polar opposite: the one who put his world in balance. He was so truly and deeply happy with her that he imagined, in his delirium, that Sandy could not but be happy as well, to see him so happy. There could be nothing wrong with what he was doing, not even in Sandy's eyes. He had an inspiration about greed, about one life not being enough, about being able to live two lives, and then when he woke up by Paulina's side he was suddenly overwhelmed by the need to go to the airport, get on the plane, and be in the kitchen at home with Sandy.

'I love you,' he said to Paulina. 'And I will see you soon.'

'That's why you're a good man,' she said. 'But there's no rush. I will be here. Or there.'

12

In Dorothy Ellen O'Oagh's one hundred and twenty-eighth year, our father changed his routines. He spent his week with Sandy and Adam and Evie, who were now entering secondary school, and he spent his week with Paulina and Adam and Evie, who were in primary school, but he did not move on to the scarred woman and the third week with his third set of us. Instead of moving on to where we were waiting for him to sit on the end of our bed and take us to preschool and play with us and love our mother and cook dinners and be our father, instead of all of this, he went back to the town where Cicada Economopoulos lived.

'Men!' One word was all it had taken. He could wait no longer.

He checked in to the Holiday Inn late in the afternoon, in springtime, out of his usual season in that part of the world. The jasmine in the air made him dizzy and melancholy. In order to come here he was taking a risk with his work. There were facts to be verified and authentication processes to be carried out elsewhere, and for the first time in more than thirty years he was delegating the direct task. He passed it off to two younger colleagues (one would not be enough) and did not tell either of them where he was going. He was so fully trusted that no one questioned his whereabouts. He was like a boss. He could do what he liked: even nothing. Even play hooky.

He lay on his bed and read the manuscript of the novel Paulina was currently working on, her fourth since the publication of *Wonder of Wonders*. She seldom released her work to him until the last stage before she sent it to her agent. The process, he had found, was a ritual. She would thrust the manuscript at him with a look both desperate and casual, and ask him to read it quickly, with the assurance that she didn't care what he thought. He would take it away and read it while he was flying to one of his other families. Then, two weeks later, he would return to Paulina with his suggestions. She would fly off the handle, accusing him of having no idea what she was trying to accomplish and of reading it like a schoolboy, without any sensitivity or tact or even a brain. He would say, So why did you want me to read it? She would storm off in a huff. Nothing more would be said of it until, some weeks later, Paulina would sit him down as if in a conference and say she had been thinking about her manuscript and had had a couple of ideas, and what if she made such-and-such changes to it? Knowing that they were precisely the changes he had suggested, he would bite his lip and nod and say, Yes, Paulina, I think your ideas are good ones. It didn't matter to her that he said the ideas were good; it mattered that he said they were hers.

But as he read her fourth novel in the Holiday Inn, he found it impossible to concentrate. Paulina's style was becoming more recherché over time, as if, with her growing stature as a novelist, she had to create a private place into which she could flee from her readers, or make it so hard to follow her that only the supremely committed could get in. It struck him that she was now writing less to communicate than to break off communication, to desert the world of readers. But perhaps this was a distortion of his current mood.

Nevertheless, he did not put it down and watch television or go for a walk, but continued to give his fantasies free rein through the mechanism of pretending to read Paulina's manuscript. He was not unaware of the symbolism, in his act, of infidelity, but nor was he equipped to stop it. It was ever thus.

He had decided that if Cicada Economopoulos was in the bar tonight, then she must be there every night, which would mean she was unworthy of his attention, a bored, boring small-town girl who could imagine no better way of wasting her youth and beauty than upon a passing parade of salesmen. Our father wanted this, for to see her exposed in her squalid ordinariness would release him.

If, on the other hand, she was not here, that would, might, surely did mean that Cicada only came to the Holiday Inn on those nights when she knew John was there, which meant that she structured her activities around his visits, which meant that he was a figure of some importance to her. If this was the case, then—then he exalted. The thought that Cicada might be coming here to show off to him, even if it was to torment him, gave him unthinkable, unspeakable pleasure.

So he tried to tell himself that when he went down to the bar tonight, he was in a win-win situation. He would either be freed from Cicada or put in a position of tremulous power over her. Whether she was there or not, he would gain an insight into his condition.

•

As rehearsed as he was, to a fever pitch, almost to paralysis, he could not have anticipated what happened when he went down to the bar. In fact, he did not make it to the bar.

By the time he exited the lift on the ground floor, our father could not recognise his surroundings. Or rather, he recognised them but not from the places in his memory where they should have been catalogued. The lobby, through which he had walked countless times, was high in colour, almost day-glo, with shadows as black as ink, and as he paused to look around he had a terrifying sense that he was not living this scene for the first time, but was revisiting it from a dream he had had, possibly the night before, possibly from some other time. He did not recognise the lifts. He did not know if he had just come out of them. Instead of turning right and entering the Lakeshore Bar, he followed some instinct that told him to exit through the front revolving door of the hotel itself. Outside, when he was in the light cast by the fluorescent-lit porte-cochere over the parking apron, he again sensed that he was retracing his steps from a dream. He crossed the road, without checking for traffic, and found himself in a petrol station. Again—from the dream. He had been here inside his mind. He walked to the front counter and bought a Mars Bar. He never ate Mars Bars, but was compelled by some kind of logic from the dream. He recognised the Mars Bar in his hand. He recognised the face of the young Sikh manning the counter. He recognised every imprint the interior of the petrol station was making on his eyes. When he stepped outside, he did not know how he had come to be in the petrol station. He saw the Holiday Inn across the road and felt that he knew it only like this—just like this, from this precise point in space—and only from his dream. He could not recall ever having been inside it.

He did not unwrap or eat the Mars Bar, but put it in his pocket. Something told him that in the dream, he did not eat the Mars Bar. He turned left out of the petrol station and walked along the footpath towards a shopping mall a half-mile away. He walked. To his side was a newly-turfed area that was part of the industrial park complex beyond it. The path branched off into a park created for the lunchtime use of the workers. There was a gazebo and a small hedge maze. He recognised these things.

John Wonder's heart began to race. A sweat broke out on his face, on his whole body. He looked at his shirt. He did not know where he had got this shirt, or when he had put it on, but it seemed familiar from the dream. The dream was now ominous to him. It was not that he felt something evil was about to happen. It was that the vast immensity of his dream space seemed to have eaten him up, that it was too large, that he was a microscopic speck against the Grand Canyon of this footpath, this road, this link of hotel car park, petrol station and shopping mall. What happened next—he walked towards the mall—was also in the dream. He was stuck in here, trapped in a space exponentially greater than the world of grooves and ruts and evasions he had carved out of his usual reality; instead, now, he was wandering lost in a dream that was huger than anywhere he had known, he was tiny, he was lost in eternity and infinity, and a fire suddenly broke out in his chest and spread to his face and he was burning with tears, he could find no way out of this, he did not know how he had got here or what he was meant to do next.

13

The first years with Paulina had been the most tempting time for him to see his situation in the standard way: he was having a conventional affair, married in one city, keeping a woman in another. His options were bordered by a simple matrix. He could keep the situation going, or he could break it off with Paulina. He could leave Sandy. He could do one thing, or the other thing, or neither. He was walking a path made smooth by millions. There was nothing unusual about it.

Paulina had affairs with other men. She told him ('In my country, six million men and women is having extramarital affairs, you idiot, that is more than pay income tax'), and our father did not ask for more information. Of information, he received ample. While his sense of justice told him it would have been hypocritical to ask Paulina to account for her actions in his absence, it was his basic avoidance of conflict, call it cowardice, that prevented him from confronting her. Not that he was tempted: our father was not the jealous type. He had to watch his own step too vigilantly to be worrying about what his women were up to.

It also suited him to allow Paulina her 'own space', because her independence ventilated his sense of obligation. If he didn't ask for full disclosure from Paulina or Sandy, then he could tell himself that he did not owe it to them. The lies he was telling them could remain something more benign than dishonesty—something more like mystery—if and only if he permitted a similar mystery to them. He knew there was a piece missing in this deal, that piece being that Paulina and Sandy did not know they were making it. The deal was between John acting on his own behalf and John acting on theirs. Bit of a conflict of interest, no? He knew how egocentric he was being, but, without the equipment to reverse what he had done, he accommodated his conscience to the palliative of knowledge. That is, knowing he was selfish was preferable to not knowing, and a good sight closer to moral responsibility. He couldn't see any way out of lying to his women, but he would not lie to himself.

To his astonishment, in the first years when he was seeing Paulina, events fell in his favour. Paulina, obsessed with her career, was not interested in having him around permanently.

He was one of her lovers, who came and went at times of mutual convenience. She was curious about the facts that should change the world, but totally incurious about him. She had no time to wonder about Wonder. He could not help it, this was absurd, but he was flattered by the title she had chosen for her first novel, because it proved that she knew his name. He could not explain this rationally, but in his heart he was never quite sure that Paulina knew it.

Meanwhile, Sandy, whose career was also flying high, was comfortable with John's supportive role and allowed him—out of her own guilt!—a certain freedom from inquiry when he travelled. Sandy knew of his work, but had never been very interested in it. She sometimes asked herself if John was the type of man to have affairs on the road, but she was so absorbed in her own work, so turned off to sexuality unless he was at home, that she assumed he was the same way. She did not probe herself on this unspoken marriage contract of don't ask, don't tell. She assumed that because she was the first, and because they did so much together, she was the only lover he would need.

And yet our father, a man of conscience, was constantly tempted to snap the thing, break it off. But which? There was no question of leaving Sandy. He loved her. He admired her. They had a house together. She was his first love: he *owed* her. He had absolutely no reason to end their marriage. He might break it off with Paulina, but she asked so little of him, and by ending their affair he would be giving up so much. He thought categorically, our father: things were black or white. As the line of infidelity had already been crossed—he had committed the sin against Sandy once, therefore for all time—breaking with Paulina would not undo what he had done, or exonerate him, or save him, or redeem him. He was in for a penny and in for a peso. There was as little pressure to end the affair as there was to end the marriage. Neither woman knew of the other. What they didn't know couldn't hurt them. It was down to him to erect the firewall in his mind, in his heart, in his conscience. If he could maintain the firewall—and of course the physical frontier—then there was no reason, other than his own pangs and inconvenience, to change the way things were. For all those years his inconvenience and regret and sour insomniac guilt were not enough to promote change. He never made a decision to keep these two women. He put his decision off. By postponement, he made the decision to leave things the way they were.

14

Our father woke in his room in the Holiday Inn and phoned the Economopoulos home. Cicada answered. He told her who was calling, and asked her permission to meet, at a place of her choosing, for lunch. Without showing any surprise at his call, Cicada named a steakhouse chain restaurant and a time. 'Are you going to tell—ask—your father?' John Wonder said. 'No,' Cicada said quickly, assuming that John was asking her to keep their meeting a secret. 'I will not tell a soul.' She spoke in a tone of intimate acknowledgement, as if the first thing she had always understood about John Wonder was that he was a harbourer of secrets; she, too, was such a person.

Our father arrived at the restaurant first. It was a dismal franchise, not unlike the Lakeshore bar where she drank. The town, he knew, was hardly at the leading edge of nightlife or dining, but there had to be better than this. Cicada chose these places expressly, as if to make a statement, not of irony, but of *nostalgie de la boue.* Like a recreational slummer, a wealthy seeker of rough trade, Cicada's first interest was in abasing herself.

He was taken to a booth and given a glass of water. As he waited, he took his third dose of headache tablets for the morning. The episode of the previous night had left his brain feeling laid to waste, charred, as if a bushfire had gone through it. The déjà vu, or whatever it was, had lasted about half an hour. Drenched in sweat and tears, in an overwhelming panic, lost in his infinite dreamland and unable to get out, he had wandered the perimeter of the closed shopping mall. A security guard had walked up and asked him what he was doing. Forced to reply and defend himself, John had woken from his dream. 'I came for a walk,' he said. 'Well, you better go back because there's nothing to see here,' the security guard said.

The security guard had not been in the dream. That was how John knew he had woken. He wiped his face dry and walked back to the Holiday Inn. He was in no mood for the Lakeshore. He went to bed with his burnt-out feeling and woke with a splitting headache. He was sick of it. He had to see Cicada.

She was wearing an outfit he had seen at the Lakeshore: calf-length jeans, high wedges, a floral-printed blouse underneath the tight-fitting electric-blue cashmere jumper. She was wearing light make-up and no jewellery, none on her ears, none on her neck, none on her wrists or fingers. Her hair was, perhaps, the colour of itself: dark chocolate, 85 per cent cocoa.

The early part of their lunch had an air of strange formality. Cicada spoke with propriety and trained elocution, like a marketing trainee. She ordered a salad and Coca-Cola. She had Menis's smokiness around the eyes. Our father, top-heavy with nerves, fell back on the cushion of his knowledge. He told stories from his work, just as he told such stories to his children, to us. He might have wanted to impress her but really he was saying the first things that came to his mind. He ordered a minute steak, something he felt he could eat without making a mess. She seemed to be watching him, so he ate very slowly, talking much.

Surprisingly, Cicada seemed nervous. When John told her about the animal with the slowest heartbeat (blue whale, four to eight beats a minute), and the plant that had bloomed most at once (a 'Queen of the Night', or *Selenicereus grandiflorus*, in the USA which once produced forty blooms in a single evening), Cicada replied, improbably, 'I know that,' or, 'I've read that.' While he talked, she nodded as if she knew everything already. Our father could not understand why she would want to create a favourable impression by lying. He paused and said, 'Do you already know this?'

'No,' Cicada said. 'Why should I?'

So our father continued his story, but Cicada kept on nodding and saying, 'I know that.' He began to leave parts out. It was a relief. Whether she knew anything or nothing, she was bringing him to the point.

Up close—and this was the first time he had been given the licence to examine her so closely or directly—Cicada was both more and less striking than he remembered. Her cheeks and neck had a sprinkling of decorative dark moles. Her teeth were lined up as flawlessly as a North Korean army parade. Her bronze-flecked green eyes smiled coolly. She was every bit as perfect, as Platonically ideal, as he had suspected. She was twenty-nine, nearly thirty years younger than he, but she seemed younger, with her plasticky enunciation and the unlined perfection of her features. Even if everyone seemed younger these days—thirteen-year-olds were actually eighteen, and so on—there was something inexperienced and childlike in Cicada's transparent desire to match John in conversation. The more grown-up she tried to appear, the stronger the impression of youth. In her beauty, there was a slipperiness, a blankness, as if giving him nothing to hold on to. He talked rapidly, darting from subject to subject like a deer seeking shelter; even now, in the first flush, he knew that the predators were his own rank silliness—no fool like an old fool—and the potential for her to grow bored, dangers he redoubled his energies in escaping.

'So,' Cicada said, twisting the lock of hair away from her left eye (it fell straight back), passing from one topic to the next as if on a checklist, 'are you married?'

John saw no reason to lie. He decided he had seen enough and need never see Cicada again. This whole thing was a figment of his imagination. He had authenticated her beauty: she was indeed the Most Beautiful Woman on Earth. But beyond that, she was just a provincial girl saddled with a tyrannical father, leading a dull life perked by the sexual interest she aroused in commercial travellers. She had too much beauty for her needs: she was content to waste nine-tenths. John, so hungry for the extreme and the superlative, was both unsatisfied and relieved. He would not be falling into any further complications here.

'Yes,' he said.

Cicada nodded. 'I know.'

'You knew?' he said, knowing she knew nothing.

'I can always tell. And you have children, a boy and a girl.'

'Adam and Evie,' our father said, roping us into the half-truth, the one-third-of-a-truth.

Cicada gave a satisfied snort, her instincts confirmed. John fancied he could sense a matching disappointment in her, to find that he was just another married man on the prowl. But probably not. And what did he care?

'And your interests?' she said.

'You have been on a lot of, ah, *dates*, haven't you?' he said, his mouth pruning and puckering around the low word.

Cicada, sensing the insult but not wanting to let it go further, said: 'Shall we go for a walk then?'

'But our meals have not arrived.'

'Are you hungry?'

'No,' he said.

'Me neither.'

They walked in a crowded plaza. John felt the eyes of the town. Every man—literally every one—stared at her. Some walked into light poles. One, bedazzled, had to be dragged away by his female partner. The toughest of the men in the plaza, or perhaps those who already knew her, made a point of ignoring her. Every single person was reacting in some way to Cicada. John was fascinated. It was like being led through an experimental laboratory of human sexual attraction.

Though he wasn't listening to her, he picked up enough of Cicada's shaped, trimmed history. She had lived in the town all her life, and remembered her grandfather, Christos. When her brothers had all left, she took on the duty of looking after her father. Of her mother Helenna, she said nothing. The curse of Dorothy Ellen O'Oagh's longevity was the ruling myth of her family. It had formed her as much as her parents, her brothers and her grandparents. It had either killed them or sent them insane. 'But my father and I are the warriors of the family,' she said. 'We will outlive this old woman—even if it kills us!'

At nights and on the weekends, she attended classes in criminal law. She did not sleep, she said matter-of-factly. 'I go to sleep at four o'clock in the morning and wake at seven or eight. I can't sleep.'

'Fifty-eight per cent of adults report symptoms of insomnia at some stage in their lives, but for only six per cent does it last more than one month,' our father said mildly. 'Have you tried to do anything about it?'

Cicada shrugged. 'It's just me,' she said proudly, as if insomnia marked her genius. Changing the subject from her insomnia, she said she spent her days studying, writing essays and helping her father achieve what he could not by himself, under the supervision of the police. She still had two years of her law degree to go. It was taking so long because she had not got into a university course. She was studying by correspondence at community college, which took up to a decade.

Passers-by in the plaza looked at John, and he wondered how long before this got back to Menis, and what Menis would do. He remembered the man's devilish laugh, a laugh full of pleasure in the demise of men. The laugh, he thought, of misery finding itself in company.

As they came to the end of the walk—Cicada had said she had to get home by two o'clock, which was now imminent— our father wondered why she had asked nothing of why he had wanted to meet her. Was she waiting for him to reveal his motives? She showed no curiosity. Aside from asking him if he was married and saying 'I knew that' to every stray factoid he could muster, she had shown no interest in why he was here. His headache was returning. He wanted to get home. For a moment he couldn't recall which home he was late getting back to.

They came to a halt at a bus station. Wordlessly, Cicada chose this as the place of their separation. She turned to face him. She was almost a foot shorter than him, and as he looked down into her face, she shook her hair out of her eyes. She had the bodily control of a model, a dancer. She calculated every smallest gesture. But not a good model, or a good dancer: her calculation was too obvious.

He didn't know what to do next.

He held out his hand. Cicada looked at it. Her fine-boned, biscuit-coloured palm slapped his away, gently. He wondered if she was going to kiss him, but she made no move. It had been the strangest interview of his life, and also the blandest, the most ordinary.

'So . . .' She twitched her head again, like a filly. 'When am I going to see you again?'

She said it with neither welcome nor relish. In fact, she might have been talking to a tutor. She was fighting something in herself, he could see that. Her tone was hostile, but not necessarily against him.

He did not know what to say.

'I want you to know something. I have been asking myself for three years if I should approach you and talk to you. You are the most beautiful woman on this earth.'

Cicada opened her mouth to speak, but he cut in: 'Please do not say anything, that is the last word. I am someone who is qualified to make such a statement. So take it as a fact. From the moment I realised this fact, I have been asking myself if I have any reason to talk to you other than trying to seduce you. Because that was all I wanted. I could see no reason to make any kind of approach other than to make love with you. You are so beautiful, I have been overcome by love. Love, not in the way you might be thinking, but in the sense Plato put it: the desire for beauty. Life is grey when you have been around for a while. Simply by standing here and permitting me to look at you, you are giving me the gift of colour.'

He was breathing heavily. He now realised that he was standing to attention, his shoulders pulled up to his ears like a child making his first speech in front of a hall of adults. He closed his eyes to regather himself. He had been rehearsing these words for three years, awake at night, thinking it through. There was no room in his rehearsals for Cicada to speak. Nor was there any space in his dreams for the plaza, the bus station, the people of her town. If he opened his eyes, he feared that something, a tree or a car or a shopping trolley, would throw him back into the dissociative state of the previous night; he would recognise it! So he had to plough on, keep on saying what he had prepared for so long. He was a weirdo—that was what she was thinking. But that was what he was thinking too! They thought the same, he and she! You think I'm a fucking psycho! Yes, yes, I do too! He did not want to open his eyes and see her scorn, her pity, or her recognition. Better to suspect the worst than to open your eyes and see it confirmed.

'Forgive me, I don't know what I'm saying.' (This too—rehearsed! The swine!) 'I suffer from the disease of candour.' (Dad, don't make us laugh!) 'But please, listen for a moment. Please. I have seen you since you were a child, but I never noticed you until three years ago. Perhaps you changed. Perhaps I had not been looking. But there we have it. And over those three years I have fought with myself, and I am here to tell you that I have won that fight. I have no intention of seducing you—even if I had any chance of "success", so to speak, which I acknowledge I do not. But I have had to assume that I do have a "chance", as absurd as that must sound, in order to go through the requisite mental processes to overcome and reject any temptation. So, to summarise: I only called you this morning, I only came to this town, because I have proven to myself that I am *not* interested in you, ah, sexually. That is a pre-qualification for why I am here. I have proved that point to myself. And for you, to let you know that I can be your friend. I do not know what use I can be as a friend to you, that is for you to choose. But my main point is, if I still felt that I wanted to seduce you, I would never have made any approach. And now I have authenticated the fact, by which I mean, that you are the most beautiful woman on earth. And a second fact: I have authenticated my innocence. That is what I came here to say.'

And then, finished, he opened his eyes, and our father saw a look of such emotion come over Cicada Economopoulos that he wanted to rescind every rehearsed word, every phrase saved up for three years and dumped in front of her like a load of rancid garbage. Lines formed around her eyes and mouth. Soul crept into her eyes. The youth fell out of her. Confusion aged her. At last, something to grasp hold of. Her beauty, so impervious up to this moment, was completed by the quiver around her mouth and the tears filling those verdigris eyes. Thus did our father discover that everything he was saying, at the very moment he was saying it, was a lie.

He had finished his speech. He tried to conceal the dog-like panting in his throat. A cloud passed across the sun, and in the next moment Cicada's face was lit as if touched by the finger of God.

Cicada was wearing sunglasses on the top of her head. She pushed them down onto her nose.

In a diminished voice she said: 'I don't think I've ever heard anyone speak to me like that.'

The first physical contact, a slapped-away handshake. The second: her hand striking him on the shoulder, sliding, melting into something more like sorrow, down his ribs, leaving a mark like a burn.

15

Our father came home and went through his motions. He left us, and went to us. He pursued his regimen with increased vigour and diminished attentiveness. We could sense that the stories he told us were not holding his interest. We did not know why he was only able to impersonate himself. Our mothers told us he was no longer a young man, and we mustn't expect too much of him. Sandy said it with absent-minded pity—she, by corollary, was not a young woman either. The scarred woman said it with tender sympathy, and the foreboding that she might one day have to raise us on her own. Paulina, the second mother, spat it out with contempt. But it was the usual contempt. 'He will be dead before you are grown!' We thought she didn't mean it.

Paulina had always been the most difficult of the three when it came to accommodating the arrangement, which was unexpected because it most suited Paulina to be living in parallel with him, Paulina who had demanded, from the start, that he maintain his base in his home city and not live with her. In a way, the whole arrangement (was it an arrangement? An accommodation? An evasion? A life-sized screw-up?) had been set in train by Paulina's demands for parallelism, and yet it was Paulina who placed it under the most constant emotional strain.

Since those heady days when she had sold her first novel, Paulina's career as a writer of fiction had not gone as she had hoped. Although she seldom talked about it, or not with him anyway, our father knew she was labouring under a burden of disappointment.

This was hardly due to a lack of success. *Wonder of Wonders*, which had prompted her first intimacies with our father, had achieved respectable sales and unqualified critical praise. With her second novel, she had graduated from 'a writer to watch' into 'one of the distinctive voices of our time'. With her third novel, which won a number of prizes, she was 'at the height of her powers' and 'one of the must-read writers today'. Her sales, while never those of the bestselling megafauna, were sufficient to license her to quit full-time journalism and tell lies for a living.

After nearly ten years as our father's mistress, Paulina was the subject of the kind of profiles that she used to write. Of course there was no mention of him, though other lovers were implied or named. She was successful beyond her expectations, true, but success had failed to bring her what she thought it might, that is to say, peace of mind. Ambition and resentment had grooved such powerful habits in her, such driving forces, that literary success only intensified her focus on newer, higher objects of envy. Whereas ten years earlier she had fuelled herself with hatred for third-rate novelists getting published ahead of her, for her employers at the newspaper, and for certain people in her personal past against whom she would wreak revenge in her novels, now that she was 'at the height of her powers' she was more bitter than ever, only her targets sat on a higher shelf: Nobel Prize winners, equivocal *New York Times* critics, ministers for the arts who, in her mind, had snubbed her. Paulina's anger could never be quenched by the mere satisfaction of her ambitions. The greater her fame and credibility, the more virulent her fury. She steadily withdrew from society and gave up most of her lovers. She simplified her existence and concentrated her outrage into her newest project. She lived as a hermit; the only lover she continued to see was my father, for he was the only one who demanded nothing of her, neither her precious time nor her meagre capacity for cosseting.

Paulina did ask herself, from time to time, if she should excise John Wonder, and start with, as it were, a blank page. She was still in her mid-forties and enraged to the verge of combustion. But, if asked, she would have said about the strange pale man of trivia who came to her like the full moon, in his unbreakable phases, 'It is easier to say yes than no.' Of nothing else in life could 'Senora Non', as a Venezuelan literary newspaper called her, say this.

So they didn't change anything.

We did.

16

In the weeks after his declaration—Of dry love? Of redundant celibacy? Of involuted, twisted, ingrown *virtue*?—our father wondered if he had gone too far at the bus stop with Cicada Economopoulos. She did not answer her phone when he called, and he dared not leave messages, in case of Menis. His fears of the father found an echo in his fears of the daughter. He sensed that she was angry, but why? Because he had disrespected her in his little speech? Because he had made a fool of himself? Because, when she had asked him when she might see him again (but what did *see* mean? And how much had it cost her to say that?), he had not replied directly? Because he had spoken too frankly, or not frankly enough? That she was ignoring him was not in doubt, nor was the certainty that he had gone too far. What he could not get a fix on was in what direction too far he had gone.

Then, a month before his regular visit to monitor Dorothy Ellen O'Oagh and Menis Economopoulos, our father received an email. Cicada suggested they meet again at the dire chain steakhouse. She made no reference to her months of non-response. Nor did she mention their last conversation. And when he met her, he found that, as far as Cicada was concerned, the previous conversation might as well never have taken place. At this lunch, they discussed the same kinds of things as at the first. Cicada drank water and our father a glass of wine. He tried to entertain her with stories of trivia and human extremity. Cicada claimed to know it all already. Cicada complained about her life and about the curse of Dorothy O'Oagh. She wore a floral blouse of a material so thinned out by washing and wearing that it looked like dried autumn leaves that would crumble to the touch. Her hair was darkest black, streaked with volts of blue. To her chest she had pinned a pale pink ribbon, looped to signify a Cause. 'Breast cancer week,' Cicada said, catching him staring. 'I tell all my girlfriends to have their mammograms done regularly. I do. I have my doctor check my breasts every six months. We have it in the family.' To John, she could not have spoken more erotically if she had been breathing into his ear across a pillow. Cicada often talked about her breasts in this casual, aseptic way, perfectly aware of the impact she was having yet also feigning innocence, as if she simply liked saying the word, throwing it into conversation like a bomb and seeing who died.

During the lunch she put on a kind of show for him, flirting brazenly with the good-looking male waiter, who was not only young enough to be John's child but younger than Cicada herself. She knew him already. John speculated whether she had slept with him; there was something wounded and hateful in the waiter's eye. She dropped innuendoes, going so far as to hint at where the waiter might find her later in the night. The waiter was, in spite of his white-lipped resentment, visibly aroused (as Cicada pointed out gleefully to John between the young man's visits: 'putty in my sweet little hands'). It was a casually ruthless dismemberment. John wondered if she wanted to make him jealous, or just did it for the hell of it. By the end of the lunch the waiter was practically ready to give *her* a tip. John gave him twenty per cent, in sympathy. Cicada said, 'You're so soft, you know? You should have left him nothing.'

At the end of the lunch, they walked in the plaza again. John was once more euphoric at the effect she had on men. There was a car accident, and our father was sure it was caused by the vision of heaven strolling at his side. She put on her electric-blue cashmere jumper, and eyes began leaping out on stalks.

When they reached the bus stop, as before, it seemed the time for something significant. Already, John's brain trilled, they had their little routines!

'You know,' she said, 'you'd regret it.'

'Regret what?'

He had been telling her about a woman who murdered her husband and served up his parts as a meal to his children. Cicada loved the macabre stories, even if she claimed to have heard them all before.

'Fucking me,' she said.

There was a twitch at the corner of her mouth, but it was nothing to the hot blushes that covered John's face like poured wax.

'I beg your pardon?' he said.

'You'd regret it,' she repeated with a breeziness that seemed, to our father, who was suffering something like an embolism in the base of his throat, forced. 'For me, you know, it'd be just another fuck. But for you—I can see how you'd take it. No offence, but it's not a road you want to go down. You think you would, but you'd end up being the disappointed party.'

Our father's mouth flapped like washing on a line. He didn't know where to start. His sense of chivalry urged him to contradict her, to declare that of course he wouldn't be disappointed, and if she doubted him she should give it a try and see. His sense of wounded dignity prompted him to remind her that he had already told her he had no wish to seduce her. His sense of inert social politeness was reeling from her choice of words: 'fucking', on her lips, was a kind of brutal sacrilege, a vandalism. With so many senses open, he was confronted at a crossroads with no map: he stood stock still, said nothing. Cicada boarded her bus and waved goodbye with a scintillating smile.

Every few weeks, she began to summon him—no other verb is possible, even though her invitations were tossed out in the most off-hand way and always with the rider of 'You're probably too busy and I don't care anyway'. He shuffled his other obligations to make space for her. If he refused her once, he was sure she would never invite him again. Perhaps this would not be so, but he did not want to tempt fate. In violation of everything good in himself, of his intelligence and his experience and the last vestiges of his commonsense, our father was powerfully flattered by being in correspondence with Cicada Economopoulos. He had not felt this way since his great idol, Norris McWhirter, had taken him under his wing. He felt that the gods had smiled on him. Her beauty was epic, a form and figure that he believed came along but once a century. And yet within that perfection resided an enigma that drew him in, and in. It was the enigma he had posed that first time he had spoken with her: Why was she here, and not on some yacht?

Unable to stand the abasement of the chain steakhouse, he found better places to take Cicada for lunch. Every time, her hair was a new colour: silver, nutmeg, cyan, magenta, platinum with candy-floss stripes. She showed no appreciation, eating heartily, sometimes taking a glass of wine, yet never saying so much as thank you. Our father forgave her. He knew that Menis Economopoulos was a rough-edged kind of man, who took pride in ignoring the social niceties. Our father would have called it machismo except, in the daughter, it seemed more like hauteur. Yet she could also be easily pleased. One visit, trying to vary the routine, he took her to a circus travelling through her town. In the coconut shy and the laughing clowns and the fairy floss, Cicada took as much joy as a child. When they stood and watched a particularly sleazy stilt walker go through his rigmarole, Cicada was beside herself with giggles. The more obvious and cheap the stilt walker's bawdy lines, the greater Cicada's enjoyment. For that excursion, which was an utter torment to my father, she sent him an email two days later apologising for not having thanked him.

His emotional responses to their outings followed a set pattern. In the lead-up, he would be sleepless with excitement, rehearsing the stories he would tell her and drilling himself until he was line-perfect. His greatest terror was of falling silent with her, and boring her. She was as easily bored as a teenager, and as demanding.

Then, while with her, he was like a circus performer himself, so occupied with entertaining her that his vision was trained inwards, on his own showmanship. He barely had a chance to take her in. Courtesy prevented him from leering at her, as he had while watching her cross the room at her father's house. To look was to leer. So the thing he most desired in her, her physical splendour, was the one facet he could not behold. As elevated as he was by her company, he often wished that he could be another person, at another table, watching her from afar, able to spy on her without inhibition. Sitting across the table from him, she leant forward; but her eyes were locked on his, in mischievous challenge, saying, *We both know that you want to be staring at my cleavage, but I am not going to let you, and you, dear gentleman, are not going to let yourself.* At such moments, he wished he was a dying man being carried out on a stretcher, anyone but himself.

As much as he feared boring her, he found it hard to maintain attention when Cicada was talking. Her interests were limited to the goings-on in her town, her studies and her father, and her confined sourness was that of the schoolyard. Having spent so many of his sleepless nights worrying that she would grow tired of him, in fact he was terrified that she would grow tired of herself. Incapable of listening to her, his mind bubbled with ideas for what to do next, how to keep her distracted. She was going on about something or other when he blurted: 'Shall we go and take a ferry ride on the lake?'

She sighed (what did that mean, he wondered?) but nodded agreeably. Distraction worked on us, his children, and it seemed to worked on Cicada, so childlike. Yet for him it was only another exhausting evasion.

When they were sitting on the boat, watching snow-peaked mountains pass above the line of the town, the bow bounced against windblown ripples and threw a fine spray across the deck. Cicada came closer to him, saying she did not want to get wet.

'Tony is such an asshole, he wouldn't lend me his lecture notes for that class I missed.'

She often did this, dropping male names blithely, without description or introduction or ado, as if John must already know who this Tony, Dirk or Henry was. This was an essential component of her native arrogance: she did not bother to keep track of what John knew and what he didn't. (Our father, on the other hand, remembered every breath and word he shared with Cicada, and could replay every single meeting verbatim, so he knew that this was the first he had heard of this Tony character.) It was not Cicada's wish to taunt our father by mentioning boys' names, nor to flaunt any disrespect for their friendship. She was just a tease by nature, and disrespectful, like the scorpion who befriends the frog to get a ride across the creek, and then stings the frog unapologetically. 'What did you think I'd do? It's my nature.'

'There must be someone else you can get the notes from,' our father said, thinking of female friends. 'Bucky does that class?'

'She's useless. The boys are much more helpful.'

For Cicada, whose nature was sacrosanct to herself, her cruelty was that of careless habit rather than intention. She could be cruel, but as she never meant to be cruel to John, it never crossed her mind that he might take her carelessness for cruelty and indeed she would have been offended if he had.

"Boys," he said. 'You can be cruel.'

She pushed away and regarded him loftily. 'I am one of the least cruel people you know.' And she believed what she said with such authority that it was John who wondered if he had missed out on some crucial wisdom, if he was the inferior here, if it was Cicada who held the real secrets of know-how and experience.

At the same time, probably also by mere habit, in her thoughtlessness she was also doing something that both horrified him and drew him in further still. By casually mentioning boys' names she was inching back the curtains on a roomful of men, a city of men, a world of men, a life populated by man after man after man, all of whom, every last one, lusted after her, a world bristling with extreme and uncontrollable lust, a cage so rank with pheromones that it ruled every encounter of hers with the human world, lust, total lust, male lust and also female lust, and if not lust then envy and jealousy and the knowledge of the lust of others; Cicada might as well (our father thought) have been living on a different planet from him, because responding to lust was not something he lived with, and because she was so fundamentally desirable, he felt not only pity but admiration, he put her on a pedestal; she was somehow infinite because her world was so enlarged, and this epiphany, of her greatness, ironed out any traces of contempt for her and replaced it with something else, something altogether new. He understood why beautiful people were attracted to each other. It wasn't just vanity. It was that each understood what the other had to endure. They shared a common suffering, and being misunderstood. Beautiful people, like long-distance truck drivers and garbage men, formed a natural support group.

He suffered, too, we mustn't forget that, no matter how richly deserved.

What glued him to her, far more than their meetings, was the emotion he would experience following the meeting. In her presence, he might often have pondered why he was so incapable of listening. But as soon as he left her, his mind bubbled over with questions and suggestions and further researches. The more he revisited their conversations and meetings, the more interesting they were, the more new questions arose. These he either sent her in long emails or stored away for use at their next meeting, all his questions, all his ideas, a bulwark against silence.

If there were gods, they had created Cicada Economopoulos as a joke on men. One night he was sitting in the Lakeshore bar. The man beside him was sipping a beer as Cicada jounced by, the motion of her breasts half a beat behind the spring of her heels.

'Fuck,' said the man, whose name was Cliff, in utter desolation. He didn't have wavy hair, but his goatee beard and personal digital assistant consigned him to the commercial travellers' brotherhood. 'Fuck you, God!' he said, raising his face and laying down his device to literally shake his fist at the ceiling. He picked his device up again and poked at it nihilistically.

Our father said nothing. What could he say? But the man, Cliff, went on.

'Shouldn't be allowed,' he said. 'Should not be allowed. Looks like Debbie Harry's hot sister. What the fuck did we do to deserve that?'

By 'we', he seemed to include our father, who shrugged neutrally. He did not know who Debbie Harry was.

'Or, you know,' Cliff went on, eyeing Cicada voraciously as she smoothed her buttocks with the back of her hand before levering herself onto a bar stool to share a cocktail with Bucky and two men in suits, 'the young Ciccone. Madonna before the fall. That dago profile. The curved nose and the big dark dago eyes. Fuck it. Madonna wasn't half as hot, even when she was hot. If Marilyn Monroe was as hot as she is, she'd never have died: Kennedy would've dumped Jackie and married her.'

'You have not considered going to another bar?' our father said, to make polite conversation. He felt magnanimous. Cliff was haunted by her, while John *knew* her.

'Don't worry, I have considered,' Cliff said, his shoulders rising and falling in a miserable sigh, yet mimicking our father's formal turn of phrase. 'But it's useless. We're back here like dogs to our own sick, aren't we, buddy? Can't keep away.'

'And cannot get any closer,' John said with the consoling beneficence of the man with a secret.

'Oh, pal, I've been closer.' Cliff wiped his mouth with the back of his device-clasping hand. 'Been *a lot* closer. But it's still the same, isn't it? You spend your teens wanking to pictures of girls like her, only half as hot. Then you spend your adult life chasing girls like her, only they're *one tenth* as hot, but you chase them because they remind you of the girls in the pictures. Then you finally get drunk enough to think you're going to bed with one. They're *one thousandth* as hot, but they're all you're worth. Then the real thing—*the real thing*—comes up and gives you that look and asks for your room number and says she'll meet you there in ten, and then, you know, it all happens, you think you've gone to heaven, you're there, every wet dream you ever had is coming true, you're there, you're *in*, and what's it like?' He gave a mirthless, cheated laugh. 'It's like you've left your body and you're watching yourself from the outside, she's made you see yourself through *her* eyes, and you can't stand it, it's hell, it's fucking torture, pal. You're this fat middle-aged loser shithead, that's all you can see, what *she* sees, and it's all gone, *foof*, it's just a dream, man, and you know what you'd rather be doing? Yeah. You got it. You'd rather be the teenager wanking again. Man, I've been with her three, four times. But I don't get any closer. I'm running on the spot. Every time I end up seeing myself as that pathetic loser. Every time I wish I was a kid having a tug. I'd be having more fun, I tell you. And I do. If I've been with her four times, I've wanked thinking about her four hundred times. And I can tell you which is more fun. No contest. No fucking contest. *Fuck.*'

'Goodnight,' our father said, leaving his drink half full. He went to his room and looked up D. Harry on the internet. Her band, Blondie, had sold more records by 1979 than any previous female-led rock group. He looked up M. Ciccone on the internet. She was the highest-selling female artist of all time. He did not need to look up M. Monroe. None of them belonged on the same page, authentication-wise, as Cicada.

Every now and then she said something that cut through to the truth, of himself, of the fabric of reality. The next time he saw her, they took a ferry again. It had become another of their little rituals. She asked if they could do it, more mechanically than eagerly, as if it was the thing that had to happen next, but our father was flattered by any note of recognition or memory from Cicada. She wanted to go on the boat? Then she remembers last time! It is special to her, no matter how drably she asks!

This time the day was calm and there was no spray from which she needed him to shield her, no need to cuddle closer. She prattled on about boys and college. Our father observed how Cicada lived entirely in the present. Like a fish, or a dog, she followed her newest impulse as if that was all that existed. It would be rude to say this to her, so our father made some observations about mankind instead. How she loved to be taken seriously! If he could only forget her beauty, and unsay all he had said about it, then perhaps he would have her. She wanted only to be wanted for her brain. Preposterous. Could he want her for her brain? He had to remind himself of how much he wanted not to want her at all . . .

'Men live either mostly in the future or mostly in the past,' he said (as if she should need him to complete her education on men!). 'Most men, successful men, live in the future, anticipating what is going to come next. It is not only their instinct to anticipate but it gives them their leisure outlet. Life for them is one great gamble, and genius consists in being able to accurately predict a future in such a way that can yield them a profit. But other men, who are a kind of rebel breed,' our father went on, remembering to paint himself in the best light, 'live not in the future but the past. Our role is to verify what has happened and to keep it alive. We should be living in harmony with those who live by predicting the future, because it is our archiving of the past that informs their leaps into the unknown. Without us, they would be stupid lemmings, jumping out idiotically. But of course we are disregarded, because our role is not directly profitable. We are a cost centre, not a profit centre. And because of that, our ranks are being deserted. Fewer and fewer of us are doing the essential work of looking backwards and locking down the factual basis of the past. Without us, there can be no informed speculation about the future. But this is forgotten. And so I feel the responsibility heavily. Sometimes it seems that I am going to be the last one, the last man looking backwards.'

Cicada, beside him, had laid her cheek on his shoulder. Not just laid—it *weighed* there, it wasn't a pose. She was resting on him. She wasn't listening. His words echoed to himself. What had happened to him, to make him so pompous? He did not put an arm around her, as her posture might have invited, because then she might shift away. He would give the world for her not to move. He had got lost in another little speech, and by the end of it was hearing himself. To be in her presence, and to forget her, with her beautiful head resting safely on his shoulder, was the sweetest bliss he thought possible.

They were passing a curve on the bank and coming towards the wharf. Cicada straightened. Our father felt that she had not been listening to him, until she said: 'That's what I've always said to you. You're a spectator. You don't get involved. You're letting life pass you by.'

So brutal was this—in its inattention to the gravamen of what he had said, yes, but also in its pure accuracy, as if it had jumped a long and complicated queuing process and walked straight through the door—that he was left blinking back tears while she smoothed herself, hands running down the unspeakable curves of her body, and walked off the ferry, back to the shore, to wait for the bus that would take her home to her father.

17

When our mother Sandy sat in the bathroom and the blue
face on the pregnancy test kit smiled at her, she began to
laugh and did not stop. Like a child delighted at a magic
trick, which the pregnancy test reminded her of, she laughed
without any thought of the trick affecting herself, personally.
She was forty-four years old. She was laughing at fate's capacity
to pull a prank: that she, an esteemed medical professional,
had believed that just because she had not fallen pregnant
for the previous fifteen years she could not fall pregnant now.
She laughed in self-mockery. She laughed, too, imagining
John's face when she gave him the news. She had not told
him she had missed her period and was taking this test. There
had been too many previous false alarms, with John running

back to the bathroom rubbish bin to look at them, saying, 'I cannot stop thinking that behind our back, lying in the tissues and cotton balls, the blue face has started smiling.' It hadn't, until now.

Then Sandy's laughter guttered out. She began to think about what this was going to do to their settled professional and personal routines. She thought of the sleepless nights, the breastfeeding, the insoluble mysteries of a baby's needs. When she was sixty-two, this baby would still be in school. And then, when she thought of all the babies and children she had seen in hospitals, she gave a tearful last cough, washed her hands, adjusted her glasses and her ponytail, checked the pregnancy test kit again—its smile that of an evil clown—and left the bathroom with her half-glass of white wine to find her husband, carrying the stick aloft like an offering to a tribal sacrifice.

Dad's joy and surprise restored her optimism. His happiness was no less, and possibly even more, genuine, super-authentic, for the lurking calculation in the back of his mind that this, at last, would bring things with Paulina to an end. He hugged Sandy, exclaimed his delight and eventually, that night, made careful love with her ('It can't hurt, don't worry,' she cooed, 'it can't do a thing now,'), and the inundation of intense relief flowed from the back of his mind to the front. The next time he saw Paulina, he would break it off. He didn't know what reason he would give her. To say, 'I have been married all this time and my wife is pregnant,' would be not only uncouth and cruel but would risk invoking Paulina's boundless wrath. If there was one thing he knew about Paulina, it was that she was capable of carrying rage beyond any limit. She was MAD: Mutually Assured Destruction. If he told her he had been married since the start, she might hunt him down, or more to the point she might hunt Sandy down, and have no hesitation in bringing their happiness to an end. Or she might not care at all. That was equally likely. She would give a dismissive 'pff' and wave him away like a sandfly. Which would she do? He didn't know, and that was the problem. She might do nothing, and she might destroy him. Paulina was capable of either, but John did not know which, because he did not know her.

Paulina was undergoing a strange mid-career contortion. She spent increasing time in the United States, where she was busy with conferences, festivals, radio and television appearances. Her ethnicity and the purified white-hot accusation underlying her novels had made her something of an international spokeswoman both for the fears of the western world and for the thing that it feared. Immigrant rage, the ticking time bomb. As a celebrated writer, Paulina was meant to be capable of transforming or sublimating or expressing or conquering this rage or, put more didactically, showing her fellow immigrants that art, not violence, was the answer. Or something like that. She accepted every invitation to lecture and to be interviewed, and her fame reached its apogee.

For the first time in her adult life, however, she was not writing. Initially she told herself she was taking a well-deserved break. But as the months wore on, she wondered if she had stopped being a writer, and was instead, now, a spokeswoman for the writer she had once been. She loathed herself for the pretence and dishonesty, the imposture. She was taking everyone for a ride. The more she pontificated about issues, about the world, about a writer's life, about her own methods, the more inauthentic she felt. By the time our father was formulating his plan to break off his relationship with her, Paulina had not written for nearly a year. Now let's see white-hot . . .

Dad cancelled a visit to Paulina during Sandy's first trimester. Sandy was beaten down by ugly bouts of morning sickness, perhaps attributable to her age, perhaps to the ticket she had drawn in life's lottery. Dad looked after her as best he could, genuinely solicitous and glad that by not having the time to visit Paulina he had been able to put off the confrontation.

When Sandy was twenty weeks pregnant, Dad finally went to Paulina. His plan was to let the thing wither on the vine. He would not break it off. He could not. But he would inch away from a decision, backward step by backward step, until, he hoped, the best of all possible outcomes would take over and Paulina broke off with him. He was a coward. He told himself he was being pragmatic and clever, but even he couldn't listen to that nonsense; he was a coward.

For the next few months, the storm welled but did not break. He cancelled another visit, and when he did finally see Paulina she was angry with him. They made love, but he felt her frustration boil. Her mother, recently widowed, had moved to live near her, and Paulina complained bitterly about her presence. 'Everything turn to shit,' she said after a lovemaking session that, due to John's carefully disguised vague unsatisfactions, had been vaguely unsatisfactory. 'My mother, my work and you,' Paulina went on. 'Bad things travel in threes. You all make my life hell. There is no light.'

When he and Paulina ate together, Dad saw to it that the conversation was brief and one-sided. He let Paulina burn herself out against something or other, a fellow writer usually, or critics, or publishers, or prize committees. It was so long since she had shamed his numbers, smothered his World's Longest Neck with her Cars Kill Two People Every Minute, and inspired him to want to be a better man. Where had that gone? Had he spoilt it, by endeavouring to become a better man with an act that made him so much worse than he had been? Eventually she fell silent and smoked, and then began to talk again about her mother, who, from what John could see, was a well-meaning woman, blind to the aggression her very kindness aroused in her daughter. Everything was intolerable to Paulina. John made sure that whatever he said was unhelpful, and when that did not seem to incite Paulina enough, he began a recitation of trivia on subjects that he knew she hated—sports, theatre, the movies, trivia about trivia—so that he might, in the end, bore her into throwing him out.

By the time Sandy was set to deliver, however, Paulina had still not broken with him. Dad was astounded at her capacity to endure discontent. She would refuse to talk to her mother. She would denounce her friends. She would claim she was giving up writing forever. But she would not dump him. He had given her cause. As she had always said, she did not care if he was unfaithful to her. All that mattered was that he continue to interest her. Now that he was certain he was not interesting her, Paulina was showing another side of herself. She *didn't* care if he gave her no satisfaction, either socially or in bed or in any other way. She *didn't* care if he had given up on the relationship. He saw that, for all her bluster and outrage and potency, Paulina needed him. She would not dump him. He felt an overwhelming pity for her, which, combined with his ongoing fear of what she might do if he took the initiative, meant that by the time Sandy delivered their first baby, named Adam in memory of John's father (a name Sandy, against all likelihood, volunteered), Dad was sitting at her side in the maternity ward experiencing all the usual shocks of first fatherhood—primarily the instantaneous tumble into unqualified love for a new human being, yes,

he was experiencing that he was a new father, he was ours
for life—and yet at the same time wondering if Paulina was
all right and if he could fit in a lightning visit to her in the
three days while Sandy and Adam would be in hospital. That
was the only gap in his schedule he could foresee. After that,
when Sandy brought Adam home, loomed a new regime.
For now he was still in the old.

And so, when Adam was two days into his first feeding
problems and Sandy was racked with mastitis, after spending
a night awake on a stretcher bed by their side, when Sandy
said, forgivingly, 'Go home and sleep all day and take a day
off, we'll need you when we come home,' John went to his
car, in which he had a bag packed with a change of clothes
and toiletries, drove to the airport, and boarded the first
flight to Paulina's city.

And when he arrived there, with Adam not forty-eight
hours in this world, Dad found Paulina in her kitchen, drunk,
wielding a butter knife.

Immediately he feared the worst. She knew. And if Paulina
knew, she would kill him. This was the price of Paulina's
love (in a deal he had struck, between himself and himself,
in his own imagination). He tried to calm her and pretend
he did not know why she was in this homicidal rage. He
kept his eye on the butter knife. She was powerful enough
to kill him with that glorified spatula; and because it was so

blunt, she would make it hurt all the more. She shoved him away with her free hand.

'But what is it?' he kept saying. 'What is it?'

And this was how Paulina told him that she was pregnant. *This*, he learnt, was white-hot. This was Paulina angry, what she had always promised him, the real molten core. Dad thought then that she intended to drive the butter knife into her own belly. But no: the knife was what she intended to use on *him* if he so much as hinted that she have a termination.

'But how,' he said carefully, 'do you know the child is mine?'

She threw the knife at him. He was unsure whether it was the blade or the bone handle that bounced off his shoulder.

'That's why you are the only one left, you asshole!'

Dad next visited Paulina six weeks later, when Adam was finally sleeping through, when Sandy went back to work, and when a long day care centre took over Adam's supervision for three days a week. Dad told Sandy he had to resume his normal working and travelling routines. She kissed him: they would work their way through this together, as a family. Motherhood clearly became her. Life was one astonishment after another.

On that visit, Dad and Paulina, who was thirteen weeks pregnant, went to a registry office and were legally married. As it was in a different country to that in which he had married Sandy, he gambled on getting away with the illegality.

All he had to do was sign a form saying he was not married. Who was going to investigate? If someone found out about him being married in another country, breaking the law would be the very least of his problems.

The reception took place in the house Paulina had grown up in, which was now owned by her cousins. It had a cement courtyard surrounded by whitewashed walls, and two long tables were set up for the thirty guests, all of whom were connected with Paulina. Jasmine climbed over the rooftop and perfumed the air. Our father did not understand the speeches, but there was a lot of laughter accompanied by faces grinning at him. He nodded along and raised his glass merrily, as if he was taking the joke well, whatever it was. Paulina made a speech in her own language, and patted her belly while making a toast. The laughter took a long time to subside, and men and women and old folk came up to give our father bruising claps on the back.

'For Latinos,' our father said to Paulina later, after the dancing and the cake, while they helped her cousin clean up, 'they were taking the unconventionality of a pregnant bride very well.'

'What you mean, for Latinos?' She stood braced with a tea towel wrapped in her hand as if preparing to whip him. As usual, he wished he had not spoken. 'You mean Catholics have to be scandalised by fucking before a wedding?'

'They seemed to enjoy the speeches,' he said, trying to change the subject. 'Why were they always laughing at me?'

'Eh,' Paulina tossed her chin in the direction of his groin. 'They congratulate you for your manhood. Against all appearances. They are surprised. For a gringo, you don't look like you have the seed.'

After the wedding, he and Paulina did not have the chance for a honeymoon. She, like Sandy, was beset by illness through her pregnancy. Unlike Sandy, Paulina took it in poor spirit. Already of the belief that the world had it in for her, she took morning sickness as simply more confirmation. She hated being pregnant, hated the shape it was turning her, hated the strange moods and appetites. She could not bear the smell of our father. She was losing control of her body and, she suspected, her mind. But at least she was writing again.

Dad rented her a little house with a garden and three bedrooms. Into one of them, he moved Paulina's mother. Before he left to go back to Sandy, he paid the first six months of Paulina's rent. Paulina was relieved to see the back of him. He was no help, and the reek! How, she wondered, had she failed to notice that before?

18

Our father had been seeing Cicada Economopoulos for nine months: once a month for the first three, six times in the next three, and ten times in the next three. A sequence of triangular numbers. More and more he was delegating his duties to colleagues, and pursuing a frenzied regimen of cover-up and clerical fudging to paper over the fourth crack he had opened in his life.

Far from regretting it, he gloried in it. If he had to give up anything, Cicada would be the last of his secrets. Those nine months seemed to stretch deeper into his past, so that he could barely remember not knowing her. She had the capacity to bend time itself, to erase its passage.

He was truly growing into the silly old coot he had long suspected might be waiting for him, foolish arms extended, his destiny.

Not since the springtime had he undergone another episode quite as extreme as that which took place when he wandered out of the hotel to the petrol station and shopping mall and lost his mind. That terrifying half-hour must, he reflected, have been a stress reaction, a spasm brought on by the tension of finally meeting her. And yet the flashes, or fits, or whatever kind of seizure they were, had not gone away altogether, and although their intensity was declining, their frequency was increasing. Often he would pass through a membrane of time and space and not know where he was or how he had got there. After the first attack, these passages had been brief and untraumatic. He would stay in position and wait it out. He would swallow down his panic. The effects of the attack—the confusion and the tearfulness—might be worse than the attack itself. He had nothing to fear but fear. He thought, too, that he had discovered an escape hatch. When his surroundings seemed to come out of his dreams, when he moved into that other dimension, he urged himself to find or do something absolutely unfamiliar, break the mould. He would shout out an obscenity, or intentionally stub his toe, or speak aloud in Japanese: a shock tactic against himself, like the putative victim of a mugging who commits a wild act to convince his attacker that he is insane, and not worth the risk of assaulting.

The tactic worked, although the headaches, and the after-feeling of having been laid to waste, persisted.

One attack had been disturbing, however, during his last visit to Dorothy Ellen O'Oagh, on the occasion of her one hundred and twenty-ninth birthday. As he sat beside her, pound cake in his lap, listening to her breathing, observing the doctor and his processes of measurement, our father must have drifted away into a kind of coma of his own. He remembered leaving Mrs O'Oagh's home and starting his hire car, his head full of the impending meeting with Menis Economopoulos—full of the anticipation of seeing Cicada in her old guise as her father's servant. By mutual agreement, he and Cicada kept their encounters secret from Menis. Of course they risked being seen in the town and the news being reported to the old man, but Cicada said her father was so at war with the other townsfolk that he had no friends or informants, and anything he might hear about her—'Take it from me, he's heard a lot worse'—he had resolved to disbelieve. 'He has decided that everything he hears about me is a lie,' Cicada said. 'I couldn't wish for a better father.' So when John went to interview Menis, Cicada would bring the drinks and snacks, just as in the old days, and John would affect not to notice her. It was all agreed. Except that he couldn't resist the urge: he had so few occasions to take a good look at her, to spy on her, it drove him mad, as being her friend had brought him too close, had squashed his focal length, so that he never got to see her at all.

Anticipation, then, about visiting the Economopoulos household was flustering him as he left Mrs O'Oagh. Then he remembered having forgotten his official leather-bound Authenticator-in-Chief's record book inside the mansion. From there, for an unspecified period, everything was a blank. The next he knew, he was striding back across the lawn towards his car, holding his notebook in one hand and a silver teaspoon in the other. Or rather, he became conscious of the teaspoon as it flew out of his hand and landed on the lawn. He stopped as if turned into a pillar of salt, staring in horror at the silver glint. He recognised it as part of Mrs O'Oagh's table setting. But why was it in his hand? What had happened in there? Obviously he had picked up his notebook. But had he greeted Mrs O'Oagh again? Had he talked to the staff? Had anyone supervised him as he went into the ancient lady's room? Had the teaspoon been lying there, on a side table, by the teacup he had used earlier? Why had he picked it up? Had someone given it to him? Had he stolen it?

As he picked up the teaspoon and put it in his pocket, the shudders set in, the panic and the tears. This was different from the other attacks. A stitch in time had broken, and he had been swallowed by the rent. He sat in his car and took his face in his hands and sobbed quietly. He was no longer disoriented now, just devastated. He had blanked out for five, ten minutes, perhaps more. He had stolen a teaspoon. What was going on with him? Was he losing his mind? What was going on?

It was an awful feeling, truly terrifying, akin to when he had the attack in the petrol station, the sense that he was adrift in a limitless sea of dreams. He felt minuscule, a species of microplasia. He had had such nightmares when young, feeling he was microscopic in size and lost in his environment, but this was different, somehow irreversible. Everything was *now*. *Now* followed him into a corner and surrounded him. *Now* offered him no alternative but itself. He was in decline, and what was worrying him was that he did not know where he was declining to. There was only *now*.

He collected himself for the interview with Menis Economopoulos, and all went to plan, though our father sat through it with the familiar scorched-earth headache. Menis was more defiant than ever. As Cicada had said, her father was now, after all these years, a greater threat to public safety than before his house arrest. The difference was, whereas he had expressly threatened only Mrs O'Oagh before, now he was a generalised threat, a bundle of violence about to unravel randomly and take revenge for ancestral agonies on absolute strangers and innocent passers-by. As Menis unleashed frothing screeds of resentment, our father winced under his post-episode headache, a pain so arid that not even the sight of Cicada's tight-wrapped figure thrusting reverberantly across the carpet could cheer him.

Later, Cicada met him at the Lakeshore bar at the Holiday Inn. She wanted to meet at night this time, breaking their routine, and she wanted a drink. The change portended delicious danger to our father, who swallowed four strong headache tablets and had a long bath in preparation. Although she liked to address him as 'my friend', to remind him that that was all he could ever be, and although, in her disjointed speculations about life and love, whenever she thought our father was getting any ideas above his station, as it were, she would interject with something like, 'But it will never happen between us,' he could not help harbouring the fugitive hope that something might . . . *occur*. It was like a disease. Funnily enough, considering he thought of Cicada as a person of low-ish morals, the reason she cited most often for never entertaining the notion of sleeping with him was that he was married. 'I would never do that to another woman,' Cicada said, as if shoulder to shoulder in the feminist struggle. 'I know what it is like when a man has cheated on me, and I wouldn't dream of inflicting that on a woman.'

'Alfred Kinsey found that fifty per cent of males and twenty-six per cent of females had had extramarital sex at least once,' our father said. 'More recent studies estimate the figures as having dropped by half. Obviously there are wide cultural variations. In six cultures, extramarital sex by women is considered univ—'

'Fuck that,' Cicada interrupted him. '*I* am my *own* culture.'

So desperate, in his quiet and complicated way, was John Wonder to be honest with her that he was sorely tempted to explain that the marriage he had told her about was not what she thought it was; that it was triplicated, and as it had multiplied the institution had weakened its hold on him. In other words, that he had not one wife but three, and because he had three wives he was not bound in fidelity to any one of them.

A disease! But there were clots, submerged cysts, that pulled him short of such a revelation. One, he thought it would be hopeless. If he could convince Cicada that he was not bound by marital fidelity, he felt sure that she would come up with some other reason not to sleep with him. Two, he had never told a soul about his marital and family arrangements, and as shockingly lonely as that secrecy had left him—and as much a part of the explanation as it was for why he was here, with her—the maintenance of that secrecy was the very fibre of his soul, the gravitational force holding him together. He could not contemplate confessing it all to Cicada, even if such a confession were to be, so to speak, the clincher. He would never know how she might use it against him (he felt sure, in his bones, that she would).

And finally, what stopped him short of trying to seduce Cicada was that he was still rigidly sustaining the fiction that he was not interested in her for the purpose of seduction. She fed him the 'You would only be disappointed' line from time to time, as if she knew he was only pretending not to desire her, and so it had become a kind of competition between them. She wanted to *win*, by forcing him to admit that he wanted to sleep with her. He wanted to *win*, by continuing to deny it.

At the Holiday Inn that night, our father learnt something new: Cicada Economopoulos was a drinker. Nothing else could explain her ability to consume four glasses of red wine in the first hour while remaining upright, lucid, full of vitality and argument. He knew drinkers who could hold their drink. He was married to three.

Her hair, tonight, was Royal Blue. Like her father, she ranted about the Economopoulos family's enemies in the town, and about the 'sheer spite' Dorothy O'Oagh's heart had shown by continuing to beat. 'She doesn't want to live, we don't want her to live, nobody wants her to live, and yet she keeps fucking living,' Cicada said.

Then she ordered more wine. Dad was on his first glass, still, and she rubbished him for being a slow drinker.

'Gutless,' she said when he placed his hand demurely over his glass.

But gutless about what? Afraid to get drunk with her? And if afraid, afraid of what consequence? He removed his hand and allowed her to pour.

Cicada droned on, the magnificence of her face and her figure in perverse, inverse proportion to her animating passions. He was a middle-aged man worried, like all middle-aged men, that he had seen too little of life, hoping to grasp a last taste before the long winter set in. His position was as old as the hills. And it was old in two ways. Not only was he a sad old man taking one last lunge at youth, but he was a sad old man who gained happiness from being mistreated by a beautiful young woman. She ridiculed him by her very presence, by the way she flirted with the barman and made eyes at the salesmen who were beginning to filter in. It would be pathetic enough if, as a reward for taking all this punishment, John Wonder was getting to sleep with her from time to time. But she denied him that too—or he denied it to himself, which was even worse, compounding masochism onto sadism, denied it to himself to deny *her* the chance to deny it to him.

Yet still, while he was getting so little in the bargain, while all he got was a kind of reflected glory for personal use only and the philosophical enrichment of being so close to perfection, of seeing what made beauty tick, at least it was clear that she had something to give him.

On her side, though, what was it that she expected to get out of him? Why did she continue to ask him to come and see her? Was her existence that tedious? Of course she might have enjoyed keeping him on a string and exerting her sexual power for its own sake. But she had so many outlets for exerting this power—and here she was doing it in front of him, beckoning the first pair of salesmen over with her searchlight green eyes—that it was clearly superfluous to be doing it with John.

What did she want from him? He had no money, no power, no way to advance her cause. What was her cause anyway? He could see nothing but pure randomness in Cicada's attitude to the world around her, and within it the ghostly form of himself. She lived in a small town with her father, studying law, waiting for Mrs O'Oagh to die. In the inevitable boredom this produced, she flirted with men. She abased herself deliberately, by dressing poorly, by drinking in the worst bar and eating in the worst restaurant, by posing as a member of the sales rep class. She thumbed her nose at her own attributes. All that was settled. But what did she think John was going to do for her? Why play him like this? Was it just for her own cruel fun?

Soon she was putting on her show for the two commercial travellers she had attracted to their stand-up table. John stood mugging painfully, his shit-eating grin widening and his shit-taking eyes crinkling as the conversation grew lewd.

The effects of drink finally descended on Cicada after the seventh or eighth glass, came down like an avalanche. This epic beauty, this Michelangelo's model, this porn star, this pageant queen, this Miss Universe, was swearing and rolling her eyes and playing drinking games and telling stories about cocks she had sucked that she couldn't get into her mouth because they were the size of Coke cans, telling stories about giving boys a 'passata smile' during her period, telling stories about having run out of men to fuck in this town so she had to prey on 'blow-ins' to avoid repeating herself.

John, chillingly sober, took it. And it was something for him to take, he knew that. It was all directed at him, staged for him. That knowledge was the only thing that saved his compassion for her: that this was not really her, but instead a kind of theatre that he was meant to interpret. Even the salesmen, who were as drunk as Cicada, knew restraint, and neither was game to make a move on her while John was there, as if acknowledging prior rights. How dumb they were! But it was true, the centre of gravity in this silly charade lay between Cicada and our father, and the salesmen knew they were extras. Still, extras can occasionally score a main part if they get lucky, so, like all extras, they hung in.

By eleven or twelve o'clock it became too humiliating even for our father, with his world-record-worthy tolerance for humiliation. He believed he had learnt his lesson. When Cicada stumbled off to the toilet, he bade goodnight to the two salesmen, whose names he had never asked, and slipped off to his room. He had no interest in making sure Cicada was all right. He wanted only to let her know that he would not take this anymore, that he was not a vegetable.

He lay on his bed awake, fully clothed, to the end of the night. He did not sleep. He expected, every second, the bang at his door and the scream of abuse, or the cry for help. She'd been raped, she'd been hurt, she'd taken her pleasure with the salesmen, both of them, and now she wanted to have a cold shower in our father's bathroom and a cup of coffee and a long cry with him. She wanted to lie chastely by his side in his king-sized Holiday Inn bed and confess her deepest secrets. She wanted to accuse him. She wanted to reveal the truth about the Economopoulos inheritance and Dorothy O'Oagh. She wanted to ask him, John Wonder, to come and live in this town and look after her, be her husband, be her protector, and if he could only manage to be here one week out of every four, that would be just fine, just fine.

There was no knock. Our father lay awake, waiting, through the night and deep into the next day. He waited like a corpse. He waited like a stone. There was no knock.

19

After the first Adam, Sandy's Adam, there was Paulina's Adam. After Paulina's Adam there was Sandy's Evie, named after John's mother. After Sandy's Evie there was Paulina's Evie.

While Sandy chose her children's names, our father could never fathom why Paulina was so compliant when he put the names of Adam and Evelyn forward. Paulina suggested no alternatives. She was compliant in nothing else; but perhaps he was insistent in nothing else, and the names were her concession to that single strand of metal in his weave. Paulina did not know and did not ask why he wanted those names. Paulina never asked him a single question about his parents or his past. She was quite curious enough about the rest of the world, but had a blind spot when it came to him. Him she took for granted.

But why? Why again? The first time, Sandy, who had no family, wanted us in some way to know our grandparents, and offered our names to allay the guilt our father bore in their memory. But the second—why? Did he need to honour them *again*? Did he bear *that* much guilt?

It has taken us time to work out why, but work it out we have.

Motherhood, fatherhood, parenthood, blurred those years when he breached his half-century. He was alternating weeks between his two families. He considered himself an enlightened father: he fed the children, changed their nappies, bathed them, played with them, took them for walks. He did everything their mothers did for them. He taught them and scolded them and cheered them and held his patience with them. With us. He strapped us into our baby capsules, into our booster seats. He hovered over us if we were near a road. He delivered us to birthday parties (but never stayed). If we could remember, and we do, we do, we remember him as a pale yet warm presence, shy yet amusing, sombre yet light of heart. A restrained, private dad who could laugh and joke with us but with nobody else. A good father. What else?

He was stunned by what motherhood revealed to him of Sandy and Paulina. Why did babies not hold world records for feats of strength, for their astonishing power to transform adults? Against all expectations, it was Sandy who fractured under the pressure and fatigue. Sandy, who was such a trier. Sandy, whose overachiever's mouth had proved itself in offices, churches, parks and graveyards, determined to be the best at whatever she did. Sandy, who could not abide the indignity of falling short, was the one to bend under motherhood's shockwave of demands. The mastitis in Adam's first week was the start. She fell ill during the pregnancy with Evie and could not cope with the toddling Adam, who was bringing home colds and infections which jumped to Sandy as if coming home to Mama. She spent three years red-nosed and wet-eyed. She tried to bear up and devote herself to her work, her motherhood, her standards, but could not. When Sandy spoke of the children, it was in a mood of complaint or struggle. Her moments of joy were lonely crags in a grey sea of onerous toil. Little gave her pleasure. She tried, always, to be stoical. But trying did not get her far.

And so, with such a grumpy mother, raised mostly by dour nannies, we greeted our part-time father, when we saw him, like Santa Claus.

Although Sandy battled with his absences, she never asked him to change. She took her large portion of single parenting as another challenge that she must attempt to shine at. She had survived being orphaned and sent to boarding school. Not only survived, but excelled in adversity. She would survive this. She would excel. She resolved to drink less. She drank more. But she did emerge from her illness and depression, she became strong again, until she had an iron core. She recovered from the collapse of her post-partum years to re-emerge as a disciplinarian.

This was the time, if he had any heart, for him to give up Paulina. For Sandy's sake. These were the years when he let Sandy down.

But could he? To leave Paulina would have been to leave her children, his children, us. And Paulina, it turned out, he never loved more. Paulina, who had been such a complainer when her life was a procession of well-received books, became, when her life descended into the drudgery of mothering, a doting, spoiling, laughing soak of indulgence. She gave up writing—what a relief to her!—and her mother came to live with us. Paulina's mother, whose English was minimal but sense of obligation great, eradicated every germ of antagonism she felt towards our father. This mighty effort on the mother's part combined with Paulina's joy in Adam and Evie to produce a household that was, while poor, happy. Paulina played with the children and said yes to whatever we wanted. Whereas Sandy believed in consistency and routines and rules, Paulina believed in whimsy. Her only consistency was her absolute liberality. Whatever we wanted, we got. It simplified her life, she said. It was how her mother had raised her. Against these two voices, full-time mother and grandmother and decades' worth of maternal folklore, our father could have said nothing, even if he had wanted to. He had got the names; Paulina got everything else. Given a fait accompli, he entered into the spirit of Yes, and said, 'Paulina, you do whatever you want.' It was easier to say yes than no.

Thus did our father renounce any claim or opinion or decision-making power or influence over the raising of his children. Sandy, hardened by suffering, governed her children strictly. Paulina, softened by love, permitted everything. Dad was loyal to both of his families, and beneath that, loyal to his secret. To intervene on the key issues of parenthood would risk confusion. Had he advocated controlled crying for Sandy's children, or was it Paulina's? Was banning television what he had argued with Sandy about, or Paulina? Did he take the proactive position on toilet training with the first Adam and Evie, or the second? Only when he was putting us to bed, and telling us stories, was he prepared to set rules.

But confusion was beginning to gather on our father's horizon. Keeping track of things, keeping the compartments watertight, difficult enough before children, was now compounded by fatigue and the sheer number of people involved. Commitments, commitments. He had to keep things simple. He had thought ahead. When he had pictured crawling with us on the floor, dandling us on his knee, teaching us to swim in the toddler pool, crying at us in alarm if we looked like straying towards a pond or a road . . .

his nightmare was if, in his protective reflex, his overriding instinct of love, he called out the wrong name.

It took us a while, but we worked it out.

Our capacity for forgiving him, as our mothers keep telling us, is so monumental that it has passed through the phases of heroism and admirableness, and is beginning to approach something pathological, even sinister.

But even we have trouble, a great deal of it, forgiving what he did next.

THREE

Redeemer

20

Cicada teased him for 'deserting' her at the Holiday Inn. She chided him for getting her 'plastered' before leaving her at the mercy of those 'trashy' salesmen. But all in good humour. Her idiomatic language, to a man who flinched from idiom, was a playful taunt. Cicada was impishly evasive about the night in question. Our father, taking the bait, could not help asking for details. Cicada's email assured him, 'My friend, you REALLY don't want to know.' He assured her that he did. But did he? Did he really?

Cicada phoned to tell him that the most embarrassing thing about the night was the next morning, when Menis had come into her bedroom to ask her to make him his breakfast. Cicada's friend, 'this Guy guy' sprang to attention when Menis came in, fearing the worst, 'wearing nothing but a T-shirt'. Menis addressed him evenly, asking who he was and if he had had a nice time with his daughter. The two men stood half a metre apart. Cicada watched them from her bed, 'almost wetting myself', this guy Guy half-naked, Menis knowing he was half-naked, both attempting a polite morning conversation while ignoring, as she put it, 'the elephant in the room'.

'Really, it was so funny, John, you'd have been rolling around if you'd been here.'

'Yes, that is funny.' John, as adamant in his pretence as Menis, agreed with how funny it was.

He heard nothing more from her until a few days later, when she sent an email saying it had 'gone bad' with that Guy guy, who had 'gone all icky' over her, 'a little too keen for his own good', though she didn't know why he would be keen, as she'd 'spewed all over him while giving him a BJ, I mean if he had any self-respect he'd have run like his hair was on fire'. Instead, he had forgiven her and sent her flowers and asked her on a date, so Cicada didn't like that guy Guy anymore and wanted to get rid of him. 'As usual they get hung up, you know, if I don't give them the death-knock,' she told our father, as if he would know her long history of having to let down these poor losers who didn't realise that they were one-night stands.

Our father played his role well, too well. Cicada needed a confidant. Or 'confidante', as she put it by email.

But yes, our father was playing the role of Cicada's girlfriend, which meant listening to the tales of her many, if not varied, sexual adventures. (On one point they didn't vary: she never fucked a married man. 'Or at least, no married men that I know are married.' With a positively vile laugh.)

Our father and Cicada Economopoulos were emailing, telephoning or texting each other nearly every day now. He had bought a new phone. Now he had four, each registered in a different country. When days passed without a call from Cicada, he was beside himself with anxiety. He worried that her latest one-night stand might have turned out to be a depraved sexual animal, a rapist, a murderer, she had pushed her luck too far. That was what our father told himself. Really, he might have been frantic with rage. Really, Dad? Really. Then, when he did not hear from her for a further day, he told himself that she deserved the violent end that had surely come to her.

Cicada picked up salesmen in the Holiday Inn. She fucked them for a night, sometimes in the hotel and sometimes at her home, it didn't matter to her, they just fell where the night took them. She picked up men in other bars around her town. There was no rhyme or reason. 'I fuck who I feel like fucking,' she wrote. 'Sometimes it's young guys, sometimes old guys, it's just when I'm in the mood. Never planned.

Sometimes the uglier the better. I HATE good-looking guys, or young ones who are UP THEMSELVES. Want to teach them a LESSON.'

And on it went. Our father, now given an open window onto Cicada's sex life, could scarcely believe what he was reading. Not only was she allowing herself to languish on as unfitting a stage for her magnificence as could be imagined, but she was wantonly throwing it away, giving up her silverware for free, perversely, even with a touch of evil, to the least deserving. If what she was telling him was true, Cicada was becoming more than a statue of the female physical ideal: she was an avatar of her era. She was, in her own words, 'a slut, but who wants to be some princess?' She said she might have fucked every eligible male in her town. 'Literally every.' And she was proud of herself. This incredible beauty, who could have swanned into a palace, who could have landed a trillionaire, who could have bargained her assets for any life she wanted, was snubbing all that with a fanatic's zeal, to deliberately quash the very language of 'landing' or 'bargaining' or 'assets'. To fritter away her sexual power was to vaunt that very power. What power is greater than the power to throw it away?

Her stories grew more squalid. She seemed to be competing with herself to supply John with an escalation of awfulness. She picked up an amputee and let him fuck her with his stump. She picked up an ancient cancer sufferer from a nursing home and let him 'fondle my breasts while we watched a porno together'. She enjoyed a ménage à trois with her friend Bucky and the piano teacher they shared, 'Literally!' Then they sacked him, as lover and teacher. 'I only ever give them one turn, or two if they're very good or I feel sorry for them,' she wrote. 'But after that, even if I like them, that's it. I won't see a man for more than two weeks. By the way, I'm thinking my breasts are too round. Bucky has nice long ones, I like them more. Is there an operation you can get?' She was not ruthless, she said, because she hated men. In her typical faux (yet also true) humility she explained: 'It's because I'm so boring, they're going to drop me, I've been dumped so many times I don't want to let it happen again. So I retaliate first.' 'How could any man dump you?' John asked, in spite of himself. 'Don't worry,' Cicada emailed back. 'I might have particularly round breasts and skin like honey, and I might be their all-time dream fuck, but you don't understand men like I do. They get bored so quickly, and if they don't get bored they get boRING.'

It was a punishment for John to hear this, but take it he did—because at some level he did not believe what he was hearing.

He was certain of only one thing. She was lying to him.

Our father knew his liars, and for all the carefree and jovial manner with which Cicada paraded her degradation, he could see through her guile. She was a hard-core liar, but unlike most of them she was a *bad* liar. However much she lied to him, he was lying more. His secrets were buried deeper than hers.

Our father went along with it, lied back to the liar, and was greatly consoled once he convinced himself that none of it was true. She might not be virgin, but she was chaste. She went home each night to her father and did not do any of these things, did not fuck any of these men. Not a single one.

Our father's need to be the concealer and not the dupe was engulfing his being. He was, after all, the Authenticator-in-Chief.

21

Parenthood, fatherhood, gave him what it gave all parents: true love, love unquestioning, love unaccountable. Love unambiguous. Love indivisible. Our father, that dry enclosed man without a hint of sex appeal, that scholarly numericist who lived not in the world of passions but in the world of trivia, of facts that needed to be nailed down lest they fly away, a world in which the importance of the facts was secondary to the importance of there being facts, things to ascertain and verify and authenticate, a man who preserved human memory—this man was a delusional romantic. He believed there was such a thing as true, unbreakable, indivisible love, and now he had found it in his four children, his two Adams and two Evies. At last, our existence gave him something to believe in with the devotion of a fundamentalist. His love for the children was the bed on which he could rest his questing heart.

But alas, love is the one fact that never stands still. He measured it, he pinned it down, he contained it, and then he lost it. Little children grow, and love shifts its shape. We can say this. We felt it. It was our first discovery of the perfidy of the adult heart. Our father grew habituated to us. Love receded into brief outbreaks amid the gruelling routines. Did our father love us less, as we grew from helpless babies into demanding snot-caked toddlers, and from toddlers into personalities that he would often look at with wonder—not the wonder of love, this time, but of *Where the hell did they come from?* Did he love us less? Could he, as the revelations of fresh fatherhood receded into the past, have simply grown tired of us?

That is our question. If we were not good enough for him.

We continue to forgive. He was, is, the only father we have. We are left with no choice. It is him or nothing. We can as soon stop loving him as we can stop loving our own lives, because the two are inseparable. We only have one, and so our choice is either love or death. When we see the faithful family of some politician caught in a scandal, some eminent personage who has taken the fall, the family accompanying him to court, standing behind him at the microphone, we know that the questions are not, *How can they support him? How can they still judge him favourably after what he has done?* We know that those are not the questions at all, for they have moved beyond judging their father. They are not on the stage for him. They are there for themselves. They are clinging to their own existence. They, more than he, are fighting for their lives.

The shackling of children and father was never mutual or reciprocal. We loved him because he was our only father. Ordinarily, a father would love his children because they are his only children. Blood has bound them together.

In our father's case, it was different. He believed he could bend fate to his will. He thought he still had the power to multiply.

By the second half of his fifties, when he could not hold back the guerrilla surges of what he had done and what was left, when he lay awake in the dark, he came to the realisation that what he needed was redemption. He had lied to two women. He had two sets of children whom he kept unknown to each other. He was a narrowly-built mid-twentieth-century machine. He had been raised in the religion of free will, which he thought he was still able to exercise.

Undiscovered, at large, he thought he had another chance. He was omnipotent, superhuman, absolutely insane.

Redemption? Yes, Dad, sure. Come to us. We will redeem you.

But no. He sought redemption without having to sacrifice his secrets.

No kind of redemption, really: just intentions that he could tell himself, for a time, were good.

22

Three weeks before Dorothy Ellen O'Oagh celebrated her one hundred and thirtieth birthday, our father was busy with preparations. As happened every fifth year, interest in Mrs O'Oagh's age metastasised beyond the world of trivia. Television, radio, print and online media converged on her little town to report on the wonder of her longevity and to record the moment when she managed to lean forward and give a little puff that, with the help of a discreetly-held off-camera blow-dryer, would extinguish the single candle on her cake.

The reporters would also converge on Menis Economopoulos, the villain of the piece, who was enjoying a groundswell of notoriety, even admiration, for the duration of his temporary restraining order and his refusal to rescind his past threats. He would give a press conference, as he had done previously, in which he would regretfully confirm that his dearest wish, the vessel of his desire for freedom itself, would be Mrs O'Oagh's passing. Then the police chief and the governor would be interviewed, explaining why the house arrest of Mr Economopoulos had to continue. The reporters would hammer them with questions over whether it was necessary to imprison such an old man, who, in the view of a new generation, was a vaudeville act, a simulacrum of revenge rather than the real thing. Wearily, the police chief and the governor would ask the reporters if they would like to take responsibility if, on his release, Menis Economopoulos went and carried out the threat he had repeatedly uttered since before they had been born? He had the motive and, of course, the wherewithal. All he lacked was the opportunity. Did the reporters want to give him that too? Did they want to be complicit in the murder of a helpless old lady, not just any old lady, mind, but the oldest old lady on earth, a world record holder?

Our father would watch this circus with a weariness that would exceed even the weariness of the officials, because he, unlike they, had seen this exact press conference so many times before.

Still, the event provided an occupation and a complication for our father. His recording of Mrs O'Oagh's age and his interview with Menis Economopoulos, both of which were routine annual affairs, would, on this auspicious anniversary, be performed in front of cameras and microphones. He had to rehearse and refine and cooperate with the demands of the broader media. He was something of a celebrity himself for the day, as no-one else was qualified, from an independent third-party point of view, to voice an opinion about the prospects, statistically speaking, of both Mrs O'Oagh and Mr Economopoulos.

His attacks of the not-knowing, as he called them, seemed to be manageable. But the more firmly he kept a bridle on them, the more they seemed to leak out sideways, so unexpectedly that they were again triggering the tearful panic of the first attacks. The more control he asserted, the more he lost.

Around this time, he began to suffer episodes of being unable to recognise his native language. In a newspaper he read the word ANYONES and sat there stumped, for his brain had converted it into a Spanish word, incomprehensible. ANYONES, he wondered. What does that mean? In his mind he was pronouncing it *an-YO-nees*, to rhyme with *mejillones*. He was so flummoxed that he began to sweat and tremble, butterflies filling his stomach. Eventually he worked out what he was reading: a word in his native English. But in the ensuing weeks, the episodes continued. The word PICKY leapt out at him treacherously in Polish, as *PIS-ki*.

Was he reading a Polish name, that of some deracinated nobleman? Who was this Picky? The panic rose in a wave, coated him with sweat, and then receded. It was just the harmless English word.

And so on.

Amid the busy preparations for the one hundred and thirtieth birthday, and having just visited Cicada, our father was not expecting to see her again until the carnival had come and gone. He had recently visited her town and listened to her latest episode of depravity and debauchery—somewhat inattentively, it has to be said—and been comforted by his strengthening belief that she was making it all up. He felt he had the upper hand in the pantomime, but it was wearing thin. He wanted to know what was going to happen next.

But he wanted it to happen on his timetable, not hers. His timetable was a pyramid of a thing, a tower of Babel, a modern wonder of the world. Hers was that of a thirty-one-year-old single woman. She had to respect that.

She did not. The last thing Cicada was going to respect was the mysterious elsewhere-obligation of friend John Wonder. Cicada was the most desired and beautiful woman in her town. According to him, her town might as well be the whole world. According to her, it was. And so what she said went.

He was with us, his children, when his mobile phone rang one evening and he crackled to his feet and moved stiffly out of the room, out of the house, onto the street, where he said the reception was better.

'I'm in the bath,' she said.

'How did you get this number?'

'I'm in the bath, on my own.'

'That makes a nice change.'

'Listen, no joke. I feel like I've got bugs crawling all over me. My stomach, my breasts.'

'Bugs. What kind of bugs?'

'It doesn't matter what kind. They're not real bugs. I can see they're not real. But I can feel them. They're ghost bugs.'

'Why don't you get out of the bath?'

'No, that's why I got in. To get rid of them, wash them off.'

'How did you get this phone number?'

'John.'

'Mm?'

'I need you to come here. Why can't you be here? I'm going mad. I'm going crazy. Why the fuck can't you be here? Where are you?'

And to her credit, or to his, she had him. John's heart sped up, like a ski jumper before leaving the earth. He looked at the front of the house—the house his wife and children lived in. He was not going to do this.

'I cannot,' he said. 'I shall be there in three weeks.'

'Three weeks?'

Cicada was crying. She was raging and sobbing. 'Don't make me beg you, John,' she wept. 'I've got bugs crawling all over me and I haven't taken any drugs and I haven't drunk and I haven't had a fucking cigarette in a fucking week and a fucking half, and I'm going mad, and I *need you*. I fucking need you, John. Please don't make me beg you.'

'So what,' he started to say, is in it for me? But he cut himself off. He did not speak that way. What was happening to the way he spoke, to the conversations he had? His language, his dignity, felt like it was dissolving in his mouth.

'I am a long way away and by the time I get there you will be better.'

'So that's the reason you won't come?' she hissed. 'Because you don't think it'll help if you do? What if I tell you it *will* help! What if I tell you I need you here because you will save my life! What does it matter if it takes you a long time?'

In so many years, his whole life really, of doing this, maintaining the separation of his lives, he had never dropped one obligation in favour of another. Always he had managed to keep this scene, this very scene, at bay. It was his cardinal rule: once he was gone, he was gone. No backsliding. No tearful begging. No compromise. He had sustained it through three marriages and six children. He was not going for her, just as he had not done it for the other three. The other three loved him; when he said no, they respected him. They did not ask him to choose, even though they did not know what it was, other than his work, that he was choosing over them. That was the measure of their love: the woman with glasses, the dark-skinned woman, the scarred woman. The first love, the soul mate, the redeemer. The measure of their love was their respect for the privacy of his trivial pursuits. The primacy of facts. The overriding necessity. Against that, here was this little trollop, this liar, this tart without any respect or decency or honour or kindness, simply demanding that he come to her like a lapdog because she was having what was no doubt a reaction to too many late nights and drinking and drugs.

No respect.

'John,' she said in a voice he hadn't heard before. 'I promise you: if you come, I will tell you the truth.'

'The truth?' He held a fist to his mouth and coughed. His knuckles were white. 'You have always told me the truth.'

'Don't be a fuckwit, John. That's my promise. From now on: the truth. And let's see where it takes us.'

'Your meaning.'

'Meaning whatever you want it to mean.'

'You do not want to play this game with me.'

'The truth, John. Both sides. We let it all fall. You. Me. For once in our lives. The truth.'

Our father looked again at our house. She was asking him to do what he had never done before, and for what, really? For what? Our house mocked him. The unkempt facade, the peeling paint, the overgrown moss, the screams of children's fights from within. We had friends over. With their parents. Their parents who never asked our father what he did. The unspoken agreement between our mothers and the parents of our friends: not to delve too deeply into Mr Wonder's whereabouts.

'You gave me this number,' she said. 'You said call any time. Don't you remember that, John? Don't you remember anything that has happened between us?'

'As you wish,' he said. 'I shall come.'

23

While his personal attitude to his work was incorruptibly that of the purist, our father was employed by a commercial organisation, whose direction of his tasks obeyed the precepts of the marketplace. The basic techniques of his work remained stable, even doctrinal, but the material he was called on to verify went through a number of changes that reflected the popular appetite for facts. Norris McWhirter had stated, 'A fact is a fact, there is no gainsaying that,' unaware of the metre and rhyme that turned his homily into a motto, and of course he was correct, but not all facts were of equal weight and certainly the priority of one fact over another was as fluid as the weather.

Around the time he became a father, John Wonder's clients, or bosses, were directing him increasingly to the subjects of crime, villainy, roguery, infamy, notoriety. The buyers of the information he authenticated were showing an unprecedented interest in the world of wrongdoing.

The Last Word sent him around the world to authenticate crime. He brought us back some wonderful entertainment. We were entering an age where the more gruesome the story the better, so in a way we were a focus group for the wider audience. We relished the story of the impostors, such as the African business student who impersonated a famous footballer and convinced a leading manager to play him in the premier league; and the American housewife who passed herself off as a Middle Eastern virgin writing a bestselling memoir about witnessing an honour killing. There were the men and women who faked their own deaths, who orchestrated art frauds, who confidence-tricked their way from harmless prankery into grand criminality. Our father, for reasons which won't surprise, was drawn to those who lived double, treble or quadruple lives. He told us of Anne Bonny, who posed successfully as a male pirate in the eighteenth century until another impostor, Mary Read, also posing as a boy, fell in love with Anne and uncovered her. James Miranda Barry was born a woman and had a child at a young age, but then, for nearly fifty years, posed as a man, serving as a military surgeon with great distinction throughout the British

Empire, becoming physician to a governor, fighting duels, even throwing a rival out of a window. Her reluctance to box or to seduce women were the only clues to her sex, which was discovered in her autopsy after she died of influenza at sixty-seven. There was Archibald Belaney, a lonely English orphan who went to America and reinvented himself as Grey Owl, a Red Indian chief, a role he played for more than thirty years until his death of pneumonia while on a speaking tour. He wrote many bestselling books about life as a Native American. These fascinated our father, and us: great fantasist adventurers like Louis de Rougemont and Lafayette Ron Hubbard; Arthur Orton, the Australian horse thief who claimed to be the heir to an English fortune; and Sarah Wilson, the escaped convict who posed as a member of royalty until she was caught and sent back to servitude, but then, swapping places with an innocent woman of the same name, ran away once more, married, and settled down to live a long and happy life in obscurity.

Our father passed on to us his relish for these magical acts, often asking if we thought the impostors believed in their masks or knew they were actors. For us, still young, these questions were too complicated and adult to answer. But our father enjoyed asking and ruminating on them, often losing the thread of the story he was telling and sitting silently on the end of our bed, astray in his thoughts.

Authenticating the 'criminal enterprise', as he described it, led him to a variety of felonious types. He told us about insurance swindlers and death fakers, judges and politicians corrupted by romantic obsessions, snake-oil salesmen, thieving magicians, horse ringers, resurrectionists and recluses, safe crackers and double agents and tax dodgers. It was all in good fun, we thought, but inevitably, with crime, it starts with a small thing and leads to a larger one and soon (our father hastened to remind us) someone gets hurt. Once he had done with the lovable rogues and quaint criminals of the distant past, our father was asked to authenticate crimes of a more contemporary nature. He had to engage with Holocaust deniers and seek statements from serial killers, passion criminals, homicidal doctors. The work turned him dark and for a while he would not tell us about the new things he had learnt, instead running himself like a repeat television channel in the low season, telling us old stories, harmless chestnuts he had told us before, rather than expose us to the evil he was having to venture into. Within himself, he was beginning to rebel. Our father eventually came to object to much of what he was doing, recording superlative criminal acts for mass entertainment. Roguish girls faking a life as a pirate was one thing, but authenticating the known facts of the Yorkshire Ripper was quite another.

In his long professional life, there had been one certainty: wherever our father went to authenticate a record, he would be welcomed and loved. The world, it could seem, was swollen with record seekers, hopefuls who had spent their days practising their special skill or planning their record attempt, perfecting that one thing nobody else had done. And then they would write to The Last Word, and wait. Finally, in answer to their prayers, he would come. Long-awaited, he was always met with smiles and gifts and the warmest hospitality.

When the focus of his authentication shifted to criminal deeds, this was no longer the case. He travelled to meet victims, investigators, witnesses and, sometimes, perpetrators. The former were reluctant to talk to him, and received his visits with caution at best, hostility at worst. The last of that group, if they did consent to talk to him, could not be trusted: a true criminal saw the Authenticator as another leg to pull, another opportunity to convince a credulous assessor that the accusation against them was false. So in this new line of work, our father was dreaded, tolerated or exploited. No longer was a feast ready for his arrival; no longer was he garlanded with the joy of the hopeful; and he missed all that. He missed the love. He began to yearn for that simple, smiling, unconditional love like an addict who is cured of his addiction and yet, years later, is brought to his knees by the craving's return.

His qualms were heard at the highest level, and after a time he would be offered relief from the duty of compiling and authenticating details of criminal acts. The Last Word did not stop publishing them, as the public demand kept growing, but our father would need to be taken off the case, like a burnt-out detective.

Not, however, before he found the woman who, he believed, might save him.

His last assignment on what he had grimly come to call the 'crime beat' involved meeting a police archivist who had helped him find information previously. Wanda Wilson was a prematurely wrinkled woman in her early forties whose generosity and good humour belied her careworn looks and the often gruesome nature of her occupation.

At a function following a criminology conference, Wanda, who believed our enigmatic father to be a single man, sat him next to someone she wanted him to meet. Wanda fancied herself a matchmaker, and she felt great tenderness for this gentle, secretive antiquarian John Wonder, who had conducted himself in her archives with tact and reserve and responsibility. She trusted him and liked him and decided she had to do something to cure his all-too-transparent loneliness. So, at this function, Wanda decided to set him up.

Of Thai and Chinese descent, Kim was a colleague of Wanda's who worked part-time in the counselling section of the police department. The country in which they lived was, needless to say, oceans away from the places where our father kept his family with Sandy and his family with Paulina.

He sat next to Kim without any notion of Wanda's plot. Because our father was so consumed by the concentration needed to balance his many secrets and stop his worlds from intersecting, he never thought about how casual acquaint- ances might perceive him; he would never have thought kind-hearted Wanda would see him as a single man who needed to meet a good woman. So he fell for the ruse blindly. Kim, whom Wanda had forewarned, or forearmed, was ten years younger than our father but centuries old in experience. Her face was slightly pitted by adult chickenpox. Kim's qualifications for the job of counsellor to the victims of sexual crimes included a bachelor's degree and a doctorate in her subject. She had a third qualification, which was less well known. Kim had been the victim of rape not once, not twice, but countless times during her early adulthood. She had been brought to this country as a slave, her passport stolen, indentured to repay her expenses by means of prostitution. As a prostitute she had lived in the borderlands of the realm of sexual crime. Did such a crime as raping a prostitute even exist in this country? But Kim had been assaulted repeatedly, day after day, assaulted in the exercise of her work but also assaulted by the very nature of that work. Every job she did was an assault, for her speciality, in the galaxy of sexual genres and subgenres, was in fact 'rape'. Some men wanted to be whipped. Some men wanted to whip. Some men wanted to be dressed in nappies. Some men wanted women who were pregnant. Some men wanted dwarfs. Some men were dwarfs. Some men wanted giantesses. Wearing glasses. With short hair. With long hair. With red hair. With no hair. Some men wanted mothers. Some men wanted daughters. Some men wanted babysitters. Some men wanted girls dressed as school students, or nurses, or teachers, or dentists or science fiction characters. Some men wanted women with abundant breasts and no pubic hair; or women with flat chests and abundant pubic hair. Some men wanted to be fellated through a hole in a cubicle. Some men wanted to fellate through a hole in a cubicle. Some men wanted other men. Some men wanted other men who looked like women. Old men wanted young women. Young men wanted old women. (Old men rarely wanted old women.) White men wanted black women. Black men wanted white women. Men who were American, English, Australian, Russian, French, Czech, Japanese, Chinese, Italian, African, Arab, Indian, Pakistani, South American, Eskimo, Aboriginal and Maori wanted women who were Chinese, Indian, South American, English, Aboriginal, Arab, Japanese, Italian, Australian, American, Eskimo, African and Pakistani. And that did not start on the world of specific combinations, re-combinations and permutations of all the above and the numberless sex acts, of locations of the act and locations on the female body, that were wanted in the finite but numberless universe of men living lives other than those they started with. Some men wanted to be the first to do a thing. Some wanted to be the last. Some men refined their tastes down to an art form. Some men would not stop until they had done everything. Man and his superlative dreams!

Some men wanted to commit violent sexual assault. For those men, there was Kim.

So far, her story (she was telling all this to our father quite matter-of-factly over grilled fish and crème brûleé at the criminology conference dinner) was tragically ordinary. Women were brought from poor countries and subjected to this kind of debased enslavement every day. What separated Kim from this historic crime was that she made her way out of it to become a crusading advocate and, while risking deportation as an illegal alien and also risking her life, launched a series of criminal court actions against not only the clients who had assaulted her but her former employers and their agents in both the country of her origin and of her degradation, setting off a trail and a hunt that eventually netted the resignations in disgrace of political and business figures and the criminal convictions of pimps (sometimes the same persons) on both sides of the ocean. No defendant was able to maintain the legal argument that paying for sexual assault was less culpable than doing it for free. They might have been exonerated had Kim been *paid for* being assaulted, as receipt of payment would constitute consent; but as Kim was never paid, being held instead as a slave, then she was, legally speaking, a victim of assault, and her clients became, due to her action, criminals.

'I had no idea I was talking to a hero,' our father confessed, humbled by what she had told him. She was small and fine, not pretty but intelligent and intense, compelling his attention by how, in that tiny frame, she contained so many lives' worth of experience, so much dreadful memory, so much history. Some people, he recalled from his travels, were like this: they contained entire eras of humanity in their experience, through trials of sadness and displacement and suffering. Most were broken by the time he interviewed them. Those who survived were not only proof of Nietzsche's dictum about what does not kill makes stronger, but they radiated that strength in their eyes, in their speech, in their bewitching stories.

'You say there is no number to how many men did this to you?' he asked.

'Finite,' Kim repeated, 'but numberless.'

Unworthy to look her in the eye, he stared at the white scar on her right cheek. When it frightened him too much, he stared at the dimple in her left. Kim was hard at the edges, but our father, by the end of that night, had entered a new dream; he had found the World's Bravest Person.

It was always a dream for him. Life, what we call waking life, was only an interruption to where he truly lived, in the dreams that held sway over him. Sandy had provided him with one dream, that he was blessed by fate, that his first love was his enduring love, sufficient for a lifetime. Paulina had held out another dream: of intellectual and spiritual challenge when he had grown soft and complacent. They were a Hegelian pair: Sandy was the thesis, the pure opening statement, and Paulina was the antithesis, the questioning of all he had stood for, the accountability. Unable to choose between one life and the other, he had attempted to live both.

Kim was synthesis: a reconciliation of his opposites. Against all commonsense and morality and ethics and expectation and wisdom and goodness, Dad found himself falling into another dream: a dream of reparations, a dream in which he could make good all his wrongs. He understood, through meeting Kim, that what he had done was wrong. Insofar as he had thought about it—which he could not afford to let himself, fully, do—he had told himself that he was being kind to both Sandy and Paulina by splitting himself into two; he was sparing them from losing him. That first decisive step, setting up house with Paulina yet not breaking with Sandy, was, he believed, an act of love. He still loved Sandy. Loving a second woman should not mean ceasing to love the first. Love did not have to be divided. Love could be doubled. He was an enlarged lover of those two women. But now, in his monstrous lonely arrogance, he dreamt that he was as much an avatar of a human type as was Kim. Just as she embodied the suffering of woman, he dreamt that he embodied the misdemeanours of man. In fact, of all males, all the criminals whose darkness he had ventured into, a part of him suspected that he, and his type of crime, was, if not the worst, if not as heinous as those which caused actual physical harm, somehow universally emblematic of the ways in which men wronged women. He was the World's Biggest Coward. Thus he was able to dream that he could speak to Kim as something of an equal. More frightful arrogance; more dreaming; more good intentions.

Kim had more secrets than he. But by now he was in the full throes of solipsism, in a hall of mirrors; around him he saw different distortions of himself. One such was Kim.

He paved his own road to hell.

Kim knew that Wanda was setting her up with this man who, as far as she could tell, was single. He appeared gentle and scholarly and kind, not the type of man she was used to. She asked him if he wanted to come home with her, and our father followed the precepts of his dream. What happened next was always what had to happen next.

FOUR

Fall

24

Cicada no longer had bugs crawling over her. She was drinking red wine in the Lakeshore bar of the Holiday Inn. Her hair was the colour of rancid butter. He sat next to her and ordered a non-alcoholic cider. Then he changed his order to a straight tequila on ice, a drink he had last tasted when he was sixteen years old and sitting on the centre console of a friend's car that was about to be driven through an intersection into a street sign and a tree. Miraculously, the car had stopped a foot short of the tree and the street sign had folded in half and sheared through the middle of the windscreen and between John's legs. He had vowed never to touch tequila again.

'The truth,' he said.

'Dare!' Cicada laughed.

Our father was not in the mood for frolics. He was tired from his journey and had left behind some important obligations.

'Such as?' Cicada grinned, touching his knee with the back of her fingers, letting her hand rest. 'More secret agent work?'

'I am not at liberty to tell you.'

'Not at liberty,' she said mockingly, finishing her drink, placing it on the bar and brushing her hair out of her left eye. She was wearing a lavender halter-neck top, denim cut-offs and sandals strapped Roman-style around her calves. 'We're not off to a very good start, are we?'

His traveller's tension ebbing out as the tequila tide flooded in, our father soon had to admit he was enjoying Cicada's company, the first time he had done so. She was courteous and respectful and, after her initial teasing, grateful to him for coming. She held back from probing him on his 'other obligations'. 'You're a married man, and your marriage is your own business. Honestly I don't care about your marriage or your children. You've been honest enough to admit that you're married when you knew it would have been to your advantage to lie and say you were single. You wouldn't be the first. Ha!'

'When I told you I was married,' he said, 'I did not realise it was to my disadvantage.'

'Didn't you? You thought I was the type of girl who would do such a thing to a married woman? Traitor to my sex?'

'No.'

'So would you have lied, if you'd known?'

'Do not flirt with me, Cicada. We've been down that path. You know I have no interest in . . .'

'In fucking me.'

She wiped her mouth with the back of her hand. She was wearing no lipstick. Unusually for her, she was wearing no make-up at all. She looked younger, more girlish, both plainer and more hypnotically beautiful. Her outfit, he estimated, must have cost no more than fifty dollars at Kmart.

'I thought we were here to speak the truth!' She laughed gently.

'Please,' he said. 'I have come a long way. Can we talk about why you wanted me?'

'I think you know why I want you,' she said. 'You just haven't looked under your nose.'

In spite of himself, he looked down. He saw only his lap. 'You rang me in a state of panic and desperation. I felt sorry for you. I felt . . . I suppose I felt that you needed me, and so I rearranged my obligations for you.'

'I love you, John.'

He stopped what he was about to say, a clot of teenage words spurting out of his sick heart and onto his lips, and blinked at her. Her eyes glittered. She was a bad actress,

Cicada, but this time she was both acting and painfully, manifestly genuine. She wanted to cry, and left to her thespian devices she may or may not have been able; emotion took care of the rest.

'And I love you too,' he said mechanically, too wise to be tricked. 'You are the most beautiful woman in the world. When I am with you, I feel that I have been singled out by the gods.'

Cicada did not deny it. This also was something he loved in her. She was not impressed by being told how beautiful she was. She was deaf to his superlatives.

'You mean you've never felt singled out before?'

He drank his tequila. He did not remember it tasting as good as this before the car crash.

'You poor gorgeous man.'

'I love you,' he mumbled. This time, he was not lying either.

John and Cicada looked at the floor, as if for something dropped. Technicolour yawn, the pattern of their declarations, imprinted for eternity.

'You do?' she said, her voice tiny.

'Forever,' he said.

'Then you know why I wanted you to come.'

'I do not.'

'You do. You're just not looking.'

'I do not know what it is I can do for you. I have never known why you talk to me. I have never been able to see what you get out of . . . this. I cannot see what is in it for you. I cannot read your mind. So please. Tell me what it is you want me here for.'

She took his hands in hers. Never had she held him like this. Her small palms were hot and moist. He was vexed at himself for, at this of all moments, ending a sentence with a preposition.

'John?'

He took a breath, dived into her green eyes.

'All these men,' she said, 'they're never satisfied with fucking me. They want to own me. That's why I hate them, that's why I use them up and spit them out and treat them like crap. They can have me, but they can't *have* me, know what I mean? When they wake up in the morning, I am always awake first, waiting for them. I am the leader in this game. I just want them to know that they own nothing. That's why I cut them off. In your case, my dear friend, I am offering you what I offer no other man. You won't fuck me, but you will have what every man who fucks me wants. You will *have me*. Get it? You and I will be twisted around each other like this.' She pushed her crossed fingers under his eyes, to force him to look. Perfect fingers. The Platonic ideal of fingers. 'We'll share this secret. I will belong to you and you will belong to me. We have a pact to tell each other the truth about everything. See? I love you. We love each other. This is love. My love.'

'You are the most beautiful . . .'

'Shh,' she whispered. 'Shut up. Just think. Just . . . don't make me say it, John. Please don't make me say it, because if you make me say it then I can never let you see me again.'

25

He betrayed us with a gesture of kindness towards a woman who deserved no less, yes, but also more kindness than he could give. His first visits with Kim were a period of as little introspection as our father had known since childhood, when he had locked himself away from his warring parents inside his dreams of highest, fastest, longest, vastest. Kim's personal history, and the miracle of her gentle mercy, reduced him to a fleck on the ocean of cruelty that passed for man's relations with woman. In falling in love with Kim, Dad felt he was atoning. His crime was monumental: he had the hide to believe that he was atoning not only for himself, but for the men who had violated Kim in her past and, beyond that, for Man. Cresting middle age, he had entered his last flush of megalomania.

He grew to know Kim in infinitesimal increments. He never knew her fully. She only let him into her life story by story. He extended his work on the encyclopaedia of criminality he had been commissioned to authenticate, withdrawing the resignation he had proffered a few weeks earlier. Now he was prepared to investigate all crime, no matter how awful, if it meant being in the same city as Kim. He would imbibe the evil and the darkness and the horror; it was all compensated by the love he could give her.

Kim's gift for kindness defied his imagination. Her first reflex, in any situation, was in the direction of the right and the generous. She forgave his disappearances and waited faithfully for his return without asking for an explanation. At the moment when he would have been prepared to confess, to at last, finally, lie next to a woman and say, 'You are not the only one, I already have two wives'—and yes, Dad was prepared to do this for Kim—she did not ask it of him. He opened his mouth to confess and she placed her finger across his lips. 'Our secrets are our secrets,' she said. 'I remember everything that has happened to me. I have forgotten nothing. I have given you the barest of outlines. But I do not want to hurt you, John Wonder. I do not want you to know the horrors men are capable of. Please, do not tell me your own secrets, no matter how heavily they may weigh on you.'

'But I want to tell you,' he said, lying in her arms.

'You must not. You may not.'

She took his hand and placed it on the drum-tight rise of her belly.

He did not take a lot of persuading, it has to be said. In Kim, he never saw another human, but he did see the universe. She allowed him to imagine everything that had happened to her, to women. Another dream: another denial: another refusal. But can we condemn him? He chose the most terrible ways to betray us, to lie to us, to live as if we did not exist. And then he made more of us.

26

The solution was so obvious that he laughed at himself for not having worked it out a year ago. What Cicada saw in him. What she wanted from him. What she would share with him. How she would belong to him.

How he would belong to her.

He did not see her during the week leading up to Dorothy Ellen O'Oagh's one hundred and thirtieth birthday. Cicada was absent when our father visited Menis Economopoulos to find the old man in an uncommonly cheerful mood. Menis had been revelling in his newfound cult heroism. 'The tables are turned,' he burbled, rubbing his hands together. 'I knew that the world would eventually come to my position. I just had to live long enough.'

Our father saw it playing out. Menis, in his house arrest, was being cast by the media as some kind of Nelson Mandela, a man who would hold out until the end of time in the service of his principle. The principle was murder—or it had been murder to an earlier generation—but now it seemed to have been rewritten as euthanasia, an altogether more popular cause. The ageing of the population was becoming such a source of anxiety to the young—Who was going to house grandparents who lived forever? Who was going to feed them? Who was going to foot their infinite medical bills?—that there was a concurrent public debate, formerly unspoken, now shouted from the rooftops, about 'what to do with those who refuse to die'. It had become one of the leading social and political issues of the time. Health budgets were sinking public finances. The aged, the unproductive hyper-aged refuseniks, were a drain and an anchor on those who worked. They were a millstone around the neck of the present and, worse, the future. Dorothy Ellen O'Oagh became, during the week of her one hundred and thirtieth birthday, a 'news peg', that is, a personification of society's anxiety—no, anger—towards those who refused either to live or die. A tabloid television program about her was titled *Madam, (please) shit or get off the pot*. No sensitivities were spared. Spokespeople for the young, the old, the gratuitously old and the egregiously old were pitted against each other on forum programs. They shouted and ranted, the young at the sheer selfishness of the old, the old at what they saw as the homicidal impatience of the young. Aged-care facilities were filled to overflowing. Cultures where the old were looked after at home by the young were breaking down, because the 'young', for the purposes of caring, were now in advanced old age themselves, ninety-year-olds being expected, in line with tradition, to look after one-hundred-and-ten-year-olds. And what then? Seventy-year-olds expected to look after both the ninety-year-olds and the one-hundred-and-ten-year-olds. It all landed on the fifty-year-olds, who would be expected to relieve the state of the burden of caring for two and sometimes three generations of deadweight.

These were the burning issues of the time, but our father heard a message meant for his ears only.

How could he have overlooked it?

To share a secret, first we must make a secret.

Love is procreation.

By the eve of the birthday, Dorothy Ellen O'Oagh was being portrayed in the media as an albatross of villainy, a greedy old witch sucking the life out of the heroic Menis Economopoulos. Our father was even drawn into the debate as an 'enabler' of her tyranny, part of the 'life industry', or 'Big Life', that conspired with Big Pharma to 'string along' the unnecessarily old. He had to go on television and radio and the internet to explain that he was not personally responsible for keeping the world's oldest woman alive. 'My role is to authenticate,' he said, reading a written statement and refusing to answer questions. 'The Last Word is not a body that seeks to influence history. Rather, we are a keeper of records. I do bring her a cake each year,' he added, 'but I do not think it sustains her. I have not seen her eat a crumb since her one hundred and seventeenth birthday. I do not think she has taken any nourishment other than that which is administered intravenously for some years now.'

His statement, far from placating his critics, heightened the frenzy of criticism. This John Wonder, this 'Authenticator', did not seem to understand that by measuring Dorothy Ellen O'Oagh's age he was not only giving her an incentive to keep on living, to stay 'in the way', but he was 'sending the wrong message' to all the other hyper-longevitous clogging up the works, assuring them that their selfishness was a virtue, that longevity was something to keep on striving for, that they were setting records in the same way as the strongest, the fastest and the highest—who, by the way, were inhibited from going stronger, higher and faster by the constant cuts to government and private funding for athletic pursuits due to the overwhelming needs of the aged, particularly the hyper-aged, the record-setting aged most of all, who were, to restate the point, an anchor tied to the foot of the entire drowning human race.

Our father did not respond to the criticism. He presented a facade of bland dignity, on his organisation's behalf and in keeping with his lifelong reticence and fear of the limelight. And he was afraid: he was afraid that if he allowed himself to sit down and take questions, he would break down and admit that he wanted Dorothy Ellen O'Oagh to die as desperately as they all did, probably as desperately as anyone in the world outside of the Economopoulos family, possibly even more so.

Mrs O'Oagh's house, due to its propitious position by the lake, was now worth many millions. But since her ownership pre-dated operative changes in taxation law, and due also to a special award made by the local authority twenty years earlier, when Menis Economopoulos had been placed under arrest and she was held up as a paragon of victimhood, she paid no land taxes, council rates or any other public duties.

On her birthday, a picket formed outside this priceless white elephant. A crowd of hundreds formed a line, linked arms, held candles and sang into the night. They held up placards saying FREE MENIS and ENOUGH IS ENOUGH and LET HER GO—OUT. For mercy's sake, the public mood was saying, or at least those parts of the public mood that found voice, Mrs O'Oagh must be made, or allowed, or encouraged, to cease breathing.

On the big day, our father sat with Mrs O'Oagh and her physician before a battalion of klieg lights. She wore a new dress, dove-grey with mother-of-pearl buttons and long billowing sleeves, sheer stockings and grey leather shoes with high heels. High heels!

Breathe Dorothy O'Oagh continued to do, to the groans of the sweating cameramen and sound technicians. There was silence but for the sound of her rasping, silence as the doctor velcroed the blood-pressure strap around what remained of her withered upper arm. Silence as the doctor put his stethoscope to her etiolated chest. Silence as the doctor murmured figures to our father, who inscribed the data into his leatherbound notebook. And then, breaking the silence, the rough and ready voice of a best boy: 'Fuck's sake, man, somebody put a pillow over her face and give us some footage.'

There was no laughter, only disgruntled murmurs of concurrence.

Our father thought the technician was beseeching him, personally.

Dorothy Ellen O'Oagh's webby eyes flickered, then sprang open. Our father had not seen those eyes for three years. He had forgotten how opaquely dark they were with their cataracts, like black coffee with a single droplet of milk swirling in them. They were trained, as best as he could tell, on him.

Her lips moved as if she were trying to talk. Our father looked at the doctor, who lengthily busied himself with packing up his equipment. He didn't want to be seen as another enabler.

Our father leant closer.

In a rattle—but not, alas, a death rattle—Mrs O'Oagh's words came out.

Then her eyes closed again and her mouth wrinkled in upon itself.

'What did she say?' the television director cried out. 'Did we get any of that?'

Our father, who had dreaded this moment, being put on the spot on live television, shook his head. 'It was private,' he said.

'Private?' the best boy, a man older even than our father, shouted with a sneer. 'You her dad or what?'

Our father shook his head and sighed. 'If you have to know, she said—' he swallowed and blinked away his emotion '—she said the pillows are in the hall closet.'

There was a puzzled silence as the television people, never the quickest on the uptake, divined the entrails of Dorothy Ellen O'Oagh's gnomic utterance. It was the best boy, the first interjector, who again was there before anyone else.

'Well come on, mate, you need us to give you a map as well?'

What, our father wondered after the circus had moved on and Mrs O'Oagh was thirty-six hours into her hundred and thirty-first year, was her life anyway? Could an ancient body showing a minimum of vital signs, while not being in a coma, be any more valuable than that of an embryo that we regretfully but necessarily put to death because its parents will not be able to bring it into the world with love? Our father was no opponent of abortion, in fact in some cases he supported the idea on a retrospective basis . . . But he was shaken by the turn of the public mood against Dorothy Ellen O'Oagh, not simply as a matter of practicality, but as a question of the very nature of existence, of life and its worth. Questions of 'quality of life' seemed terribly obsolete when it came to Mrs O'Oagh. Her life had had no meaningful quality for forty years. But it was a life all the same, and it was in nobody's power to end it. For her nursing staff to stop feeding her would be murder. For her doctor to administer a lethal injection would be murder. For our father to go to the hall closet and bring her a pillow would be as complete a case of murder as if he did it to a child in the flower of her youth. Murder is murder, and no law had yet been devised to make an exception. Voluntary euthanasia was the preserve of those who wanted to die. Dorothy Ellen O'Oagh may well have wanted to die, but was incapable of satisfying the legal tests to allow a mercy killing to proceed. Whichever way he looked at it, our father could see no way of breaking the impasse.

Only love could set Mrs O'Oagh free.

He went to Menis Economopoulos's home next to watch the television interview taking place there. Menis was engaging and expansive, like a Third World dictator exiled by a gang of thugs and thieves: Menis was the lesser of two evils, surely. He enumerated the benefits of 'putting her to sleep', as he phrased it, not only for him—'What could it matter to me any more?'—but for the public morale. In fact, as he was lionised, Menis seemed to identify his own welfare fully with that of the community at large. 'What is good for me,' he said, 'is good for you. All of you. I do not matter. This is a matter of urgency facing the entire body politic.'

He was asked what he would want to happen if, say, he fell off the plateau of rude good health he was bestriding in his early eighties and became a 'vegetable' like Mrs O'Oagh.

'For one,' he said, waggling a despotic finger and sucking his cigar, 'I have waited many years. Once I have prevailed, I will display the same determination and regimen of exercise that has kept me in such good shape for so long. And for two,' he said. 'For two? I have forgotten what for two was. All I want to say is that if I ever lie and fester in the path of youth, my loved ones will know what to do.'

This set off a series of questions about Menis Economopoulos's family, which he refused to answer.

'For me to know and for you to find out,' he said with a wink and a puff.

As he stood in the background watching this, our father wondered where Cicada was. Like a cigarette held to the soft skin of the palm of his hand, Cicada burnt a hole in him. Normally she would be attending to her father. But this situation was far from normal. What would happen if she was exposed to television? How many attoseconds before some news director or celebrity presenter took a glance and discovered, in this godforsaken place amid this godforsaken tabloid story, a world-historical beauty whose physical presence demanded an offer of a contract, a proposal of marriage, or a kidnapping?

Menis, our father concluded, must have hidden her away. And Cicada would willingly have hidden. She did not want her beauty recognised by television, by celebrity, by the greater world.

She wanted to belong to John Wonder. She wanted John Wonder to belong to her. She wanted John to be free of his lies. She wanted her father to be free of his temporary restraining order.

And somewhere, elsewhere, we watched the television clips in our different places, in our different houses.

Sandy didn't watch, being too busy at work, but we did.

Paulina had no television, she didn't believe in it, but we watched it at a friend's house.

Kim sat and watched it with us. We knew what was happening. It was our father. He was a famous and important man. Here he was at his work, the most important work in the world.

We were exceedingly proud of him, and told everyone at school the next day—in all of our schools, in our different places, this was what we all had in common, the bragging rights—that our dad was the man in the television set and he was *our dad*, nobody else's.

27

Kim gave birth to twins, a boy and a girl. She was living in a small apartment overlooking a railway line. Kim earned little from her work as a shopfront counsellor, and the children required constant medical attention. The girl suffered from a complex of congenital conditions affecting her sensory apparatus: she could not hear, feel, taste or smell. The boy had been born with muscular dystrophy, a cleft palate and a hare lip.

At first, Kim would say nothing about their biological father. All she told John was that they were the product of an assault before she met him.

'Even when I was becoming middle class, when I was a citizen of this country and I was working my way through university and I was turning myself into a *doctor*,' she said, 'the assaults continued. My only regret is that sexual assault is not a finite quantity, and I cannot soak them up for all of womankind.'

'This was after you . . . retired?' John asked.

'Men who rape, they find women who have been raped. There is an animal signal that comes from me, that says to such men, This is a rape woman, a woman to attack.'

Our father did not want to know what that said about him.

'Who was it?'

'My doctoral supervisor,' she said. 'And that is the last you will know. You can go and fact-find, Mr Fact-Finder, but you will not find him.'

'Oh?'

'He has been disappeared.'

'He has disappeared?'

'My English is perfect.'

Our father waited, but no further explanation was forth-coming. He did go and fact-find on Kim's supervisor, but all he could discover was a university statement saying that the supervisor had resigned for personal reasons and left to travel overseas. No academic postings or publications had been recorded in his name since then. It was believed he had gone to India to study the Vedas in their original Sanskrit.

The boy and the girl remained unnamed for a long time while Kim decided. She called them 'Boy' and 'Girl'. And then she named us Adam and Evie. This also was how our father knew he had found his redeemer. Kim did not know Mr and Mrs Wonder's names.

Dad sold some assets and shifted some funds and moved our mother Kim and us into a more comfortable house, away from the railway line. He paid the rent and took care of the medical bills.

Kim did not want the formal recognition of marriage. But she finally had the children's names registered.

He had three families: a highwire act. In the second year of this arrangement, when his existence had turned into a breathless race from one commitment to another, an incident occurred that threatened to finish him. He was walking from Kim's house to the nearest taxi rank, to hurry off to the airport to come home to Sandy's family. He had told Sandy he was in one place, and told Paulina he was in another place. There had become almost too many lies for him to keep track of, and the finest disruption to his routine would bring questions that he could not easily answer. He was walking down the suburban street towards the taxi rank when he witnessed an old man being mugged and kicked by two teenaged boys.

As a matter of practicality, our father scrupulously avoided getting involved in anything superfluous to his routines. His life had to be covert. His first instinct, then, as he saw the boys jumping up and down on the old man's ribs, was to scurry on with his head lowered, to pretend it was not happening. Sure, he could have helped the old man, but our father had to keep his priorities at the top of his mind.

Yet the sight of the bashing, the pimply, cawing cowardice of the teenaged boys, so infuriated him that he turned back and chased them away. He phoned an ambulance and waited with the old man by the side of the road. A crowd gathered, and people asked the Good Samaritan who he was. Our father brushed off their inquiries, looking at his watch. When he saw that if he waited any longer he might miss his flight and be met at the other end by all sorts of uncomfortable questions, he disappeared.

The spotlight likes nothing more than a shadow, though, and as he told nobody his name he became an instant mystery celebrity in Kim's city. Stories abounded of the Unknown Samaritan. Far away, as he was keeping an eye on the internet for news stories of the old man and the bashing, our father came across descriptions of the Samaritan. Nobody who had seen him could remember quite what the Samaritan looked like. There was an identikit photo that looked nothing like our father. He felt like a criminal on the run, except that the big news was that the old man was a reclusive millionaire and wanted to offer a substantial reward. He made a personal appeal to the Unknown Samaritan. The police, simultaneously, were calling for witnesses to the crime, namely him, to come forward. A humdrum mugging went viral due to the wealth and eccentricity of the victim and the mercurial disappearance of the Samaritan. News reports of Samaritan claimants, and the outrageous impersonations they were willing to perform, fed the cycle day after day.

When our father returned to Kim's city three weeks after the mugging, he kept his collar turned up and a hat pulled low over his face. He dreaded being identified. When he saw how Kim was struggling to meet her children's needs, and how little he could help, he began to think about the money. He racked his brain trying to work out how he could claim the reward but avoid publicity. It might be achievable, but he didn't trust this internet machine. Its lips were too loose. One slip and the whole thing was over: John Wonder would be world famous as the Unknown Samaritan, but to two women, in faraway cities, he would have to answer questions about why he had been where he said he wasn't, and what he was doing with the money. Putting his hand out for the old man's reward could turn out to be his one fatal error. The old man would ask him why he didn't want publicity. The old man would hold back the money until John confessed. His confession would be the price he would have to pay to receive the reward. It was not going to work. It was a cosmic trap laid for him by a crafty old god.

Then he learnt from the television that someone else had claimed the reward. He saw a picture of the claimant in the newspaper. The man looked substantially more like the identikit picture of the Unknown Samaritan than John did.

'What a wonderful man,' Kim said.

Our father agreed. The picture showed the claimant with the old millionaire, arms around each other's shoulders, thumbs aloft, saviour and victim in perfect harmony.

•

We saw our father sleeping. It seems a miracle to have thus breached his privacy, but we did have a domestic life, of sorts, the mornings when we crept into his bedroom and found him asleep with one of our mothers. It breaks our hearts to remember the naked creases across the back of his neck while he slept: three of them, intersecting, like braided twine. To think that those wrinkles were carved in his skin from every time he twisted his head to glance around and check that he was not being followed. Wrinkles made from every time he looked to the stars above, to check what side of the world he was on, to get his stories straight. Every time he nodded to a flight attendant on his way through the skies. Every time he nodded to agree with his wife or to encourage his children. Every time he authenticated. Every time he did anything, he deepened those three wrinkles. Like a river, they carved their banks. An unending river. We were in three separate strands, we three groups of children, but those wrinkles stayed with him across all the different lives he led. They were more his intimates than we, or his women, were. The vulnerability of him, while he slept, brings tears to our eyes. And the intimacy of those wrinkles. As if they were his real children.

Another thing, while he slept:

When he was with our mother Sandy, he lay on his back, on his side of the bed, and she slept with her arms around him. In sleep, Sandy clung to him like a lemur to a tree.

Every love is a reaction against a previous love. When he was with Paulina, he lay on his side, facing away from her, and she lay on her side, facing away from him. Their skin did not touch while sleeping. They did not want the clinging.

And when he lay with Kim, while he slept, he clung to her. Our father, holding on to Kim for dear life. We crept in and there was the back of his head, with its wrinkles that were made not only when he was with us but when he was with the others, and even when he was with Cicada, the delicate exposed wrinkles that would stay until erased by death. The wrinkles, the most private of his private parts, that he did not know were there, and that he could not stop us from seeing. He could no more bring them under his control than he could bring back his arms, which, in sleep, were reaching with animal need for Kim's shoulders. His legs bent towards hers, one knee clasped over her thigh. She, lying on her back, holding his hand to the hollow below her throat, a quarter of a smile on her lips.

We crept out again.

28

After Menis Economopoulos's television performance, our father left the town. He did not see Cicada, who he surmised was in hiding from the remnants of international media roaming for a few more days and the celebrities and hangers-on who attended Menis's festivities. John did not need to see or hear from Cicada. The two, in their pact, had gone into a kind of lockdown, they were a sleeper cell, and they would have no communication until the job was done. Cicada was a law student after all, a criminal law student as well as a young woman with a fertile criminal imagination. She had not asked him to commit a crime. Should the worst come to the worst, he could not prove anything against her. But it would never come to that. They were locked down together.

Already, in the preparation, he felt her presence, a warm vibrancy, as if she were nestled in his arms.

He came home to us and Sandy, for a week.

He came home to us and Paulina, for a week.

He came home to us and Kim, for a week.

He sat on the ends of our beds and told us stories from his work.

We told him we had seen him on the television.

Then he had to go.

•

Cicada was not at the Lakeshore bar the night he arrived.

He checked into the Holiday Inn as a couple: Mr and Mrs Wonder. 'My wife,' he said to the featureless young man at the desk, 'will be joining me after.'

'You mean later,' the man said.

John smirked. Stupid young man. Cicada would lie and say that she had slept with him. How John loved her lies. How he looked forward to the moment Cicada came to join him. After.

He had not been drunk in three years. He got drunk that night, on cheap red wine, in her honour. She was not there, and nor were any salesmen. He was in the bar alone, drinking. Even the barman had gone back to reception and left our father with the bottle.

The next day, he drove to Mrs O'Oagh's residence. He used his passcode to enter the newly-built security gates and parked his car on the forecourt of her house, beside a nurse's car. He greeted the nurse in the doorway. She let him in and offered him a cup of tea. He followed her into the entrance hallway. She was a handsome woman in her seventies. She wore high heels, which bulged her calves beneath the hem of her white uniform as she walked away from him to the kitchen. Her uniform hugged her strong, swaying hips. Our father thought: she is young enough to be her patient's granddaughter. He had a pound cake in his hand. The nurse: it must be she, he thought, who dressed Mrs O'Oagh in stockings and heels. Who got her up nicely every day. Who put her in her pyjamas at night. He wondered if it had been the same nurse all these years, who did such lovely things. He must ask her.

While the nurse went off to make the tea for him, he paused in the entrance hallway and took in the view of the lake, which sat like a primeval bubbling swamp under the evening mist. He heard the nurse stumping about in the kitchen. He thought, A watched pot never boils. And a life, if you observe it vigilantly enough, recording its movements thoroughly enough, may never come to an end.

That was all. The next thing he knew, he was getting back into the car. He was fumbling his key into the lock. But it was not his key. It was a small silver fork, an antique dessert fork. It came from the same set as that teaspoon he had once found in his hand, falling out of his hand, in fact, as he had stumbled into wakefulness outside Mrs O'Oagh's house in almost identical circumstances.

He drove fast to the Holiday Inn and went straight to his room. He showered and changed and sat on his bed watching television. His brain, as always at these times, felt like a landscape scorched black by bushfire. He fingered the silver fork in his right hand, turning it over and over as if it might bear some evidence, give him some clue to what he had done.

But he would not have used a *fork*. He knew where the hall closet was. If he had done anything, he would only have followed the plan, wouldn't he?

Wouldn't he?

He drifted in and out of sleep in front of the twenty-four-hour news channel. No news, good news. As he coasted towards a numb stupor he entertained himself with his favourite fantasies of Cicada: how he would bring her to this room, this very room, and unravel her from her electric-blue cashmere sweater. In the fantasy, he never made love with her or even touched her. It was a strange passage between daydream and dream, and yet for our father it retained a certain lawyerly deniability: if he didn't touch her body, he wasn't being unfaithful, was he? As if it mattered. As if he wasn't so far gone that nothing mattered. When we think of his fantasies, at this late hour, our faith trembles.

When he woke, he expected to see news of Mrs O'Oagh. But then, he wondered, it would take time to reach the news organisations. It would require the nurse to find her, the doctor to confirm her death . . . and what would happen next? The police, yes, the police. And then how did the police release such information? How long did it take them? He didn't know. It was now four hours since he had left Mrs O'Oagh's house, or rather, as he could not remember leaving it, he could count four and a half hours since he had arrived there and sat with the nurse waiting for his cup of tea. The last he could recall. The watched pot, not boiling.

Still nothing came up on the news.

He tried to reach Cicada, by email and by text and by phone. That she was not responding was almost reassuring: she at least was sticking to the plan. But soon, as each minute passed without news of Mrs O'Oagh, he felt the first rustling of panic. Something was happening, some police investigation occurring without his knowledge. Surely they would come to see him. The nurse would mention him. He was ready for that. But he was ready for that *now*. He was not ready to wait for it. He wanted it all to proceed—the arrest, the interrogation, the phone calls, the lawyers, the charges, the bail, or the discharge, the lack of evidence—he was ready for all of that but only, he discovered now, on the condition that it happened *immediately*. It was the waiting that he could not stand. The waiting was the torture. He had never imagined this, never taken it into account, even when he seemed to have war-gamed every last detail and contingency.

And of course he could not have taken into account what had happened, which is that, due to his little episode, he did not know what had happened.

He tried Cicada again: phone, text, email, instant messenger. He phoned her home number, which he never did. Menis Economopoulos picked up and answered with a violent growl.

'What?'

As if he was expecting someone.

John hung up.

After eight hours, with night well fallen, he had still received no knock at his door. Nor had anything appeared on the television news channel. Perhaps he had done nothing? Perhaps, during his dark episode, he had changed his mind and not gone through with his plan? He wondered if some mechanism of goodness, or conscience, or cowardice, had taken over his body and conducted him out of the house without having gone to the hall closet, without having done it. The invisible hand of some god he had neither believed in nor deserved. Perhaps he had been saved. This was why there was no news—because nothing had happened! And the reason Cicada was not answering him was that she had decided to cut off relations with him. He had disappointed her once too often. It was over between them. So be it, he thought. I must have been crazy, I must have been suffering some kind of episode all along, what was I doing, what kind of spell was I under, that for this common little small-town trollop I was prepared to make myself a murderer, and not for the trollop's physical favours, just for some idea of sharing a secret with her, for some promise of spiritual intimacy. What kind of idea do I have of love, that I would be driven to take a human life for *that*? What was I thinking? What on earth was I thinking?

And just as he breathed easier and reconciled himself to a future without Cicada, reeled himself back to normality, or the version of normality that could reside in maintaining three separate families, *ah, the simple life,* just as he thanked his good fortune and the benevolent automatism that must have taken over him, the item came up on the news and a slab of knuckle and meat knocked at the door to his room.

29

If she had known it would end this way, Cicada Economopoulos would have spent her life in a nunnery and never spoken to a man. Swear it. Which was what her papou always told her she should have done. But of course she couldn't be a nun—she'd have ended up corrupting the Catholic church—and so her papou had done the next worst thing, which was to imprison her in the house with him, to give company to his misery, and bottle her up and pressurise her desires and turn her into his lab rat, with the result that instead of what he wanted he got its opposite.

But that was that. That was her so-called life. Now she had to deal with this: a man in a hospital bed, staring at the ceiling. A mad old man she barely knew, he dragged her into this—okay, she did know him, but she wished she didn't.

She looked for a nurse, for someone to talk to. She didn't want to talk to John. She had worked as a nurse once, in an old people's home, on her school holidays. She didn't mind cleaning bedpans, she sort of liked bodily functions. What turned her off was how the men, and some of the women, always grabbed at the zipper down the front of her uniform. God, she went to work in a nursing home to escape from that kind of thing.

He'd been like this since he burst into the house. Wild-eyed, zombie, awake, wired. Totally freaked out. Her papou thought John had come in to attack them, and picked up the golf club he stored by his bedside in case of intruders. Papou always said that if he swung hard enough, he could stay beyond the intruder's reach and take him with one blow. If that blow failed, however, he was in strife. So the key was, strike your hardest with your first swing.

Anyway, she'd calmed Papou down. She could see that John meant them no harm. What he meant to do to himself was another thing. He hurled himself, weeping, on the parquet floor. Cicada and Papou looked at each other. They were not exactly rich in the gifts of charity and care. All they had done for twenty years was look after themselves. Since her brothers had gone, it was just her and her papou, and her and her adventures, and if there was one thing she was not responsible for, it was men.

She and Papou managed to pick John Wonder up and seat him in an armchair. Papou, slowly putting two and two together, went off to his study. He had started on the bottle of French champagne he had saved for twenty years in anticipation of this day, and he wasn't going to be diverted now. He was two glasses in and not drunk enough. He laughed—of course he was in a good mood!—gave John Wonder a pat on his sandy head, and disappeared.

Which left Cicada with him. He was still blubbering and apologising, but over what and for what she didn't know yet. Sure, she knew the general subject—but this was a night for celebrating, right? This was the night of liberation. She was already a bit pissed herself, having cheated a little to be honest, opening a bottle of claret her papou had presented her on a birthday, all those years ago . . .

This was a night to spend with Papou, but John was putting a dampener on things, falling all over the kitchen table, bursting into tears, spoiling the moment, draining her until all she wanted to do was flash him her tits or give him a feel, anything to shut him up and send him on his way.

He'd been bent over at the table for quite a while. She'd given him a pat on the head to hurry him along, but he didn't realise that it wasn't a good idea for him to hang around here. Questions would be asked.

Questions had already been asked, but it had gone well. Dorothy Ellen O'Oagh had expired—God be praised!—from natural causes that very evening. There were no suspicious circumstances. How could anything be suspicious about a one-hundred-and-thirty-year-old witch dying? A witch everyone, the entire world, wanted to see the back of? There was nothing suspicious about it, unless John managed to bugger it up.

He'd already done his best to bugger things up . . . but let's not go there, she thought. Let sleeping dogs lie.

He'd gone back to his hotel room, where the police had found him. They wanted to let him know the old lady had passed on, so he would not have to come and record her birthday anymore. Let him know? Sure. John didn't know. Silly old John. She wasn't sure why she'd involved him in the first place. She knew he'd get the wrong message. She just wanted to see how far he'd go. He was a man. Men did what she wanted, always. It had only struck her recently that this one, this John Wonder, was obsessed with her in a different way from the usual ones. There was something terrible in his loneliness. They were all lonely, one way or another, and bored—that was the one thing they had in common with her—but this guy was different. She couldn't put her finger on it, but ever since they'd begun talking, after so many years of knowing each other, she'd felt that he presumed a kind of intimacy. It didn't help her that she wouldn't fuck him. If she'd fucked him, just once, the usual way, it would have all been over. But she hadn't fucked him, because he was married. That was the truth. She never fucked a man she knew was married. There were so many other guys in the world, and they were all pretty much interchangeable, why complicate things by getting mixed up with married ones? She'd done it by mistake a few times—when guys had lied and said they were single—and it always ended up messy. So she had this one rule. No married fucks.

And the other thing she'd said to him was true, too. If she fucked John, he would have been one in, what, a thousand? And for him—know what it was?—he was like a virgin. He would never get over it. Not only would it scupper his marriage, it would send him totally nuts. She wondered what his wife did for him. No, correction: she never wondered what his wife did for him.

Not that she figured (seeing him weeping at her table, seeing him catatonic in the hospital bed) he needed any help. Going nuts that is. But still. No way was she going to fuck him. But still. It would have finished things off and saved her from this. But still.

In her kitchen, he had begun babbling nonsense about being in the Holiday Inn when the police came and informed him that Dorothy O'Oagh was deceased. The police thought he would want to know. For his records. Police understood that. Maintaining records, bureaucracy. John was on their level. Scumbags. That is, men. All types.

Only he didn't seem to comprehend what was going on. He didn't realise that he had a watertight alibi. It couldn't have worked out better if she'd planned it. Mrs O'Oagh had died of natural causes, and he had been with an alibi witness when it happened. There was nothing to worry about. Cicada told him that, but he was just crying and crying, wanting something, babbling about 'truth'.

'Truth'? Truth was, she wanted to get back to her bottle of vintage red. She didn't appreciate him rocking up the minute she'd opened it. A kind of nightmare: you anticipate this moment for years, how you're going to sit there and savour this bottle that means so much to you, means everything, you're going to toast your freedom, with Papou—and just when you're uncorking it, this person turns up who you know too well to just turf out, but you don't like well enough to invite him to share it with you.

It really pissed her off.

The truth was, she'd always told him the truth. That was what he couldn't handle. Of all men, he was the one Cicada had been most candid with, most honest, most herself. That was why the part of her that liked him, liked him. She always told him the truth. There was nothing more to it. She was a slut, she didn't regard herself as out of the ordinary, she hated men who went all gibbery over her, she was suffering from near-terminal boredom, she loved her papou. That was all there was to her. And she wanted to be a criminal lawyer.

It never seemed enough for John Wonder. He wanted her to be some kind of miracle. Men!

He never got it. She was already giving him the truth. And it wasn't enough for him. He had appetites for an army. But he didn't know himself. That was what she'd seen in him at the start: the poor guy was in his fifties, and he just didn't know the first thing, the most obvious thing, the very basic thing, about himself. No fool like an old fool.

'I,' he said. 'I did it.'

'No you fucking well didn't.'

His chin trembled. 'I did it. For you, Cicada.'

'You did not. You were with . . .' She couldn't speak. Fuck him! She inhaled. 'You were with—her nurse?'

'I . . . I cannot remember. But I . . . I must have done it, just as we planned.' He paused and then stared at her. 'Nurse?'

And then the bastard had had a kind of fit, a breakdown, a full-on nervo, right there in her kitchen. She'd had to call her dad in. Menis was smashed now, he'd finished his champagne. He was all for picking John up and leaving him out on the street for a car to run over, a hit and run.

'That episode is over now,' her papou had said, dismissing the last half-century with a curt wave of his hand. 'Another reason I am celebrating: I no longer have to sit down and answer questions from this man once a year!'

But Cicada couldn't let him lie on the street. He was too pitiful. She'd called an ambulance. By the time the paramedics had arrived, he was weeping and rolling around and saying he didn't know where he was, who he was, what day it was, how he'd got here, where here was. Nothing. He was totally lost. He didn't even know who *she* was. That was what got her in the end. A man, looking at her desperately, without the foggiest idea who she was.

She had to respect that.

So she'd gone with the paramedics to the hospital, and here she was. She had to fill in forms, but she didn't really know anything about him, she wasn't next of kin, she wasn't even a friend really, he'd just been at her house, she didn't want to take responsibility, he was just some old man.

The guy at the hospital triage—she knew him. She'd fucked him once. She didn't remember his face or his name, but there was this way he was looking at her. She knew that. The way they always were. Cock holds more men in servitude than any cotton planter or Pharaoh ever dreamed. More than religion. Cock could make them march to war if it wanted.

In this whole town, her papou was the only free man left.

She answered the hospital's questions and told them what she knew: the patient worked for an organisation that certified facts such as those this town was famous for. She sat in the reception while they phoned The Last Word. It took them a long while. The head office was in another country, in another time zone, and they had to go through international directories.

But they got through. They put her on. She spoke to some guy and told them that John Wonder had collapsed and was in hospital in this town. The guy was flirty over the phone. Jesus! He asked how she knew John. She wouldn't bite. She just said his next of kin had to be contacted, his wife, whoever, but his wife, yes, she knew he was married, his wife had to be told.

This was Cicada's last debt to the institution of marriage. She wanted John's wife to know where he was and to come and take over his care. She wanted his wife to take him off her hands. She wanted to go home and celebrate.

'We're not sure if he is married,' said the flirty guy at John's office. 'We have no family details for him at all.'

'Well he is,' Cicada snapped. 'So why don't you get off your pimply arse and find his wife?'

The guy laughed her off. One of those guys. From a continent away, she could smell them.

'Look,' he said, 'we'll just sit tight. When one of our field authenticators doesn't go home for a time, we eventually get a call from the family. They come to us. We don't need to go to them.'

Yeah, keep pulling on it, Cicada thought.

'So,' he said. 'Cicada. Where did you say you are right now?'

She knew it. She was so pissed off now she wanted to go somewhere and drink for a week. For a year. However long it took before bloody John's bloody wife turned up.

30

We have been in the shadows, undifferentiated. We were just a mass to you, Dad, weren't we? We were just 'the children'. Just Adam and Evie.

Well? Weren't we?

One week after he left for Cicada, for Menis and for Mrs O'Oagh, his wife Sandy, his first love, our first mother, took a call from his office in his home city.

'We have this number as the next of kin of John Wonder,' the office administrator said. 'We are calling to tell you he is all right.'

'What do you mean?' Sandy said. 'We're not expecting him at home for another week.'

'He's all right,' the office administrator went on. 'We received a call from the Holiday Inn in F_____, where he has been working. They said Mr Wonder was in hospital. He and Mrs Wonder had checked out of the Holiday Inn, but he is being looked after.'

'What did you say?' Sandy said.

'We can tell you the name and number of the hospital,' the office administrator said.

'No, the other part.'

Sandy would take the children out of high school. We would all go.

Next to call our father's office was Paulina, angry that he had not been in contact. She spoke to the branch office of The Last Word in her country. She spoke to a human resources assistant who had not been told that Sandy had already been informed. So the same message was repeated: Mr Wonder was in hospital in F_____, but he had checked out of the Holiday Inn with Mrs Wonder and was being looked after.

'How bad is he?' Paulina asked. She assumed the part about 'Mrs Wonder' was a mistake, the usual fuck-up from John's stupid trivia company.

'We don't have enough information,' said the human resources assistant.

'You never do,' Paulina spat.

She took us out of school and boarded a plane.

Three days later, Kim had a premonition. She had seen our father on television, on the occasion of Dorothy O'Oagh's one hundred and thirtieth birthday. Kim had followed the story closely. She was not expecting John home yet, but when she heard on the news that the world's oldest person had died, of natural causes, she knew that John would be there. Something in her gut told her that he needed her.

Kim called the branch office of The Last Word in her country.

'He's in hospital,' she was told.

'I knew it,' Kim said. 'How bad is he?'

'We don't have a lot of information,' she was told.

She did not wait to be told that he was in the care of Mrs Wonder. She boarded a plane. She took little Adam and Evie with her, even taking into account the troubles of travelling internationally with them. They needed to see their father.

We did.

Sandy arrived first. She checked into the Holiday Inn and went to the hospital. She read his charts and talked to the doctors. She took a position by his bedside. We sat beside her and played hand-held video games. Dad's eyes were open. When we passed, he showed no sign of recognition.

Sandy had been there for three days when there was a sound of argument in the corridor. Feet scuffled, and a wild-looking grey-haired Latina in a muumuu appeared in the doorway, flanked by two preadolescent children. Their skin and hair was dark, Sandy thought, but their faces were terribly familiar.

The Latina glanced at her. Then, when she saw John lying in the bed with his eyes wide open, she let out a ferocious scream that brought the hospital security guards.

Things grow confused from there. There were many interviews between Sandy and hospital staff, between the Latina and the police and government bureaucrats. Sandy still couldn't piece together what she was being asked, what was happening, because the hospital staff and the bureaucrats and the police couldn't seem to piece it together either.

Then another woman arrived. A dumpy Asiatic woman with a wise pockmarked face and two young children. One was in leg braces, the other a victim of some kind of genetic irregularity. Sandy felt the tears rising. She felt so sorry for these women. It was always the ones with the sick children who were abandoned by their husbands, who ended up in the hospitals on their own.

The third woman went straight to the desk. Sandy was waiting in a seat with Adam and Evie. The Latina had been taken to another area while the administrators interviewed her.

The Asian woman said: 'Hello, I am here to see John Wonder. I have been told he is in this ward.'

'Okay,' said the nervous staffer. 'And you are?'

'I am Kim Wonder. I am his wife.'

'You?' Sandy stood and leant (she could not walk) towards the woman. 'You are the Mrs Wonder he was in the Holiday Inn with?'

Kim looked up at this tall, broad-shouldered, official-seeming white woman in a business suit.

'I have never been in a Holiday Inn,' Kim said. It was a lie. She had been in plenty of Holiday Inns with plenty of men. But she wasn't talking about those anymore.

Sandy was in pieces. She was never the strongest or the fiercest. She was merely the brightest, and that was not going to get her far enough.

Paulina, after threatening the staff and causing arguments, had been taken over by a special manager. We tried to ask her if we could have a fruit juice, but when we finally caught her attention she glared at us with murder in her eyes.

Kim was begging to be allowed to see him.

Cicada was the last to arrive. The hospital reception area was a bedlam of weeping women and wailing children and arguments and confusion and staff running to find supervisors when, finally, this creature straight out of a pornographic centrefold, blonde, long-haired, made-up, busty, in too-tight jeans and an electric-blue cashmere jumper strode in as if she had a mark on the floor.

The orderlies, the nurses, the doctors, the administrators, the police: all stopped. The male ones stayed stopped.

She waved them aside, like a celebrity.

31

Cicada had never had such a laugh. Three on the go! Who'd have thought the old guy had it in him? Bit of a dark horse, JW, old J-Dub. Three! All with kids! In a weird way, she thought to herself, she'd have been more inclined to give him a mercy fuck if she'd known. If he was married to three different women in three different countries, raising three different families, and all totally unknown to each other . . . well, he was beginning to interest her.

When she'd first arrived at the hospital, she did not go to the desk. She turned to go down the corridor to the ward where John's body lay.

Then she paused, and looked around the reception area. She took in the Asian woman at the desk, trying to reason with the hospital staff and also with her restless children, poor things, something not quite right with them.

Cicada took in the grey-haired cubic-shaped Latina in the far corner of the room, checking her watch, sighing noisily, kicking the back of the chair in front of her. Two more kids staring at a TV with dead eyes.

Cicada took in the tall woman in the boxy business suit and bad pony tail, holding on to some more kids' hands like she was sinking and they were the last pieces of driftwood. Taking them down with her.

'Well,' said Cicada, royally amused. 'Well!'

Fuck it, Cicada thought, she was dreaming again, always fantasising; nobody thought she was a romantic but she was, the worst kind of romantic, the fanatical and hardened kind. John was in a waking coma in this dump of a hospital and these three jet-lagged wives were hovering over him like the Furies. Cicada's instincts told her this was the time to run. She no longer had responsibility for him. If there was one thing he had, it was women to take responsibility for him! So there was no reason for Cicada to hang around. And clearly the women would be happier. She could see the way they looked at her: their worst nightmare. If there was one thing in this situation she was familiar with, it was that. That was how all married women looked at her, even widows. Married women hated her on principle.

To hell with running away! Cicada was fascinated. It tickled every funny bone she had in her, and every nasty bone, and aroused her sense for Greek drama. What was going to happen when he woke up? Who was going to win? Was it to be handbags at twenty paces? How was he going to explain himself? She just wanted to be a fly on the wall. She didn't want to be part of it. She only wanted to watch. Her money was on the Latina.

The Wonder Women, Cicada called them in her head. She was intrigued by how differently each of the Wonder Women reacted as, over the course of several hours, the facts were made clear to them. Surprisingly quickly, Cicada thought, after the initial confusion, they understood. She could see this cloud of disorientation sweeping over them for the first period, as they took it in; and then there was a kind of denial or anger or whatever; but then, they *knew*. They'd had time, having been told about the mysterious 'Mrs Wonder' he had checked out of the hotel with. They all thought the other was the Mrs Wonder, when in fact it was Cicada, though Cicada, having never checked in anywhere with him, could revel (for once!) in her innocence.

But they were steeled for the discovery. To see the other women was only to have the news confirmed. Cicada thought that each of them looked relieved, as if a long-standing tumour had been removed. But in different ways. The Latina with the wild grey hair and the best-looking children was ranting and raving and saying she was going to kill John when he woke up. The Asian woman, short and stocky and composed, spent a lot of her time calming the Latina down. The Asian one had this conciliatory way, soft and quiet-spoken and level-headed, and soon she was taking the Latina off for cups of tea. Cicada saw them on the visitors' balcony, huddled in conversation, both in tears. And then they were laughing. Cicada saw the Asian woman holding the Latina's hand. She saw them looking at phones together—photographs!—shaking their heads. The next day Cicada came into the hospital to find those two, with their four children, in the play area, like some regular mothers' group. The Latina was still prone to tantrums, and at one point raced for John's room where it took two orderlies to restrain her from ripping his tubes out of him. But at other times she was quite calm and rational and even seemed to enjoy the company of the Asian woman. These two, Cicada learnt, were wives number two and three.

Wife number one was a separate case. Wife number one was older, plain and hefty, with Coke-bottle glasses and oily hair. A quiet, scary woman. For a lot of the time Cicada saw her, this woman remained aloof from the other two. She didn't say much. Just the type of woman Cicada had sworn she would never become. Wife number one, of course.

But then Cicada learnt, from the Asian woman, whose name was Kim, that the large woman with glasses, Sandy, was some kind of famous medical researcher. If a medical researcher can be famous. But the fame wasn't the point. The point was that she was this high-powered, super-brainiac doctor, with this amazing reputation in her field. She wasn't so terrifying, she was just unsociable. She sat reading text-heavy papers and stared out the window. Cicada recognised the type: the woman who thought she could think her way out of this. Her children went to the play area and spent time with the other four. Cicada felt admiration and sympathy for her, but was too intimidated to try talking to her, too scared that the woman might lash out, too sorry for her, and anyway, the woman gave no sign that she wanted to talk to anyone other than the doctors.

The doctors were not able to say much. John was suffering some kind of seizure that left him alert and awake but not conscious. He could eat, but could not understand language. He could bathe himself and go to the toilet, but could not remember what he had just done. He could listen, but not hear. He could talk, but not make sense. He could look, but not see. They did brain scans on him and found nothing. Hah! Cicada laughed. Nothing that gave them a diagnosis. They ran many complicated neurological and physiological tests, but still, none gave them any idea of what had happened last or what was going to happen next.

Of the three, Cicada observed that it was the Asian woman who directed most attention towards John himself. Wife number one sat and read and had private conversations with the doctors. She seemed utterly incapable of even looking at John. Catatonic herself. Sandra had looked at him when she first arrived, in the fog of bewilderment surrounding the arrival of the other wives, had taken it all in, summarised the detail, solved the puzzle of Mrs Wonder from the Holiday Inn, and from then on had withdrawn. She had taken care of the details of getting her children into a hotel and looked after by professional nannies and teachers, as if she was digging in for a long-term stay. Then she came to the hospital each day and avoided not only the other two wives but John himself. To Cicada, she was the most mysterious of the three. You couldn't know what was going through her head or what she was going to do when John woke up, or came back.

It was the other two, Paulina and Kim, who Cicada broke the ice with. They were sitting in the creche drinking coffee and watching their children play with Sandra's—the three pairs of children really got on well together, we were like instant best friends—when Cicada was walking past. She quickened her step to get away, to leave them in peace, as she usually did, but there was a call. The women were beckoning her. They wanted to talk.

And so Cicada became their friend. That morning at the creche was the first time, but after that she fell into the routine of joining Paulina and Kim in the mornings. Cicada drank in what they told her. Paulina was a well-known novelist. Cicada had heard of her, and had even tried to read one of her books once, but couldn't finish it. She felt flattered by being in the company of a famous person. Paulina was also the one to immediately say what she thought of Cicada—'You were his bit of fluff, weren't you?'—which enabled Cicada, with relief, to honestly avow that there had never been anything romantic between her and John, that she was the daughter of Menis Economopoulos, the man who had been under house arrest while Dorothy O'Oagh, the World's Oldest Woman, stayed alive in the house by the lake, and that she, Cicada, had got to know John over many years when he came to visit.

'If it was that innocent, you would not be coming to the hospital,' Paulina said accusingly, but not, Cicada felt, with ill intent.

Cicada could not tell them everything—they'd had enough shocks for the moment—but she did say that the death of Mrs O'Oagh was the trigger for John's fit, which he had suffered in the kitchen of the Economopoulos house. For that reason, Cicada said, she kept coming to the hospital to visit him, for she felt some responsibility.

'And you tell me—' Paulina gave her an ostentatious up-and-down '—that you are not his *puta*? Looking like this, you expect me to believe he would have had *anything* to do with you that was not about getting in your pants?'

Cicada assured her that this was the case.

Kim, the third wife, wanted to know more about Mrs O'Oagh and the background to John's collapse. Cicada instantly admired Kim. It wasn't just that these women had been given the run-around by John. Cicada didn't pity them as victims. Even though they were all John's wives, they had clearly done so much without him that they were hardly wives at all. A wife was something Cicada never wished to be. She didn't hate the wives. She just felt terrible sorrow for them. If she'd hated them, she would have slept with their husband. But she thought that to be a wife was such a pathetic lot, to be a dependant—well, it was like Cicada's own situation, only without a sense of injured justice and family loyalty. Imagine being tied to a man when you didn't have to be. Imagine voluntarily giving up your freedom. It's like a habituated prisoner who commits a crime to get back into jail. Cicada couldn't imagine it. In her naivety and complete ignorance of the world, she had seen marriage as slavery. A woman enslaved had to escape: like her mother had done. But now, meeting these women, she saw a new dimension.

Paulina's independence of mind was nothing that a man could limit. Her ferocious anger was literally indomitable. John had given her—and this was Paulina's own summation, she told Kim and Cicada—the best of both worlds. 'I got the security and financial support of marriage, I got a father for my children, a good one when he is there,' Paulina said, with her flamboyant hand motions. 'I do not have a man in my house standing over me telling me what to do or asking me what I been doing. He is like a good friend who come in and solve problems. Because I stay married to him.'

Cicada struggled to follow Paulina's words, her logic. She wanted to ask: *Are you sure you're a writer?*

'But love,' said Kim.

Paulina said she had no hope of, or belief in, perfect love. 'I believe in me and my art and my children.' John was her fourth priority, so it was all for the best, she concluded, that he was only with her occasionally. 'The best of all worlds.'

Cicada dug Paulina's lack of sentimentality. Kim, on the other hand, was still in love with John. 'I thought I had found the perfect man,' she said. Unlike Paulina, who worked her rage through her system at rapid pace, Kim was openly perplexed at the betrayal. She couldn't understand why John had done this. It didn't square with what she knew of him. She loved him more intensely now—hence all the time she spent at his bedside holding his hand—but she also wanted answers. She wanted him, on his own, to confess to what he had done and explain why. She had her own ideas why, because she, of the women, was more interested in working John out than any of the others were. But she desperately wanted him to wake up so that she could put those ideas to him. She was, however, Cicada remarked, strangely *unhurt*.

Kim understood her. Cicada was used to being suspected, scrutinised and hated by women. She assumed John's wives wanted to kill her. But one day in the hospital creche, as Paulina was piggy-backing Kim's son and making a tunnel with her legs that the other children could run through, squealing with delight, Kim said to Cicada, 'In all this, I feel the most sorry for you.'

'Me?' Cicada's hand rose to her hair and pulled it away from her eyes, her instinctive tic whenever she felt uncomfortable. It fell back down. She searched Kim's face for hostility or sarcasm, but Kim was gazing happily at the children.

'It can't be easy for you,' Kim said.

'For me?' Cicada was so shocked she could say no more. Why should this woman be feeling sorry for her?

'Just living,' Kim said, 'when you look like you do. You must never have had a normal relationship with any person. A woman like you, you turn them blind. They see something else. I pity you.'

Cicada never cried, but now she was swallowing a tremendous surge from her chest into her throat. 'I . . . my father loves me,' she said. 'My mother . . .'

'Hm.' Kim did not look at her, to allow her the privacy of her emotions. 'You may be lucky one day. You may lose your looks. Then you can start living life.'

Cicada wiped her nose with the back of her hand. Never had she been read so lucidly.

'Do you know the worst thing a man did to me?' Kim said. As they had grown to know each other, Kim had candidly told Cicada of what she had endured in her life, down to the abomination of having been men's rape fantasy. Kim knew that Cicada was a woman she could share such things with. Cicada could not guess that there could be worse. 'A man I knew, he wanted me to pretend I was a whore,' Kim said. 'You have to think about that. When you are a whore, every man wants you to pretend you are something else. You have to pretend you are enjoying it, or not enjoying it. But you are an actress and you must play the role you are asked. It is understood that the role will involve more genuine emotion than you are feeling. You must put it on. But there was one man who did not want me to act more real than I was. He wanted me to act less real. 'Scream like a whore!' he said to me. If I seemed like I was enjoying it, he would stop until I screamed like I was only pretending to enjoy it. He would not be satisfied until I could scream like I was faking. I had to fake the faking.'

Cicada took Kim's moist, plump hand, raised it to her mouth and kissed it.

'You wonder why this is the worst,' Kim continued. 'How can this be worse than rape? I will tell you why. It was a *theft*. This man was trying to steal me from myself. I might rehearse my moans with other girls. We might laugh and imitate each other. A whore, when she is relaxed and with other whores, they entertain themselves by putting on the whore-like screams they use on men. This does not make sense, but when we were play-acting our screams, *Oh God, it's so big, oh God!* this was when we were most ourselves. And that is what this man wanted. He wanted to steal my self. He wanted to trick me into giving him something I valued. And that is what the cruellest man does: tricks a whore into giving more than he has paid her. This was the father of my children.'

Cicada, suddenly, understood why Kim was saying this to her. Cicada knew such men. Cicada knew how it was to be such a woman.

'This man,' Cicada said. 'It was John?'

Kim smiled. She had terrible skin, Cicada thought, but the most dazzling smile, a smile she could not help, a smile that could not be stolen.

'No, not John. John was good. I am talking about the father of my children.'

As she asked more questions, Cicada realised what a singular soul Kim was. Kim's children were not John's, but John had fathered them. They were the most adorable little things Cicada had ever seen. She learnt of how they had been conceived, and she flew into a rage of her own. This teacher, he was the man Cicada hated most. Paulina joined in, saying she had written about such men in her books and they always died painful deaths. Cicada said most men were bastards, and she had the sample size to speak with authority. But Kim had far more experience than even Cicada, and she was the most forgiving; 'John is now the father of my children,' she said. Cicada found it hard to believe such a merciful soul could exist on this earth. There was something otherworldly about Kim, but with her quiet ways and her plain, careworn face, Cicada could not help loving her. It was the strangest feeling, for Cicada did not, as a rule, love anyone. Loving a stranger was anathema to her. Yet she found herself loving Kim and needing to see her each day.

'And so,' Kim said, looking searchingly at Cicada, 'did our husband have anything to do with the old lady's death?'

Cicada looked at Kim, and across the crèche at Paulina, who was playing with the children, the cherubs. Angels. It had been so long since Cicada had done anything good for anyone else. Had she ever? She didn't know. She did not know.

So she told them.

32

Her boredom was world-record-sized. Most Bored Human: she'd have accepted that. Boredom such as hers, can you wonder why she would screw with a man's head? He was so hooked on her, she couldn't help speculating on what she could make him do. She didn't think he would go through with it. But when boredom reaches a certain point . . . you can't control the consequences.

He came back to town and kept trying to contact her, but she didn't want a bar of him. What if he did do it? What if he accused her of soliciting? Sure, Cicada wanted the old bat gone, but she wasn't so stupid as to commit a criminal act. Not when she was a year out from finishing her law studies. How stupid did he think she was?

Probably no more stupid than every guy thought.

And so she'd given him a wide berth when he came back. She still didn't really think he'd go through with it. He wasn't the killing type. She'd fucked a few criminals in her time. No murderers, but a few bashers, a few hard men, a few standover artists, quite a few who'd done time for crimes of violence. She liked hard men. Liked the danger element. Cool. But John wasn't one of them, and in all her studies—the books she read, the life she led—she knew that he wasn't going to go through with it. If you have five suspects for a murder, you don't go for the one who has the strongest motive or the best opportunity. You go for the one who's killed before. The ability to commit a violent act overrides all other bases for suspicion. That was what she knew. That was the type of street-smarts she was going to bring to her practice of criminal law. When she fucking graduated.

But still, you could never know for absolute certain. So she camped in her car near the Holiday Inn and watched and waited until he made his move.

She followed him to the old bat's belfry. She saw the nurse let him in. She went to the kitchen window and watched him sit there, silly old fart, sipping his tea, making polite conversation.

And so Cicada had been there at the window, watching John drinking tea with the nurse in the kitchen and holding his pound cake. She could see his resolve slip. He might have gone there thinking about the pillow in the hall closet, but now he was talking with the nurse, frittering the time away.

The window was open: Cicada could hear everything.

'You have nursed her all these years? Strange that I have never met you,' John said.

The nurse nodded.

'But I feel that I know you,' John went on. 'The way you have dressed her. Cared for her, so well. All these years.'

Then the nurse spoke words Cicada would have put into her mouth.

'But you do know me,' the nurse said.

And now he was nervous, laughing hysterically, totally losing the plot. Cicada began to feel sorry for him. Not in a good way. Sorry for what a sad old fool he was. He'd been sucked in by her, taken her far too seriously, actually thought he was going to seduce her by stiffing the old bird. Of all the idiotic idiots men were, he had to be the greatest idiot of them all! What a bloody fool! And now he was losing his bottle. He'd come in here to do a job and he was failing. He was failing at being a failure. How pathetic was that? Honestly. She'd had enough of him.

What had she said to him? How had she brought this on? Confessing that she loved him? But she said that to any dumb fuck when she was drunk. What did it mean, in the middle of having her ass drilled by some prick with his eye on the soft-core in-house porn channel, that she cry, 'Oh, you fucker, I love you!' She did that to mess with their heads, to stop them watching TV, to get them back on to *her*. 'I love you'? What's cheaper than that? Surely it couldn't have been that.

It must have been the other. That night she said she loved him and he said he loved her. When she set him straight.

'My friend,' Cicada had said to John, 'you keep missing the *point*. You can't measure beauty or love like they're quantities. It's what they can make a man *do*. How large is beauty? What a man will do for it. How great is love? Love can only be measured by what a man will do for it.'

What a man will do for beauty. That is its power.

What he never understood, and Cicada did: power. Love is power.

Fuck him, the fucker.

It was making her queasy to see him crapping on with the nurse, almost like he was there to pay a social call. For a second Cicada thought the nurse was flirting with him. Slut. Probably was. And John was flirting back. It was making Cicada want to puke. Then she saw the nurse open a bottle—vodka? Some clear spirit?—and flash it at John, who raised his eyebrow. The nurse emptied the two teacups in the sink, and poured a measure of the spirit into both. She and John toasted each other.

'Helenna,' John said. 'It is so good to meet you at last.'

'John,' the nurse said. 'My ex-husband is a madman, but we are not bad people. We are not a bad family. We do not,' she laughed, 'steal cutlery from people's houses!'

Cicada was ready to vomit, but she had a thought. She hadn't seen the old witch for so many years. Or Mrs O'Oagh. Seen her on TV, of course, but not in the flesh. Before she left—and having seen how John was not able to kill a fly—Cicada went along the side of the house and climbed through a hedge, until she came to the lit window around the corner from the kitchen. Had to be the sitting room where the old trout sat rotting away.

Cicada pushed her face right up to the window, and there she was.

The size of an acorn, practically. The old bat. She'd shrivelled into nothing. She had an oxygen mask. She was wearing a print frock and sitting up in an electric armchair. The television was on, but her eyes were shut.

Cicada watched her for a long time. This old shell—what kind of a human was that? What kind of life? Was it, technically, life at all? If John had rediscovered his bottle or his madness or his stupidity or whatever it was that drove him, if his cock woke up and started giving orders and he came in here and snuffed her out—maybe he'd grab Cicada's mother and they'd do it together, put themselves out of their misery, do the old bat in and then fuck like rabbits on the floor in front of the corpse—would it really be murder? How could you call it that?

If she could have had anything, in that quiet moment as she spied through the window, Cicada would have wanted to speak to Mrs O'Oagh and tell her about all the pain she had caused Cicada's family. There were Papou's parents but also her brothers. Every Economopoulos, ruined, gone rotten while they hung on the family tree, then fallen off, dead. Stone dead. And what the old woman had done to Papou. And what she'd done to Cicada herself. This shitty so-called life Cicada led, chained to her father, getting her jollies out of blowing salesmen in the Holiday Fucking Inn, just dying, literally dying, of boredom—all caused by the acorn sitting in that electric armchair, nine-tenths dead, but not so dead that she couldn't ruin a few more lives as she went out. In her stockings and her high heels. Her high fucking heels, which Cicada's mother had left her family to go and put on every day . . .

How Cicada hated her.

And—ah! Her powers!

Cicada always had power. The power over men, the power over women. She willed them to do things. Sometimes she wondered if she was the witch, the one true witch.

A goddess.

That's what they called her.

And here—her power . . .

The old bat suddenly convulsed like she was in an earthquake. Cicada pressed her face closer to the window. Mrs O'Oagh was—this was the most unbelievable part—she was *sitting up*. And now she was trying to *stand*! Her eyes were still shut. But her face was turned to the window. It was like Cicada's presence had her on a string. The old fossil couldn't have got out of her chair under her own steam for the best part of twenty years. It was incredible, like Cicada was watching a stuffed animal in a natural history museum suddenly start moving around in its glass case. *And she was the cause!*

Then the eyes opened.

The eyes were older than one hundred and thirty. The eyes were as old as everything. The whites were dark and bloody, and the pupils were white.

They were looking at her. In the window.

Cicada smiled. She didn't mean to be mean, it was just what she did. She had a billion-watt smile. Why not use it?

Mrs O'Oagh blinked once. Slow motion. Not even a blink. Her eyes shut, then creaked open again. You could almost see flakes of rust fall off the hinges. Then her face folded into a kind of frown of recognition. Like she was seeing Cicada's grandmother. Or grandfather. Or both. And like she was remembering now, it's all coming back, the contract she signed with Cicada's grandfather Christos Economopoulos, her obligation to die and pass on the house to him, and after all these years it was coming back to her, that was what she was recognising when she looked at the face in the window, Cicada knew it. The Economopoulos apples didn't fall far from the tree!

Mrs O'Oagh's lips opened and closed. There was a word.

Then she fell to the floor in a tiny little heap of ash, like she'd not collapsed but dematerialised. On the rug there was a pile of frock, a tuft of hair, and precious little else.

Cicada decided to make herself scarce. She scuttled back around the corner and through the hedge. She got past the kitchen window. At the sound from the sitting room, the little party of Wonder and Helenna had broken up. Cicada's mother, Saint Fucking Helenna, was running through the house in the direction of the sitting room. As she passed the last lit window, Cicada caught a glimpse of silly old John.

Old coot. Standing there in the kitchen like he owned the place, fingering a silver fork like he knew antiques and everything.

That was the other thing about him she got sick of. The great know-it-all.

•

'So our husband did not have anything to do with it,' Kim said.

Cicada shook her head. 'The old duck really did die of natural causes.'

'If seeing a ghost can be called natural,' Kim said.

There was a long pause while Kim and Paulina took in what Cicada had said. While Cicada took it in herself. What an extraordinary ending to her and Papou's seclusion. What a way to break through to freedom.

But for the Wonder Women, Cicada realised, it was not an end. They were not hearing the ending of a story. They were hearing the beginning of another story; and this, in turn, they hoped, would set off another story what they would do with John, what they would ask him, what he would say to them, when he awoke; which then would be the beginning of another story, what would happen next now that John's betrayal was in the open. Stories were like that, Cicada thought, always beginning just when you thought they were ending.

'What is the word?'

It was Paulina speaking. Her eyes were narrow, sparkling black coals, fuming with not the usual anger but the novelist's curiosity. Of course. Paulina wanted to know the word.

'What word?' Kim said.

Paulina nodded towards Cicada. 'The word the old woman say before she die.'

These beautiful women, these wives, these sufferers from an imprisonment Cicada scorned and feared and despised, these survivors of the imprisonment and the perfidy that went with it. Marriage. She could not stand back from them. She could still do some good with her life, even if it was too late to undo all the bad.

'Angel.' Her voice was a whisper.

Paulina nodded. Cicada could see she was taking it in, storing it away, reshaping it.

'Angel?' Kim said.

Cicada nodded. 'Angel.'

'She been waiting for God to take her away,' Paulina said. 'John tell me this. Every time she see him, she hope he is God, and she is disappointed. When she see you, she understand at last. She need an angel to come and take her.'

'That was the word,' Cicada said.

Paulina nodded again, briskly ecstatic. She took out a notebook and pen and began scribbling. 'That is the word!' she snickered. 'That is the word!'

33

Oh Father, where art thou? *Who* art thou? We file into his hospital suite, two by two, like animals into the ark of his forgetting. His eyes are open and he seems to see us, but we know that he is carrying us across flooded lands into storms and squalls without compass or map, without any idea, and what he cannot hide in his eyes is his terror. He has lost his hiding places.

He does not seem to be the father we knew. The special pool of light that illuminated us, that spot in the darkness just for us, has been extinguished. In our tight little families of four we were destined, we were singular. Now we are six children with three mothers, we are not special but a species. We are humdrum and clumsy. We are ordinary as we plod along with the masses. That light has moved away and we are on our journey to be adults, unremarkable and unnoticed.

But before your light leaves us, Father, before we join the massing tide, there are things you ought to know. We are not simply we, not a stream of Adams and Evies tumbling in packets off the end of your production line. No, Father, we are not a complicated system of transactions and obligations for you to meet as you rush off to another. We are present even when you are absent. We live and deepen, like the braiding of wrinkles in the back of your neck, whether you are allocating your time to us or not. Even when you are with us and dreaming of the next place you have to go, we will insist on our presence, and you will listen. Keep your eyes open, Father, and try now to see what you have missed.

Adam, the first Adam, Adam I, son of Sandy, has inherited his mother's practical sense and inquiring mind. Adam was able to use the remote control of the television and play his own programs before he was two. Adam was able to add and multiply and subtract (but not, oddly, divide) before any other child in his school. Adam had a warmth and sense of hospitality that ensured his popularity among boys and girls his age. Adam enjoyed the company of adults, too. Because there was so often no man in the house, Adam sat down with his mother Sandy when her friends came over, and assumed the head of the table. This was a four-year-old boy. He sent quizzical looks the adults' way and laughed at their jokes. Adam never wanted to be young, to be a child. He was scared of roller-coasters but pretended he was not. He was scared of sports but pretended, when forced to play, that he had a headache or a stitch. Whenever children were playing something that he was not good at or was scared of, Adam convinced them that it was a boring thing to do and they should be doing something different. Adam came first or second in his class. Adam tormented his younger sister for many years, until she started tormenting him. Adam loved his mother.

Father, how much of that did you see?

Evie, the first Evie, Evie I, daughter of Sandy, was a troubled child who woke up crying in the middle of the night. Evie competed mightily with Adam, intuiting at the youngest age that the highest goal in a girl's life was to outdo her elder brother. Evie's competitive sense was even stronger than Adam's, but because his gifts in the classroom, in reading and writing and numbers, were so evident, Evie had to think up some new way to outshine him. Evie was the first girl in her class to be sent to the principal's office for misbehaviour. Evie walked around playgrounds telling girls she hated them and would not be their friend. Evie's only friends were the boys who did the things that Adam was scared of doing. Evie was braver than Adam, and she teased him for that. She scorned his manhood before he knew what manhood was. Evie made up stories about her father that she told the other girls at school: that he was James Bond, that he was a secret agent, that he was *so* cute. Evie was always the first to the door when you arrived home, but the first to her mother's lap when you left. Evie knew which side her bread was buttered. Evie was destined for incandescent success, or failure. When Evie found out she had another sister—two sisters, both called Evie—she suffered the most. The first thing she did, when she got back to the Holiday Inn from the hospital, was to sneak out behind the air-conditioning control room and smoke a cigarette.

Father, you saw none of that.

Adam, the second Adam, Adam II, son of Paulina, was a complicated little boy, kind and gentle yet capable of outbreaks of unreasoned destructiveness. His mother called it his 'Cuckoo Clock'. Adam loved to hug her and hug his grandmother and he cried inconsolably every time his father left home. With his father, Adam's gentleness came out and he loved to rub his hand against the grain of the shaved prickles on your cheeks. Adam did not do well in school. He stared out the window and seemed to be listening to voices that were not coming from this world. Adam was extremely small for his age, and was treated by other children as a baby, a midget, inferior. Consequently they indulged his pointless innocent stories and then, when they were bored, punished him. He was no good at ball games. They soon teased and ignored him. He invited many friends to his house and they always enjoyed themselves and played robustly, and Adam's piping voice was heard shouting as raucously as theirs. But he was never invited to their houses. Adam was never popular. He collected information and spilt it out in gushes of factoids that interested no-one but himself. He had a bottomless curiosity about *things*, such as trains and countries and volcanoes. He loved to compile lists. He could connect any two facts and use one to explain the other; from before he knew the word, he disbelieved coincidence. He saw so many things that others looked through, he was running towards some synthesis of ultimate knowledge, yet he was not capable of seeing himself the way others saw him. The high and the great occupied him while what was most obvious, his place in the group, his local politics, were invisible. Consequently he suffered. Other boys chased after him, pinned him down and poked at his penis. It made them laugh. When he asked them to stop, they poked harder. He was so small they did not have to listen to him. He told no-one but eventually, at home, told his mother. Paulina found the boys and told them if she heard a story like this again she would kick their teeth so far down their throats they would need to send their toothbrushes up their assholes to brush them. The boys did not poke Adam's penis anymore, nor play with him at all. Yet he conquered that, too, because his boundless curiosity looked over their heads; he was off with the angels, in the distance, in a place where he knew no fear.

And in his own place, too, for all the suffering, he knew no fear.

Father, you saw none of this.

Evie, the second Evie, Evie II, the daughter of Paulina, could play the same game for a whole day without eating. Evie could sit with a single crayon and draw a picture for hours, embroidering until there was no more space on the paper, then find more paper, never thinking that there might be something else to play. Evie was a fussy eater, changing her mind about foods from one day to the next. Evie was prone to terrible tantrums and when her mother lost her temper at her, Evie would lose her temper to a higher pitch, until it became an arms race, a competition, a duel to the top which Evie knew she could never lose. Evie played make-believe with such conviction that she could not hear her mother talk to her. Evie adored her grandmother and played her off against her mother. Evie had few friends at school, but from time to time would attach herself to one girl and want to invite the same girl to her house, or go to that girl's house, every day. Evie attached herself as if for life and then detached herself with unforgiving finality. Evie was highly gifted but did not do well in her classes. Evie had an icy stare that went above and beyond children's things. Evie seemed set for a life of question marks, one to watch, one who could go this way or the other way. Evie suffered from asthma and sometimes had such bad attacks that she needed to go to hospital. She asked her mother if people only had a certain number of breaths allowed in their lifetimes. When she was having an asthma attack, Evie worried that she would not make it to adulthood. Because she had undergone such pain, she had an uncommon eye for those in need. When a boy or a girl fell over and hurt themselves, Evie was the first to tend to them and find help. When lollies or gifts were being handed out, Evie was the only child to think of putting one aside for someone who was not there. Evie had the gift of compassion and was a victim of bullying but was also the most resistant to it. Of all the children, Evie seemed the least bothered by whether her father would turn up or not, the least thrown off her stride when he left or came. Evie carried on, didn't miss a beat. Evie marched to her own secret drum.

Father, all this you missed too.

Adam, the third Adam, Adam III, the son of Kim, suffered from muscular dystrophy. He spent a good deal of his early childhood in hospital. He was a good-natured little boy who pretended his trips to hospital were adventures and rarely asked when he was going home. He was endlessly fascinated by what was going on in the hospitals and treated the nurses as his aunties, and for that he was loved. Adam battled on at preschool and then school, and was an enthusiastic supporter of others, seemingly cut out for the role of cheerleader-in-chief, spectator supreme, without whom no success can be fully enjoyed by those who are achieving it. Adam had a nice group of friends, who included him in their parties and outings. Adam took his first steps at twenty-six months. Adam was toilet-trained and talking before he could walk. Adam could kick a ball with both his right foot and his left. Adam could pat out a musical rhythm in perfect time, and sing beautifully. For a little while he gave up music and singing, feeling that they were less than manly pursuits and that he would be seen as inferior because of them. Kim encouraged him to stick with them, as manliness was only in the eye of the beholder. Adam refused stoutly to sing or learn music. His mother gave up encouraging him. Some months later, Adam took up the violin and joined the choir.

Father, you saw none of this.

And Evie, peewee Evie, Evie the third, Evie III, daughter of Kim, unborn when her mother brought that new man into their lives. Evie knew him as a white ghost who tickled the pads of her feet. Evie knew him as a friendly monster who spoke with a strange flat voice. For a time, Evie clung to him and ignored her mother. Her mother was always with her when she went to hospital. Her father never was. So she associated her mother with the bad things and her father with the things that were not going to hurt her. But in the middle of the night, when she screamed because she saw death, it was her mother she screamed for. Little wonder. Her father was never there.

You were never there.

You were so good to us, Father, when you tried. But truly there is no substitute for the brutal fact of duration. For every nappy you changed, there were half a dozen that you left for someone else. For every story you told us, there were more stories being told to us by others. For every ball you threw us or every board game you played with us, there were three, four, five, twenty balls and twenty games being played with us by a person who was not you. Often it was our mother and often it was someone else. This is what we want to say to you, Father. You were good and you were kind and you were always striving to make it up to us, but an apology cannot constitute a life, and as contrite as you felt and as special as you tried to make your time with us, life did go on without you, and it will, it will. When we needed you, you taught us not to need you. Some think that is good and perhaps that is what you told yourself: you gave us the gift of independence. But when you withdrew yourself, you could not withdraw our need. And need unmet by a father will find somewhere else to go. So we have been in the habit of needing, not being needed. Which is not, perhaps, what you had in mind.

Did you have anything in mind?

You have left your mark on us, in us, Father. For a time we will forgive you. Then we will hate you. We will do both in our different ways, and cut it in more ways than you can count, because we are complicated beings, Father, we are not just The Children, we are ourselves, we are violent and hurt and hurtful human beings, yes, independent of what you are and were and of what you want from us, but you know what you have left, what your legacy is, what your mark on the world will be: it will be six humans who, when they come to the pathways in their lives where they are met by a kindly presence, a storyteller, a pale figure of love and generosity, an apologiser, a purveyor of Quality Time, someone attentive to them and benevolent and magnanimous, will be blocked from that path; something will lie there that will hurt others and hurt ourselves and lay waste to all around, and that thing, that untaken path, that blocked way, will be the path of trust.

34

For two weeks he lay in hospital. More physical and psycho-logical tests were carried out. No organic lesion or injury was diagnosed. He was seen by neurologists, psychiatrists, endocrinologists, oncologists, gerontologists, cardiologists and even a dermatologist. Theories were tossed around regarding temporary forms of amnesia, a psychotic reaction to a traumatic event, an ongoing seizure and, finally, what we were all fearing, the A-word, early and sudden onset of Alzheimer's disease. But scans were inconclusive or, to state it factually, unrevealing. They showed a normal brain, free of build-ups or occlusions or warpings or thickenings or thinnings, just a normal brain, perfectly well.

Yet there are injuries of the brain that are invisible to technology, and our father's could have been one of them. When awake and alert and questioned by the doctors he was of little help. At times he was quite lucid and pleasant, but he showed no signs of knowing where he was or why. His wife, Sandra Wonder, the one of his wives who claimed wifely prerogatives, sat beside him and held what she called 'a normal conversation' about their children and her work. She did not raise any questions about what had happened in this town, and made no reference to Paulina or Kim or the other children, to Mrs O'Oagh or Menis or Cicada. Sandy acted as if nothing had changed, nothing had happened. She said she did not want to send him 'back down'. It was pure make-believe. In that sense it was, as she said, a normal conversation.

When the next person came into his hospital suite, our father recalled nothing of the conversation he had just had with Sandy. He seemed not to know who Sandy was.

This next person was Paulina. He seemed not to know who she was either.

After two weeks he was taken to a rehabilitation centre for the geriatric. Sandy, Paulina and Kim began to make arrangements for the medium-term. The elder children were sent back to their schools, with nannies organised to look after them. Sandy and Kim took extended leave from their workplaces. Paulina sent Adam and Evie to their grandmother, who exalted at the prospect of looking after them according to her own rules without having to negotiate with her daughter. Sandy checked into a serviced apartment with a flexible ongoing weekly rent. Paulina stayed in a youth hostel and began writing again; when she was in this kind of mood she did not care about her physical surrounds, she could sleep in a grave for all she cared. Kim found a welfare organisation that would look after families, such as hers, that were temporarily homeless.

Our father was not rehabilitated.

After two more months, Sandy received a letter from the human resources department of The Last Word. They regretted to say that the Authenticator-in-Chief's employment was to be terminated. This had no relation to his 'current medical circumstances', but was the outcome of a review into irregularities discovered during the previous year. Rather than conducting his researches in the manner designated by his employment contract, our father had been delegating it to other staff and covering up administrative gaps by fraudulent means, falsifying essential human resources documents and signing authentication reports when he had not been the eyewitness. The investigation had concluded that he had been grossly derelict in his duties. It pained the human resources department of The Last Word to be making this decision during a time of such personal hardship, but there was a clear breach of contract and employment conditions, and the breach was so serious that no further negotiation could be entered into, even were that possible. The letter concluded with an offer of a termination payout the equivalent of two years' full salary. This, the human resources department assured Sandy, was well in excess of our father's entitlement. The Last Word had only been our father's employer, strictly speaking, for three years. His correct entitlement therefore was no more than three months' full salary, and even that entitlement was not an entitlement as such, as he was being terminated for misconduct, not retrenched for reasons of efficiency. For that reason, the offer of two years' full salary was, in the company's words, 'generous in the extreme' but 'a token of our appreciation for Mr Wonder's legacy to the great enterprise in which we share. We trust that you will accept the generosity of our gesture in the spirit with which it was offered, and will be dissuaded from any further action.'

Sandy read it but could not understand any of it other than the fundamental fact that John was now not only adrift in a permanent squally night, lost in his sea of dreams, but unemployed.

Paulina commented: 'Not only out of his mind, but out of a job.'

Every effort was made to locate our father's consciousness. Each of his wives tried, in their different ways, to reel him back. Sandy sat patiently making conversation with him, pretending, as ever, that all was normal and the humdrum processes of daily life were the reality he needed. While he participated in these discussions, the moment the subject turned 'deeper', as she put it, beyond the glassy surfaces of the everyday, he vanished again.

Paulina went to him at unexpected times, when she was taking a break from her writing, at times of her choosing rather than his or the rehabilitation facility's. Paulina ran her own race. When she went to our father, Paulina raged and cursed at him, trying to provoke his passions. She climbed into bed with him and let her hand sneak beneath the covers, seeking to open a valve that was shutting him off from his past and his self. She managed to open something, but the valve which functioned was, like its owner, redundant.

When her efforts failed, and when even flagrantly refusing to offer him the relief his eyes sought did not bring a plea of recognition or surrender from him, Paulina was the first to raise the accusation that had been preying unspoken on everyone's minds.

'Come on,' she said to Kim in their regular council. (Sandy still only spoke to the other two wives when summoned by some official matter requiring the agreement of all three, but otherwise offered them nothing, not even small talk about the weather.) 'What you think he do?' Paulina said. 'He been caught out. Discovered. All his years of lying and, the naughty boy he is, he retreat into his shell to hide from us. He spends sixty years avoiding. Because he would start now? He is terrified. This is my medical diagnosis of him. He is too scared to speak to us and too frightened of what we will say to him. He refuse to allow his mind to open to this reality. If he cannot remember, he cannot answer for his crimes. It drive me insane. I want to kill him. If I were not a mother, I *would* kill him. With my bare hands. Not for what he done, but that's why what he now refuse to do.'

Kim, secretly, had been wondering if John's amnesic state was not some kind of psychosomatic reaction to overpowering guilt and shame. Kim, lacking Paulina's violent instincts, had no impulse to do him harm, but her frustration was no less potent. She did not think he was faking, but she was losing patience. His motives, whether any motives existed or not, were increasingly beside the point. The point was that Kim had a home to go to, a job to return to, and two children to go on raising. It was not that she did not love John or feel pity for him or acknowledge a general responsibility to do what was best by him. She faced up to these things. But trumping them was that she had to get on with her life, hard as it was, with her children. She could leave John to the others. It sounded harsh, but in her humility Kim did not believe she had the same claim on him as did Paulina, and certainly not Sandy. 'Last in, first out,' Kim confided in Paulina.

Paulina looked at her, wide-eyed. 'I think you are the last to give him up,' she said quietly.

Kim shook her head. 'I love him, but I will not wait for him. I have two children who only have one mother.'

'But you are the kind one,' Paulina said, as if Kim were a character in a fairytale.

'That might be why,' said Kim, 'I am going home first.'

Kim's decision to leave precipitated a chain of events that brings us to the present day. Until she decided to leave, none of the wives would sit down and talk about what to do next. Each, in her different way, was waiting and hoping for our father to snap out of it, to return to normal, to face facts, to confess, to acknowledge, to look his wives in the eye and apologise for what he had done. More than anything they needed his past to return to him. Just some acknowledgement would suffice. His silence, his vacancy, was infuriating but it was also ruining them, like a cancer. It was immeasurably worse than the silences he had portioned out to them in the past years.

Kim's announcement that she and her children were going home brought the three women together. With no progress behind him and none in sight, our father's stasis was pressing them to make plans.

Kim, Paulina and, reluctantly, Sandy gathered in a counselling room at the rehabilitation centre. They refused the staff's offer of a mediator. They had one request: that the patient, in his bed, be wheeled into the room while they conferred. This was Paulina's idea; it suited her sense of theatre that John would have to sit there, mute, while they settled his future. 'He have no more say than a child,' she said with satisfaction. 'He have to sit and learn what we think of him. If he is not understanding what is happening, so be it. If he is understanding—maybe this bring him back to life.'

So the three women sat around a circular table, with John in his bed pulled up at the fourth place. His eyes were open and staring sightlessly at the ceiling. His breathing rattled with the onset of bronchitis, for which he was being treated by intravenous penicillin. His health had deteriorated just that day, when Kim had told him she was leaving.

Paulina and Kim started the discussion. At first the logistical difficulties seemed insurmountable. Three wives wanted him in a place where his children could know him, in whatever form he presented himself. But where that might be was a ticklish matter. Their respective cities were all a vast distance from each other, many hours by air. Kim did not have the material resources to look after him, and with the medical requirements of her children she already had enough responsibility. Out of kindness to her predecessors, she renounced any wish to have him stay at a facility in her city.

Paulina, quite simply, did not want him. She said it would be unfair for him to live in her city.

'Unfair to whom?' Sandy asked.

'To you!' Paulina blurted. Then, her eyes filling, she shook her head and said: 'To me. Unfair to me. I do not want him and I am afraid that if I got responsibility for him then I wring his neck. I cannot stop thinking he is doing this on purpose, that's why there is a part of him that does not want to recover his memory and face up to us.'

'But your children?' Kim asked.

'We survive without him three quarters of our life. Now we survive without him four quarters. It is not too much. It is a harder adjustment—' Paulina allowed herself a humourless smile, '—if he recover and live with us. My mother cannot stand him.'

And so they looked at Sandy, the enigmatic one, the familiar stranger, who had said so little.

'You are waiting for me,' Sandy said to John, who was blinking rapidly at the ceiling. 'They have found the limits of their love for you.' Nodding at Kim, she said, 'You have known him for the least time and you know, from your experience, that you can put traumatic events behind you. That is your strength. I envy you for it. And what you are doing is kind. When I first saw you, I understood why John had fallen in love with you. You are caring and gentle, much as he is. I have not been caring or gentle to him. I have been many things for many people, but I have not been that for him. I'm a cold fish, see?' She gave a little laugh and adjusted the front of her blazer. 'When I saw you, I thought that you would be the one to have him. If he were awake and able to decide, if he were to do that one thing that we want him to do, and acknowledge what he has done to us, I feel certain that the one he would choose to be with would be you.'

Kim lowered her head and began, quietly, to sob.

Sandy addressed Paulina. 'And it's very easy for me to see why he fell for you. Men like John, men who dream, can only see life as a glass half-empty. They are haunted by what they are missing out on. This is not the men who are deserted by their women. This is the men who do the deserting. They fly to something different. You have fire and creativity. You force him to question his world of quantities. I have none of that. It broke my heart when I saw you. Before anyone told me, I knew that you were the one he had chosen after me. You take the initiative. I don't. You are active. I am passive. You live life to the full. I do too, but only in my own way, which was not enough to satisfy him. I am too much like him. My focus is on the general, on health solutions for generations. You live your life entirely on the plane of the individual. I can see that's why he wanted you. Fire. Impulse. All the things that I never had.'

Sandy's chin trembled when she thought of herself, how she had come here. Wiping her eyes, she looked at John. Here, the love of his life, the partner he had never left, the first one, the defining one, the one whose side he would join in heaven or hell, was crying for herself, crying for all those years, crying with pure rage at what he had done. He had wished away his life while dreaming of lives unlived. He never knew what he had. He had *her*.

Our father's eyes were fixed on the ceiling, or perhaps he could see through it, to the stars in the sky and his billions of ancestors.

Paulina leant forward and stroked Sandy's knee.

'But he does not desert you,' Paulina murmured. 'He still love you. He cannot leave you.'

'If only he had!' Sandy spat. 'I really wish he had left me. I could have started living. You see, that's what I can't forgive him for: not for leaving me, but for *not* leaving me. It's not love. It's cowardice. He was too scared to face up to anything, so he thought he could string things along. String *us* along. By doing so, he told himself he was a better man than if he had left me. I hate him more than I can ever imagine hating any person.'

Paulina swallowed. Silent Sandy had spoken; and her feelings for John, love and hate, dwarfed theirs. It was clear to Paulina that John could not go to Sandy's city, for the sake of either of them. Sandy would be consumed by the fight between revenge and indifference. She had no more love for him. Her children were the most grown. They would learn about John in their own ways. Sandy was not yet sixty. She had more work to do, for children, not for this man.

Kim saw that John could not go to Sandy's town, for John's sake. How terrible, she thought, for John, no matter how debilitated he is, to live under the shadow of the woman he has betrayed most of all, who hates him most of all, whom he would fear most of all. It did not matter to Kim how low John was. She still had love and sympathy for him. She could see that Sandy had none. Not a jot. Sandy and John—no, not together. It would be ruinous for both of them. Sandy was the last person who should have responsibility for him. Sandy's hatred could not be subdued.

Sandy looked at Paulina and said, 'I have a question for you.'

'Ask.'

'When he was with you, did he drink?'

Paulina nodded. 'A little. As much as I drink.'

Sandy turned to Kim. 'You? Did he drink?'

Kim said, 'He enjoyed a small glass. A little, not a lot.'

The sound of Sandy's breath, as she sighed, wavered and caught in her throat. Paulina and Kim both felt that their hearts were going to break.

'I asked the girl,' Sandy said, her eyes on the floor. She took off her thick glasses and began to clean them on a corner of her blouse. She seemed childlike. Her burrowing animal's eyes, shrunken to creased slits without the glasses, blinked blindly. 'I asked the girl if he drank when he was with her. Do you know what she said? *Like a fucking fish.*'

The three wives fell silent. Sandy replaced her glasses. Paulina jotted a note in her diary. Kim could not help stealing glances at the man in the bed. Why, Dad, did you think you were done with this world? How can you, who have dedicated your life to humanity in its multitudinous variety, feel alone? When you know so much of what humans can do, why do you turn your back on them? On us?

With a sigh, Kim stood up and cradled his chin in her palms, looking into his eyes. She moved away. Paulina stroked the back of his hand, and then pretended to give him a slap across the cheek, but she did not have the heart and stepped to one side. Sandy stood over him, her arms crossed over her ample chest. Then she reached down and put her hands on his shoulders. Then she moved her hands to his throat and squeezed.

35

Kim returned home with her children but was bringing them back in a fortnight to visit him. Paulina desperately wanted to go home, but felt she could not do so while Sandy was still there. And Sandy, nobody knew what was in her mind. When she began choking John, screaming and crying as the stoppers on her emotions burst open, Paulina and Kim just watched her. They shared a deep understanding of her need to kill him. But they could not let him turn her into a murderer. Paulina moved first, and Kim followed. Together they pulled Sandy's hands from John's throat.

Like a zombie, like John, Sandy had recovered her wits and walked from the room. Then she resumed the cold silent efficiency she had maintained through the weeks of his inertia. She had established technological connections with her workplace that were so sophisticated she could conduct much of her necessary analytical work from her serviced apartment. She had shown no sign of moving home, or of resolution. She seemed to be waiting for something to fall out of the sky.

In a way, it did. The solution to our father's care came from an unexpected quarter.

He had been in the town, now, for three months: one week stalking Dorothy O'Oagh, two weeks in hospital, and now ten weeks in the rehabilitation facility. As he was not suffering from any life-threatening condition and did not need constant monitoring for vital signs or medication, the administrators of the facility had made it known that he needed to be transferred to a place of residence. The pressure was building on Sandy and Paulina, but mostly Sandy, to make some sort of decision. The children came and went for visits and asked when he was coming home. We learnt nothing. He was a mute shell, a blind worm.

And so it was on the verge of the precipice that the solution came. From the least expected source.

Menis and Cicada Economopoulos had moved into Dorothy O'Oagh's mansion. After fifty years, the deeds and occupancy had passed into Economopoulos hands. From a distance, Menis had observed the saga of John Wonder's wives and their inability to reach a decision. Cicada was still visiting and talking with Paulina, with whom she had forged a close understanding. It seemed that John was going to be abandoned by all three women, and all six of his children.

Menis and Cicada thought he deserved no better. The man was a traitor. He knew no constancy. They, who knew nothing but constancy, scorned him. He was half a man.

Cicada, now a wealthy woman in her own right thanks to the reorganisation of Menis's assets for taxation purposes, saw no need to continue her tiresome legal studies. A refinancing of the O'Oagh mansion and a planned subdivision of the property would assure both income and growth in her portfolio for as long as she lived—even, she joked, if she lived to one hundred and thirty.

Part of Menis's subdivision plan was to convert the stables and some of the land into an aged-care facility. Menis felt that this was poetic, the dues he owed to the memory not of Mrs O'Oagh, as such, but a monument to the meaning of his life. Menis's story owed its coherence to the longevity of the human body and the vitality of age. He was now an old man himself. He dreamt of an up-to-date medical facility, on his own property, that would keep him alive forever. He believed the property and the house had some kind of mystical power, some elixir, that had kept Mrs O'Oagh alive for so long. Menis's dream was that he could sit in his new study overlooking the lake, with the best medical care in the world, and stay alive for even longer than the old lady. Big Life would keep him going. He had a number in his mind: one hundred and thirty-one. He would be satisfied with nothing less. If he exceeded her, he would finally vindicate his father and mother.

Once the plans for the high-technology aged-care facility were fully established, Menis decided, out of the goodness of his heart and at the suggestion of his daughter, to offer a room at the bottom of the property, near the lakeshore, to John Wonder. Menis had never liked the man much, but he did not hate him either, and Menis was a man of romantic as well as pragmatic sensibilities. To render the development taxation-exempt during its two-year construction period, the facility needed a minimum of one patient. Eventually that would be himself, but Menis could tolerate having John Wonder there in the interim. He saw a kind of justice in the whole mess.

Helenna Economopoulos offered to nurse John, but Menis refused. He did not want her to have to work anymore. He bought her a cottage on the far side of the lake, where she lives in retirement. Sometimes she and Menis meet and talk over a glass of Laphroaig. 'We are not a bad family,' he likes to say. Helenna nods along, but manages to avoid Cicada during her visits. Since Helenna left her family to become Mrs O'Oagh's nurse all those years ago, her daughter has never spoken to her. Cicada cannot forgive her desertion and cannot accept that her mother acted in atonement. For Cicada, loyalty to family should always have come first. Helenna has never spoken of her conversation with our father the night Mrs O'Oagh died.

As for Cicada, she lives in a separate wing of the Economopoulos compound, where she can bring the one-night stands and other flings upon which she continues to sacrifice her beauty. As she approaches forty, she has found that her tastes tend younger. She brought home twenty-one-year-olds, then twenty-year-olds, and on one occasion she had to use her influence to have the chief of police, an old friend of hers, bury an accusation, brought by a sixteen-year-old boy's mother, of statutory rape. Cicada's life continues much as it was. The cross she has to carry is the constant spectre of an overwhelming boredom, a boredom she can only allay by going to the Lakeshore bar at the Holiday Inn and drinking herself into stupidity. Her physical charms are undimmed. Kim's hope, that Cicada would lose her looks and discover a normal life, has failed to come to pass. With age, indeed, her beauty has become sharper-edged, more defined, more delineated, more satisfying to a particular kind of eye. She has become overripe, lined and past her prime, no longer girlish, a mature woman, and all the more desirable for that. She is more than ever a world-historical beauty, with a body that men will die and lose their minds for. But she does not see that, and everyone else in the town wants her to stay that way, ignorant of her true worth, for she, now, the great beauty, the town tramp, she is their talisman, she is what defines them, she is what makes their lives different from all others.

Cicada became our father's legal guardian by agreement with Sandy, Paulina and Kim. Together, once the Economopouloses had made the offer to house our father, Sandy, Paulina and Kim resolved on two actions. One was that it was best for the children that he live in some neutral territory. The wives could see him, or not see him, as they saw fit. But it would be wrong for any pair of children to be able to claim a special relationship with him by dint of having him living in their city. Many possible future conflicts were averted by having him in a neutral place. So at regular intervals the children's mothers bring them here, to the lake, to see that he is still alive. We authenticate his existence. Sometimes we play games with him or have a conversation. As our mother Sandy always knew, the conversations have to remain light and superficial and make no reference to the past or the truth. Whenever that sheet of ice is cracked, he lapses into such a state of distress and disorientation and frustration and nightmarish loss, he will yelp at imaginary bats flying past his face and duck from the very shadows; he will be adrift in a sea of non-remembering, floating oarless in a terror of the everlasting *now*. You only have to see it once for the resolve to take root in you to prevent it, as far as you can, from happening again. It is hell.

We know, now, what happened that night between his entering Mrs O'Oagh's house to sit and drink tea with the nurse, and his re-emergence with the silver fork in his hand. Helenna Economopoulos did not have to tell us.

The compartments in our father's life were not the separations he needed to build to preserve his sanity. They *were* his sanity. When he fell in love with Cicada, when he fell to the abjection he deserved and yearned for, the walls between his different parts began dissolving. And once the walls came down between all three, or now four, of his lives, so did every other retaining wall—between past and present, present and future, self- and non-self, dream and wakefulness. The walls were his sanity. Love had driven him mad.

●

Cicada, who once worked as an aged-care nurse, just like her mother, sometimes goes down to the room by the lakeshore, late at night, in her zip-up white uniform. John always wakes up when she comes. He watches her with a shameless fixity: at last he does not have to sneak his glimpses of her; finally, as she says, he can perve without fear of being caught in the act. She stands over him and conducts make-believe conversations about this and that. Her stories are openly deceitful and solely concerned with sex. She fingers the tag on her zipper as she gives him vivid accounts of the latest young man, or sometimes young woman, that she has brought home with her. She re-enacts the embarrassing moments with as much relish as the wild sex. And somehow, if he could see, and perhaps he can, the old mystery that worried him so greatly and so unnecessarily would be clear to him now: the enigma of how Cicada is so chaste in her promiscuity. She has never yet been possessed, she has triumphed over mankind in his thousands, and because she has never been possessed she is as pure as snow; and when her head rests on her pillow at night, a sight he will never see but might, from his far-off place, picture, then he would see a face that sleeps in peace. When she told him she never slept: that was her one lie. You only have to join the dots, Father, and you will know so much more than you ever did.

Now and then her hands stray to her wide hips or the generous outlines of her figure, paralysingly visible as it stretches her uniform into horizontal ridges. Her hands go no further than this, though, as she consoles the man who has become her legal ward. Every now and then she sees in his shallow blue eyes something that resembles memory, or recognition, or hope.

'I know you're pretending, you weak fuck,' she says with a tender smile. Her hair has been allowed to return to its own darkness, that of smoky night, with some early strands of the coming dawn. She takes her hands off her hips and clasps them into a prim thatch. 'You've got a long, long haul ahead of you. There's magic in this place. People around here live for fucking *ever.'*

As Cicada speaks, that look in our father's eye crosses over to what is more familiar to her; it lowers his brow and moistens the shallow blueness and tightens his fingers on his knotted sheet. She knows it too well, a feeling specific to the human male of a certain type, which can never be left behind, covered over or, indeed, forgotten.

Acknowledgements

Thanks—To those who gave life to this novel without knowing it: Chris Sheedy, Dean Frenkel, Peta Levett, Robert Benz, James Bradley, Charlotte Wood, Tom Smuts. For their work: Ben Sherwood, Larry Olmsted, Emmanuel Carriere, Michael Finkel, Nathaniel Kahn. And to those who did know: Jane Palfreyman, Lyn Tranter, Ali Lavau, Andy Palmer, Siobhán Cantrill, Josh Durham, Christos Tsiolkas, and (the only one) Wenona Byrne.